PRAISE FOR FREYA BARKER

Freya Barker writes a mean romance, I tell you! A REAL romance, with real characters and real conflict.

~*Author M. Lynne Cunning*

I've said it before and I'll say it again and again, Freya Barker is one of the BEST storytellers out there.

~*Turning Pages At MidnightBook Blog*

God, Freya Barker gets me every time I read one of her books. She's a master at creating a beautiful story that you lose yourself in the moment you start reading.

~*Britt Red Hatter Book Blog*

Freya Barker has woven a delicate balance of honest emotions and well-formed characters into a tale that is as unique as it is gripping.

~*Ginger Scott, bestselling young and new adult author and Goodreads Choice Awards finalist*

Such a truly beautiful story! The writing is gorgeous, the scenery is beautiful...

~*Author Tia Louise*

From Dust by Freya Barker is one of those special books. One of those whose plotline and characters remain with you for days after you finished it.

~*Jeri's Book Attic*

No amount of words could describe how this story made me feel, I think this is one I will remember forever, absolutely freaking awesome is not even close to how I felt about it.

Still Air was insightful, eye-opening, and I paused numerous times to think about my relationships with my own children. Anytime a book can evoke a myriad of emotions while teaching life lessons you'll continue to carry with you, it's a 5-star read.

In my opinion, there is nothing better than a Freya Barker book. With her final installment in her Portland, ME series, Still Air, she does not disappoint. From start to finish I was completely captivated by Pam, Dino, and the entire Portland family.

The one thing you can always be sure of with Freya's writing is that it will pull on ALL of your emotions; it's expressive, meaningful, sarcastic, so very true to life, real, hard-hitting and heartbreaking at times and, as is the case with this series especially, the story is at points raw, painful and occasionally fugly BUT it is also sweet, hopeful, uplifting, humorous and heart-warming.

ALSO BY FREYA BARKER

EDGE
OF
DARKNESS

FREYA BARKER

ISBN: 9781988733494

Cover Design:
Freya Barker

Editing:
Karen Hrdlicka

Proofing:
Joanne Thompson

Formatting:
CP Smith

ACKNOWLEDGMENTS

I've been blessed with an amazing group of loyal supporters. Without them most of you would not be reading my books. I would be lost without this group at my back.

Karen Hrdlicka and Joanne Thompson, my fabulous editing/proofreading team; Deb Blake, Pam Buchanan & Petra Gleason, my beta readers for Edge Of Darkness; and CP Smith for her fabulous formatting.

Perhaps less visible but equally important: Stephanie Phillips of SBR Media, my agent; Debra Presley & Drue Hoffman of Buoni Amici Press, my publicists; Krystal Weiss, my personal assistant; and finally all the wonderful bloggers, who spread the word of every new release.

Finally I'm very grateful for my readers. You take a chance on me with every new book you purchase and read, and I can't thank you enough for putting your faith in me.

I'm thankful to have you all by my side on this amazing journey!

Love you all.

EDGE OF DARKNESS

Road rash and Jack meets handcuffs and street smarts.

I am a wandering disaster.

A hedonist, a lover, a son, and a rebel.

My name is Yuma.

I'm sober enough to see the need for redemption, but too blind to realize I already found it.

I am an independent seeker.

An overachiever, a friend, a misfit, and a cop.

My name is Lissie.

I'm determined enough to find acceptance, but too stubborn to see all I need is my own.

We shouldn't get involved—all the odds are against us—but when bodies turn up on common ground and lines between duty and purpose get blurred, our future becomes clear.

FIND MORE OF MY BOOKS HERE!
(https://freyabarker.com)

EDGE
OF
DARKNESS

1

LISSIE

I LISTEN TO the conversation at the table with half an ear, but my attention is captured by the man sitting at the bar.

A biker: too-long, dirty blond hair tied back at the nape of his solid neck, slightly darker beard, worn jeans, and an old T-shirt covering his large frame. He's playing with a full shot glass, but only drinking from the tall glass.

Yuma.

He told me his name when I followed an investigative lead straight to the apartment building his motorcycle club owns and he manages. A stroke of luck, on more than one count, since it turned out to be a hot lead, but also had a vacancy sign on one of the apartment units.

Since I was in dire need of some better digs than the trailer I've been renting month-to-month once I moved here, I inquired about it.

After jumping through some hoops to qualify, I finally signed the one-year lease yesterday. It was a bit of a momentous occasion; my first real place on my own. Odd, for a thirty-seven-year-old woman, I know. I moved into one of the cabins dotting my family's ranch outside Albuquerque at twenty-four, and that's where I stayed until a few months ago when life took a left turn.

When the conversation at the table turns to one of my colleagues, Tony Ramirez, moving his girlfriend, Blue, into his home, my ears perk up. Coincidentally I'm supposed to move this weekend as well, but when Blackfoot asks me if I'm in for Blue's move, I tell him I'll be there. It's not like I have a ton to move myself. I can always bow out early and transfer my stuff in the afternoon or on Sunday.

When I look back to the bar, Yuma is gone, but the shot glass is still sitting there, untouched.

"NEED A HAND?"

My precarious hold on the queen-sized mattress I bought only two months ago slips, and it starts sliding back down the stairs. Given that the skies broke open in a late-afternoon summer downpour, I really don't want my new mattress to end up in a puddle in the parking lot.

"I've got it."

I still haven't seen who's attached to the deep voice, but I recognize it all the same. Yuma doesn't talk much, but every time he does it has impact. I've been trying to find excuses to get a little friendlier with him, and this is the perfect opportunity.

"Thank you." The bottom half of the mattress is suddenly lifted high and I can barely grab on to guide it through my front door.

"Keep going," he grunts, when I go to set it down. In the bedroom, I drop my end on the hardwood floor. "Where's the bed frame?"

"Haven't gotten around to that yet. Just drop it on the floor for now."

"You don't have a bed?"

He drops the mattress and I finally get a look at him. He's wet. As in, caught in the downpour kind of wet. It's a good look on him, even though he's making a puddle on my wood floors.

"Sure I do." I point at the mattress.

He pulls up a dubious eyebrow, but then drops the subject.

"Where's the rest of your shit?" he asks, already walking out of the apartment.

"Back of my truck."

I motion in the general direction and he takes off down the stairs, calling over his shoulder.

"Stay there."

"Yes, sir." I almost salute his barked order but he's not even looking at me.

It takes him half an hour to finish unloading the bed

of the truck I had loaded high and covered with a tarp. When he walks up with the last of my boxes, he hands it to me but stays outside on the walkway, leaning against the door opening.

"Nice truck."

"Thanks."

I grin. I love my black, heavy-duty GMC Sierra. I bought that truck early this year when the old Ford pickup I'd been driving since high school finally gave up the ghost. My family thought it was ridiculous for a girl to buy a *man's truck*, which only served as an incentive. Peter, the younger of my two older brothers, said some nasty shit, but what else is new? I can't help he blows through his money like water and can't afford one.

"Your friends couldn't give you a hand?"

"I'm new to town. Haven't made that many," I confess with a shrug.

"Saw you at The Irish the other day, looked like a group of friends to me. They couldn't help?" He pulls a do-rag from his back pocket and mops at his face, but keeps his eyes on me the whole time.

"I didn't ask. They were busy today and besides, it's not like I have a ton. I could manage." I swear he snorts, but I can't be sure since he has the bottom half of his face covered with his big hand. "I appreciate your help though," I quickly add.

The only response I get is a grunt. Then he raps his knuckles on the doorway and with a chin lift, turns on his heel and heads down the stairs, disappearing under the overhang.

Okay, so nix the hot chocolate I was about to offer him. So much for a friendly conversation over a hot beverage.

It's almost midnight by the time I have my sparse belongings put away and arranged the way I like them. The rain outside has stopped and I peek out the living room window to the river across the road. One of the many perks of this unit: hardwood flooring throughout, an updated kitchen complete with island, and a fabulous view of the Animas River.

The water is choppy and even by the light of the odd streetlight; I can see it streaming by. It reminds me of the creek running beside my old cabin back home.

I'm about to close the blinds when I hear an engine start up. A lone motorcycle crosses the parking lot and pulls out into the street. Its deep rumble still audible after the biker disappears from sight.

Yuma

I ride whenever temptation looms and it sure as fuck does tonight.

For the past three months, I've stayed in the small apartment off the office. I would sleep at the club, where I have a room, or at my place up the mountain, if I didn't think being at either of those places would send me right back down the hole I'm just climbing out of.

Some days everything is a temptation, even a hot fucking cop.

That's another thing I've gone cold turkey on— women. Or maybe I should say sex in general, since I'm afraid there were times I wasn't that discriminate. Sex and booze have gone hand in hand since I was a teenager. Part of that was growing up in an MC, where morals were loose and the law wasn't something we concerned ourselves with.

Things have changed in the past twelve or so years, since my dad handed Ouray the gavel. Fuck, was I pissed. I'd grown up the crown prince, thought my future was cemented by merit of my father's reign over the club. I played it off as a responsibility I didn't want—being president—but it stung.

Fuck that, it killed.

If I cared before, I certainly didn't give a shit after. The knowledge expectations were low anyway; I didn't even bother trying to change them. What was the point?

Momma got shot last year. Her body healed, but her mind started sliding. I got injured myself, not long after. The club was hit hard and everyone was pulling their weight to keep us afloat. Everyone except me, that is. I was too busy numbing myself with Jack and whatever else I could get my hands on.

Then one morning, I woke up and happened to catch the date on my phone. My birthday. My fortieth birthday. Fuck, when did that happen? My eyes were bloodshot in the bathroom mirror and I looked like death warmed over. Forty years old and I was fucking drinking myself into an early grave.

I got scared that morning four months ago. So scared, I drove myself to the club, still drunk, and asked for help. By nighttime, Trunk had me on a plane to Denver where I spent sixty days in an addiction treatment center.

The worst part of getting sober is discovering how low you've really sunk.

Coming home had been fucking torture. Everyone eyeing you like any minute you were going to fall off the wagon. Careful with what they say around you. Fucking awkward as hell. I jumped at the chance to take over the Riverside Apartments, needing something to keep me busy. Nights are tough, though. Momma used to say idle hands are the devil's playground; and I've never understood it as well as I do now.

I went to one AA meeting when I first came back, but sitting there, listening to everyone's goddamn sob story, had only made me more depressed. I haven't been back since.

Then the other night I found myself sitting at the bar at The Irish, ordering a shot. Fuck, that smell had my hands shaking. As some kind of personal challenge that I can lick this on my own, I kept that glass in front of me while asking for a glass of tap water on the side. I drank that. Then I spotted Detective Bucco sitting with a group of people, talking and laughing, and I knew if I didn't get out of there I'd lose my battle of wills with that damn shot glass.

It's so damn enticing to look for a hookup to keep the demons and loneliness at bay. That's what had me jump on my bike tonight. Even the fresh-faced detective in unit twenty-four—not at all my regular type, which usually veers toward stacked and easy—is too much of a temptation.

The lights are still on at the clubhouse when I come

through the gates. I'm not sure what I'm doing here, but I hope some brotherhood will do the trick.

Tse and Brick are sitting at the bar with a couple of beers. The moment Tse sees me coming in; he grabs both his and Brick's bottles and tucks them away behind the bar.

"What the fuck is that all about?" I snap, annoyed.

"You don't need to watch us drink, brother," Tse says.

"You know what I don't need? I don't need my brothers to fucking tiptoe around me."

"Good by me," Brick says dryly, leaning over the bar to grab his beer, taking a deep swig.

"Asshole," I grumble, pulling out a stool.

"You want something?" Tse asks when I sit down.

"Grab me a water, will ya?"

He tosses me a bottle and grabs fresh beers for him and Brick.

"So what are you doin' out in the middle of the night. Hot date?" Tse nudges me.

"Fuck no. I was just bored."

"Bored is bad," Brick says, giving me the side-eye.

He's about ten years older, and joined the Arrow's Edge just last year. Decent guy, from what I can tell, although I haven't had much opportunity to hang out with him. His comment is on point, though, and I wonder if he knows what that's like.

"Very bad."

"You going to meetings?"

I glare at him, about to launch a "*What the fuck is it to you*" at him when I catch myself. His gaze is steady and unwavering, dead serious. A quick glance at Tse shows him equally serious.

"No," I bite off. "Went to one and that was enough. Not big on sitting in a circle, sharing sob stories, and singing fucking 'Kumbaya.'"

Brick chuckles and takes a swig of his beer.

"More than one meeting in town, brother. Not all of them are in a church basement."

"And you know this how?"

He shrugs. "You're not the first alcoholic I know."

I'm not an idiot, I know what I am—sixty days sobering up in a treatment center made sure of that—but hearing someone slap that label on me still doesn't feel good.

2

LISSIE

"BUCCO!"

Ramirez sticks his head around the doorway and I quickly shove my private file into my desk drawer.

We share the large office space—separated by dividers—between the four detectives. It makes communication a lot easier, but it means I have to be careful guarding what I'm not ready to share. Not yet.

"Yeah?"

"We've got an issue at the new subdivision they're building near Hesperus."

"What kind of issue?"

"They've dug up a body."

My attention piqued, I scoot my chair back and shove my cell phone in my pocket.

"Let's go."

It takes us ten minutes to get to the new development just west of town. It's clear the building is done in phases. Right off the road there is a row of houses that look finished. Another small section is under construction, but it's the area where only some excavation is visible on the back end of the property, where a couple of cruisers are parked and a crowd has gathered.

"What've we got?"

One of the officers, Jay VanDyken, is waiting at the perimeter by the hole.

"It's kinda ripe," he shares. "Victim is male, my guess he hasn't been down there longer than a couple of weeks."

"Any identification on him?"

"Don't know. Waiting for the crime scene techs to get here."

"What about the coroner?" I ask him.

"New guy is on his way in."

We've been short a coroner since Doc Franco became ill, but last week we were told a replacement had been found. We just haven't had the pleasure yet.

"Let's have a look at the body," Tony announces, ducking under the caution tape.

I reluctantly follow him. Not my favorite part of an investigation, but a necessary one.

The smell hits me within a few feet of the edge of the hole. The ripe, heavy smell of death gets into everything. I know I'll have to strip the moment I get home and get my clothes into the washer before I scrub myself in the shower. Even then, I'll still be smelling death days from now.

The fact I don't do well with death is a well-kept secret. I'm from a long line of law enforcement and my father and brothers would never have let me live it down if they knew.

Yes, everyone in my family is a cop. My grandpa had been, my father still is, and both my brothers are too. The only girl in the family, and the youngest, I grew up dreaming of becoming a cop as well. Mom supported that dream—she would've supported anything I set my mind to—but she passed away when I was thirteen. Dad and the boys, not so much. I had some hope when Dad remarried two years later, but Elsa was all about the ranch and never understood my ambitions.

I'd been a cop for close to ten years before the ribbing and ridiculing finally wore off, only to turn into anger and vitriol last year. Turns out, I handle taunting better than I handle outrage. Or dead bodies, for that matter.

"Not much left to identify him," Ramirez points out.

There isn't. His face is barely recognizable as such, and I immediately consider that someone had to be plenty pissed to inflict that kind of injury.

"Whoever killed him knew him, and didn't particularly like him," I point out.

"Understatement of the year…" Tony says, pulling a pen from his pocket to move aside the jacket the victim appears to be wearing. I suppress a shudder. "…seeing as this is a bullet hole in his chest. Overkill, if you ask me."

I pull out my phone and do a quick online check.

"He died sometime in the past three weeks," I announce.

"Where'd you get that?"

"That heat wave ended three weeks ago. Daytime temps have stayed pretty mild, but the nights have gotten pretty chilly. He's wearing a coat, which tells me this happened at night or very early in the morning," I clarify, walking around the body.

"I agree with that assessment," a woman's voice sounds behind us, making all three of us turn.

A gray-haired woman dressed in jeans and a blue windbreaker is looking down on us from the edge of the excavation.

"And you are?" VanDyken asks, an edge to his voice.

"Meredith Carter. Dr. Meredith Carter."

Ah. Our new coroner is obviously a woman. Ramirez regroups quickly and holds out a hand to help her down into the hole. As she steps down, I notice her purple Doc Martens and I glance back up to her face. On closer examination, our new coroner is much younger than the gray hair implied.

"Tony Ramirez, and this is Lissie Bucco and Jay VanDyken, he was first on scene."

"Perfect," she says, pointing at the officer. "Then you can give me a hand." She tosses a pair of latex gloves at him, dons a pair herself, and bends down over the body, not waiting to see if he follows suit or not.

Tony grins and comes to stand next to me, his arms crossed over his chest.

"Do you get the sense we're witnessing some kind of

power conflict here?"

"There does seem to be some tension," I agree quietly. "Interesting."

We stand there, quietly observing Dr. Carter as she has Jay roll the body over, when Tony breaks the silence.

"So how's the new place working out?"

"Love it. I can cross the bridge and walk to the City Market in five minutes. It's perfect."

"I'm glad it's working out. Getting along with your landlord?"

I turn and find his inquisitive eyes on me.

"Yeah. Hardly see him."

Not face-to-face anyway. I've heard his bike and watched him drive off a few more times these past couple of weeks, but I haven't actually spoken to him since he helped me move in. Maybe I should talk to him about that dripping faucet in the bathroom.

Then Tony surprises me when he says, "Probably best."

YUMA

"I HOPE I didn't drag you from something important."

I look up at Lisa, who not only lives in unit twenty-three with her two grandchildren, but also works at the club. Last year when she arrived in Durango, she needed a job, and the club was in need of someone to take over for Momma, who was recovering from her injury. Momma never fully recovered and Lisa stayed on.

Right now she has a window with a crack in it,

courtesy of her five-year-old granddaughter, Kiara, who is standing in the corner of her bedroom, eyeing me with big scared eyes.

"Nothing important," I reassure Lisa, before turning to the little girl. "What happened?" I immediately feel like an ogre when her eyes well up.

"Well?" Lisa prompts her. "Tell Mr. Yuma why the window broke."

"I throwed my ball." She points at a softball lying on the ground. "Ezrah throws his ball all the time."

"Ezrah's ball is foam, baby—your ball is hard."

"I didn't know." Her bottom lip starts quivering and her face crumples.

"I can fix it," I quickly announce, not a fan of tears. "I was gonna change out some of these windows anyway. Gonna measure and head to Home Depot."

It's not exactly a lie, about changing out the windows. Last year a lot of the units got new sliding doors to the balconies and new windows, but none on this side of the building have been replaced yet. If I'm gonna do one window, I may as well do them all.

Fifteen minutes later, I walk out of twenty-three and look over at twenty-four. Elizabeth Bucco, that's the name on her lease. Except, she doesn't strike me as an Elizabeth. It's too stiff; too formal for the girl-next-door vibe she gives off. Then again, she doesn't look like a cop either. She seems normal, straightforward, and unlike most women I encounter.

It's the middle of the day and her truck isn't here. I already knew that because I watched her drive off early this morning. If I'm not fucking careful, I'm replacing one addiction with another. Her.

And I don't even know her.

I dial Ouray's number on my way to my bike.

"Yeah."

"I need Wapi for the day."

"For?"

"Getting a start on the rest of those window replacements. Could use a hand."

It's quiet for a moment on the other end before he responds.

"Thought you wanted to wait for spring."

I had told him that a while ago.

"Changed my mind."

"Anything happen?"

"Nah, just need something for my hands to do."

"Gotcha. Yeah, I'll send Wapi."

"Tell him to meet me at Home Depot with the truck. Headin' there now."

I don't have to wait long for Wapi. He drives up in one of the club trucks five minutes after I park.

"Did you bring tools?" I ask, when he gets out of the truck.

"Yup. Small compressor's in the back too."

"Good."

In the end, we were only able to get three windows and one sliding door, but what I'll need for the remaining three apartments is ordered from the warehouse and should be delivered tomorrow.

Lisa already left for the club by the time we get to

her apartment, and we get to work right away. We're just putting the second window when I hear Wapi, who's holding the window in place, whistle softly between his teeth.

"Nice," he drags out, just as I see her coming up the stairs.

"Watch it," I growl. "Off-limits."

I can feel him looking at me, but I'm too busy following her progress. At the last moment, she spots me in her neighbor's window and throws me a smile and a wave.

"Hold this," I tell Wapi and take off out the door.

I just catch her before she can close the door behind her.

"Don't come too close," she says with an apologetic smile. I automatically take a step back. "I spent the afternoon at a crime scene. I'm pretty sure I smell."

Yeah, she doesn't even try to be anything other than she is.

"Quick heads up, we're upgrading windows in a few units and I'm gonna need to get into yours at some point this week."

"Okay. Do you need me to be home? My schedule can be—"

"No," I interrupt. "I've got a key."

"Of course," she replies, looking a bit flustered, a soft blush coloring her cheeks.

It's a good look on her: a hint of innocence to contrast the invitation of that generous mouth and the mysteries behind those brown eyes.

I don't even realize I'm staring at her until she mumbles, "I really should have a shower."

"Right." I give myself a shake and force my feet to start moving. "Later."

I barely hear her response; a mental image of her in the shower has me rush back into the apartment next door.

"Who's that?" Wapi asks when I walk in.

"New tenant," I grunt, as I go back to shimming the window in the frame.

"Lucky bastard," Wapi mumbles under his breath, and I throw a sharp glance his way.

"She's a cop." I'm not sure if I'm warning Wapi or myself at this point.

We work in silence after that. Three bedroom windows are done when I call it a night. It'll be dark before we'll get the slider in, so it'll have to wait until tomorrow.

"What time?" Wapi asks when we get the tools cleaned up.

"Nine, and pick up some donuts."

"Gotcha."

I watch him drive off before I turn back to the small apartment beside the building office. Back to the quiet oppression of those four walls. When my eyes drift up to her front door, I abruptly turn around and aim for my bike. Everywhere I fucking turn, bad decisions are pulling at me.

I ride without a real purpose other than distraction, but even as the sun is starting to sink behind the mountains, I feel the need for something more burning a hole in my gut. Breaking out in a sweat, I pull off on the side of the road. I fish my wallet from my back pocket to look for the piece of paper Brick handed me a few weeks ago.

It's the schedule for meetings at a community clubhouse, not too far from the apartments, but right now I'm on the other side of town up in the mountains. Even if I hustle, I'll be late. I don't even know if they'll let me in once a meeting has started.

I realize I'm creating excuses, which is something I've been very good at. My life, until the day Trunk put me on that plane, had been a continuous stream of excuses. At the center they didn't put up with that, but it's still an easy trap for me to fall into.

Knowing I need to pull myself out of this spiral, I shove the paper and my wallet back into my pocket and aim my bike back to town.

I find a spot in the busy lot, park, hang my lid off the handlebar, and take a deep breath in. Here goes nothing.

Handwritten signs direct me to a large room, set up as a theatre, which allows me to slip into the back row without drawing too much attention. Better than the circle of chairs at the church.

"I see a few new faces," the guy at the front points out. "Maybe this is a good time to introduce ourselves."

One by one people stand up, and I sink farther down in my seat, not quite ready to do anything but listen. But the next moment I sit up straight, my eyes drawn to the person speaking.

3

LISSIE

"MY NAME IS Lissie, and I'm an alcoholic."

My knees are wobbly and I'm sick to my stomach, as I feel all eyes in the room on me. It's the first time I've said out loud what I've denied myself to be for more years than I care to admit.

I've never been a stumbling drunk, but vodka became my numbing agent of choice somewhere in my early twenties. At first it was hidden in girly mixes tasting more like Kool-Aid, just so I didn't have to feel the sharp taste of the alcohol, but eventually I drank it straight, welcoming the slow burn down my esophagus.

I never drank during my shifts, but the moment I'd get home, after dealing with the dark side of humanity all day long, my bottle was waiting for me to wash away all that ailed me. There was a lot that would stick to me—too much—but I'd never found anything that would work its magic like a couple of shots did.

I'd looked up meetings as soon as I moved here. I'd never went to any back in Albuquerque, for fear of bumping into someone who might get word back to my family. A futile attempt to hide what ended up becoming the weapon my father wielded to bend me to his will. Memories of that confrontation still cut sharp and reinforce my need to stay sober.

Which is why, after today, I needed more than my own will holding me up.

The few meetings I attended here before I sat quietly in the back, absorbing the strength of others as they shared their stories. Tonight just listening is not enough.

"Hi, Lissie," the communal mumble goes up, and I dart a quick glance around the room before sitting back down.

Somewhere behind me, I hear the next person introduce himself and I cast a look over my shoulder when my eyes freeze on a familiar figure.

Shit.

I can't escape the intensity of his blue eyes as he stares at me attentively. There isn't much else I can read from his blank expression and it makes me feel like a bug under a microscope. I straighten in my seat, barely able to focus on what is being said.

It makes sense now, the scene at the bar. It also makes things a little more complicated.

I hold no illusions I could keep the attention of a guy like Yuma. Not on a romantic level anyway, but what I'm looking for doesn't require romantic, or long term. All I need is a foot in the door and an AA meeting could be a good place to find common ground.

Unfortunately, by the time the group jointly recites the acceptance prayer and falls on the refreshments set out in the adjoining kitchen, the chair where Yuma was sitting earlier is empty.

I head straight home. Forfeiting the pastries I can do without—all they do is gather on my ass—using fatigue as an excuse with Frank, the middle-aged banker who volunteered to be my sponsor at the first meeting I attended. I'm not a blabber by nature, and the fact he spilled his life story within five minutes of meeting me had me hesitate to accept his offer. I got the distinct sense he was more interested in a sounding board for his divorce woes than he was providing a failsafe for me.

I'm still on the fence about the whole sponsorship thing. I can see the benefits for some, but I don't make friends easily because I don't trust easily. I have my reasons.

The craving for sweets is persistent, so I stop at the City Market on my way home and raid the bakery department. Good thing I have more than one size of jeans in my closet.

"Is that your truck?"

Ezrah, the boy who lives with his sister and grandmother in the apartment next door, is sitting on the steps when I get out of my truck. I stop and grin up at him.

"Yup. All mine."

"Never seen no chick drive a truck like that."

I swallow a chuckle at the *chick* label. Before I have a chance to respond, Lisa appears at the top of the stairs. When she first introduced herself to me as the kids' grandmother, I had trouble believing it. She looks way too young.

"Ezrah. Get your bony ass inside and finish your homework, boy."

He grudgingly gets up and drags his butt up the stairs, mumbling something under his breath, for which he earns a flick to the back of his head.

"Mind your manners."

"Night, Ms. Bucco," he dutifully complies.

"Call me Lissie, Ezrah. Night."

I climb up the stairs where Lisa is shaking her head, watching her grandson go inside their apartment.

"I swear that boy is growing sassier by the day," she mutters. "Thought enrolling him in regular school this year would be good for him, but I'm wondering if it's that good for me."

"Handful?"

"You have no idea. Anyway," she says, pointing at my grocery bags. "I'm sure you have stuff that needs to be put away, and I better get in there and make sure he's doing what he's supposed to."

"You know, if you ever want time off, I don't mind keeping an eye on them, if I'm home," I find myself offering.

I'm not sure what's come over me, because A, I don't have any real experience with kids, and B, I'm not usually this socially forthcoming.

"That's sweet," Lisa answers. "But I wouldn't do that to you unless I was in a real bind. Appreciate the offer through."

"No problem." I wave it off a little awkwardly, feeling dumb for even having offered. The woman doesn't know me from Adam.

"But you know, maybe one of these days you'd like to pop in for coffee?" she suggests. "Lights are on means I'm home. Just knock. It would be nice to talk someone other than a couple of kids or a bunch of grunting bikers."

"Bikers?"

"I work at Arrow's Edge MC," she explains. "But that's a story for another day."

I know Lisa and her grandkids were the victims of the American Nationalist League group the FBI had been investigating. The same group kidnapped Jamie and Trunk's little boy, River, last year. You learn a lot over the coffee pot in a police station.

"Sounds intriguing. I'll pop in when I get a chance," I promise, as I fish my keys from my pocket and open the door to my apartment.

I quickly turn on lights and take my bags to the kitchen, where I put everything but the massive cinnamon bun I scored away. Most days I'm happy for the sounds of life that filter through from the apartment next door, but tonight it only makes me feel more alone.

The massive bite I take out of the sticky pastry only

makes me feel moderately better.

YUMA

DIDN'T SEE THAT coming.

I recognized her voice, but still I needed my eyes to prove to myself it was really her. The same woman I visualized having a shower ever since leaving her apartment earlier that night.

It was her all right, even with her usual stern ponytail in a sloppy bun, there was no denying that lush ass. There may not be more than a handful up top, but the curves on her bottom half sure make up for it. Fuck if I know why, when tits have always had my attention; I'm suddenly focused on this woman's ass.

I thought the name Elizabeth didn't suit her. Hearing her call herself Lissie fits much better.

The moment I realized I was in an AA meeting drooling over her, I bailed. So many things wrong with the direction my thoughts wanted to go.

They say to avoid romantic entanglements at least until you've passed the one-year sober mark. Not that I'm envisioning anything remotely romantic. Carnal, yes, but not romantic. I'm sure banging a fellow alcoholic is breaking all the rules.

Sonofabitch, I need to get my head in check.

"Hand me a shim." I grab it from him and slide it between the window and the casing to get it snug.

We did Lisa's sliding door this morning and have moved on to her neighbor's apartment. It struck me when

I walked in, how bare it is. I already knew she didn't have a lot of furniture, but seeing the single loveseat with some kind of upholstered footstool in front of that flat-screen TV looks a little lonely. Hell, even the much smaller apartment I have downstairs is better outfitted than this one.

Aside from the bathroom and bedrooms behind doors off to one side, the rest of the apartments are all open concept; making this one look almost cavernous with the sparse furnishings. A dining table is missing and the kitchen peninsula has two simple wooden stools, which indicate the detective is not exactly equipped for entertaining.

With the shims in place, it doesn't take long to frame the living room window. Next up is the bedroom in the front. This room has more personality and what it reveals surprises me. Far prettier and more colorful than I would've expected from an Elizabeth, but perfect for a Lissie. The lady has layers. *Fuck.*

We're halfway through installing this second window when I spot the truck pulling into her parking space. A quick glance at my phone shows it's a little past four. I'd hoped to have this window done and be out of here before she got home.

She looks a little green around the gills when she walks up the stairs, barely acknowledging Wapi holding her bedroom window in place on the gallery out front. I quickly set a few shims as I hear her walking in. A thump, followed by a second one, and then a deep sigh is audible on this side of the wall.

I spray sealer in the spaces around the window and twenty minutes later we have it framed. When I carry my tools out of the bedroom, I spot her lying on the couch, watching some home renovation show on TV with the sound muted.

"You okay?"

Her head turns and she doesn't just look green around the gills, her eyes look haunted.

"Fine," she says without much conviction, before turning back to the TV.

I carry my tools outside where Wapi is waiting.

"Change of plans. The last window and those sliders are gonna have to wait."

"She okay?" he asks, trying to look past me into the apartment.

"Not your concern. You're done for today."

Without another word, I step back inside and close the door in his face. Lissie doesn't notice until I start walking toward the loveseat. Then she glances over her shoulder. Everything screams at me to get the fuck out of here, but the look I see in her eyes keeps me moving forward. She doesn't even look surprised I'm here; she's so far up in her head.

"What happened?"

I sit down on the armrest farthest from her—which isn't saying much given the size of the couch—and watch her blink a few times. A slightly sickly smell emanates from her.

"Autopsy. Not my strong suit. Especially when the body is ripe." My inner wince must've been obvious on the outside because she adds, "I swear the stench sticks to my skin. Seems every time we meet I smell. I don't usually."

"It's not that bad," I lie and she knows it. "Nothing a shower won't fix."

She immediately pushes up off the couch.

"I think I will. Sorry if interrupted your work, didn't know I was gonna be home so early."

"We were breaking for the day anyway."

Neither of us addresses the bigger elephant in the room, and when she disappears into her bedroom and closes the door, I'm pretty sure the smart thing to do would be to get the hell out of here. Instead I pull out my phone and order a pizza.

We both have to eat.

Twenty minutes later she comes sauntering in, wearing men's flannel pants and an oversized T-shirt. She seems surprised I'm still here, I just moved from the armrest onto the couch.

"Oh."

I push up and walk into the kitchen. "Got us pizza. Where's your plates?"

It takes her a few seconds to get with the game, but then she moves toward one of the cupboards, pulling down a couple of plates.

"Glasses over the sink and tea in the fridge," she says over her shoulder, opening the pizza box.

"Sweet?" I ask cautiously.

"Unsweetened."

Fucking perfect.

We eat in silence, sitting at the counter. Lissie surprises me by eating three pieces while I kill off the rest of the pie. When she gets up to put the plates in the dishwasher, I ask the question that exposes the elephant.

"How long?"

Her movements still.

"Eight months," she finally says. "You?"

"Bout half'a that," I admit grudgingly.

I watch her turn around and open her mouth for what I assume is the next question, when my phone rings.

"Yeah."

"Brother…" Ouray's voice sounds solemn and my whole body goes on alert.

"What?" I snap, the hair on my neck on end.

"It's Momma."

ARROW'S EDGE MC

4

LISSIE

I WAKE UP from another restless night.

It's been like that since Yuma stormed out of here a couple of days ago with no more than an "I gotta go." I haven't seen him or heard from him since. I eventually put his toolbox, which he'd left outside my door on the gallery, in my apartment, where it still sits.

Add to that, the case of the dead guy found in the new development is one big question mark. We haven't even been able to identify the guy. That's what had made me almost puke in the morgue, the discovery someone— with great precision—removed any identifiable marks from the guy's body. Not a tooth left in his mouth or recovered for that matter. No fingerprints, since the tip of each finger had been cut off. We know he was somewhere between thirty-five and fifty-five. We know he was five foot eleven and a smoker. We even know at some point in his life he had an appendectomy. But none of those things are enough to identify him by.

I stretch and groan at the stiffness in my muscles and fling back the covers. A quick glance at my alarm shows five thirty and I groan again before swinging my legs over the edge.

The plan for today is to try and catch some of the guys at the construction site we haven't been able to question yet, and it's easier to catch them when they get there than to chase them all over the large development. I had no idea how many tradesmen, suppliers, and contractors visit a construction project on any given day. Since we can't even pinpoint the exact day our vic was buried, we need to talk to basically everyone who's ever set foot on the site.

I step into the shower, and this time I groan because the hot water pelting down on my back feels really good. It doesn't stop my mind from churning though.

Cases like this one—where we're basically grasping at straws—eat at me. I get so invested everything else gets ignored, which is why, when I walk out of my front door with a bagel shoved in my mouth, I squarely run into a really hard, wide chest.

"Fuck me," Yuma mutters, steadying me.

I rescue breakfast from my mouth before mumbling an apology, trying not to spray the man.

"I'm looking for my tools."

No hello, sorry I ran out of here the other day. No hey,

how are you? It's enough to bring out the bitch in me, but check myself. He bought me pizza after a bad day, that's all. He doesn't owe me a damn thing.

"I put them inside. I was afraid someone was going to take off with them." Pushing open the door, I gesture at his toolbox sitting in my hall. "There they are."

I try not to be offended when he grabs them and immediately starts walking away. There's something about the clenched jaw visible underneath the scruffy beard that tells me he's not just being rude.

"Yuma? Are you okay?" I call after him. I half-expect him to keep moving and am surprised when he stops and turns.

The man has gorgeous blue eyes that, right now, look tormented. He doesn't say anything, simply staring at me.

"Yuma?" I take a step toward him, but a tight shake of his head stops me.

"I can't," he says, regret filling his voice, before he heads down the stairs, leaving me to stare after him until he gets to a truck parked below and looks up. "New windows will have to wait."

I open my mouth to tell him not to worry about that, but he's already getting into the passenger seat.

Shaking off the entire incident, I shut and lock my door, and head to work.

"So the plans were changed?"

I nod, spreading the copy of the plans I was able to get from the foreman on site this morning.

"Here, look." I point out where the current excavation is. "This was supposed to be the final phase." Then I indicate what was shown as phase three. "This section was originally marked as phase three, but…" I roll out the next set of plans. "…a little over three weeks ago, the developer decided to reprioritize the remaining phases."

"Why?" Keith Blackfoot wants to know, but I can only shrug my shoulders.

"Not a clue. Guess that's something we'll have to look into."

"Did you guys notice this?" Tony taps his finger on the revised plans. "They flipped the layout of this section. The original design had a road separating this phase from the one just south of it, but they changed it, so that now the green space is what separates the two rows of houses."

"How is that significant?" Keith asks.

"It implies whoever put that body there, likely didn't know about the change in plans," I propose. "Why else would you go through the trouble of burying someone if you know he'll be dug up anyway. If plans had remained the same, that body would have been covered by designated green space."

Keith nods appreciatively.

"Makes sense. At least if our suspect is associated with the project. We don't know that for sure. Could be an outsider trying to shine a spotlight on the development."

"True. So where do we go from here?"

"Gather info," the chief contributes. "Dig up anyone with a financial stake in the development, down to subcontractors. Knowing that will serve us in both of those possible scenarios." He turns to me with a grin. "Good catch, Bucco."

"Thanks, Chief."

The meeting breaks up and I roll up the plans I spread out on the conference table. As the guys walk ahead of me down the hallway, I catch bits of banter between them.

"Joe, can I have Bucco as my partner? She's prettier than Tony *and* smart."

The chief chuckles.

"Fuck you, Blackfoot," Ramirez grumbles.

And I walk behind them grinning.

YUMA

"HOW'S SHE DOIN'?"

Ouray is waiting for me in the hallway outside.

"Out. Finally."

It was just a matter of time.

In the past year, my mother has gone from strong club matriarch who could intimidate the meanest badass, to an old woman lost in her own little world. Four days ago, she wandered off into the woods. Nosh, my father, had been up at the gun range just north of the compound. When he dropped in at their house, just steps away from the clubhouse to check on Momma, she was gone.

We didn't find her until early the next morning,

half-frozen up in the mountains. We figure she'd gone looking for Nosh and got lost. The incident triggered a discussion no one was looking forward to and my father was outright resisting. It took Ouray, Trunk, and myself to convince him, but he finally had to concede the current situation wasn't safe for Momma.

This afternoon we moved her into a home. That did not go over well.

Nosh wanted to stay, but staff said it would be an easier adjustment for her if he didn't. I finally put my foot down and told Trunk to take him home, but the moment he was gone, Momma put up a fight. At some point she slapped one of the nurses. I had to physically restrain her so they could give her a sedative.

I thought Ouray had left as well, but apparently he waited around for me.

"Even with her mind gone, she's a fighter," he observes, as we walk to the exit.

I just grunt. I'm fucking done. Today was the ultimate day from hell, following in a long line of them. This is one of those nights I know will be a struggle. Still, when Ouray asks if I want to come back to the clubhouse with him, I decline. One confrontation a day with my father is enough.

"Just drop me at the apartment."

"You know he doesn't mean half of what he says," Ouray suggests, reading me clearer than I'm comfortable with. "Hard on him to see Momma like this. He's been trying hard to keep things as close to normal as they used to be, and I'm sure it feels like he failed."

"And his son's failed him too," I add, unable to keep the bitterness from my tone.

"That kinda talk does no one any good, brother. You did the right thing goin' to Denver."

That had been the one cutting deepest of the accusations Nosh tossed my way. Making it sound like I was being selfish, running off to Denver and abandoning my mother when she needed me most.

She'd still been occasionally lucid then, would recognize me every so often, but when I got back, two months later, she had a hard time placing me. So yes, I fucking feel guilty enough without my father helping.

"Thanks for helpin'," I tell Ouray when he pulls up in front of the building.

"Goes without sayin'. Momma's special to all of us." He turns in his seat. "You sure you'll be okay?"

I look out the front window and notice the lights in the apartment upstairs on.

"I think so."

I reach for the door.

"Call me if anything changes, yeah?"

"Yeah."

Ouray takes off the moment I get out of his truck and I stand, undecided, at the bottom of the stairs.

I stood here this morning looking up, determined my life was already fucked up enough, but here I am again. Drawn like a moth to the flame.

My name is Lissie, and I'm an alcoholic.

I've already lifted my foot on the first tread before I make the conscious decision. I pause briefly at her door, but let myself knock anyway.

"Hey," she says, a hesitant smile on her face.

I can't blame her; she must think I'm off my meds or something. Guess I kinda am.

"Hey."

For a long moment we stare at each other, but then she steps aside without a word and I walk past her.

"I made some stir-fry. I was just about to eat in front of the TV," she chatters, passing me when I stop in her living room. In the kitchen she grabs a couple of bowls and two glasses from a cupboard. "I'll get us some food. Wanna grab us some tea?"

I keep waiting for her to ask what the hell I'm doing here, but she doesn't. She acts like me walking into her apartment is the most natural thing in the world. At her request, I grab the pitcher of tea from her fridge and fill the glasses.

"Just bring them inside, I'll bring the bowls. Chop sticks or a fork?"

"Fork." I pull over the stools again to serve as TV tables. "You need more furniture."

"I know." She grins, walking up and handing me a bowl and a fork, sitting down beside me on the couch. "I was waiting to get a proper place, but I've been busy with work since I moved in here." She shifts in her seat and seems to be looking for something. "Are you sitting on the remote?"

I shove a hand under my ass and come up with the remote she takes from me, turning on the TV to a news station. She doesn't seem to expect me to talk, so I focus on eating.

"It's good."

"Thanks. Hope you like it spicy, I gave it a good kick."

"I can tell." Beads of sweat break out on my forehead at the burn.

I almost smile when she starts muttering under her breath at the news report on the current political climate. I don't have to guess where her loyalties lie.

It's not until after we're done with dinner, and I take our bowls to the kitchen, that she looks at me with a question in her eyes.

"Are you okay, Yuma?"

"No."

"Would you like to talk about it?"

I sense no pressure in her question, only an offer. I sit back down beside her, my eyes on the screen.

"I'm not a good person, Lissie." I can feel her looking at me, but she doesn't say a word. "Broken the law, did drugs, fucked anything with a pulse, been drinking to numb myself since I was a teen, and I'm a constant disappointment to the people in my life."

I'm not sure if I'm telling her this because I need to say it out loud, or maybe I just want to shock her. Either way, she surprises me when she says, "I hear you."

I chance a look at her and find no judgment in her eyes. No shock, no revulsion, no pity, and no disappointment.

"Had to put my mother in a home today. She's dementing." I snort derisively. "That's an understatement. Be more honest to say her mind's already departed."

That gets a reaction.

"That must've been so hard to do," she says softly, putting a hand on my arm.

Suddenly I really want to kiss her, but instead I get up abruptly.

"I should go."

"Okay." She doesn't urge me to stay or ask me to leave; she simply acknowledges my intent. "My door is always open. Talk, or don't talk. The couch is small but you're welcome to it any time."

She follows me to the front door where I turn to face her, but I don't know what to say. She smiles and steps close, slipping her arms around my waist, giving me a brief hug. I don't even have the presence of mind to hug her back. It's been so long.

I feel her loss as soon as she steps back, but I find my words.

"Thank you."

ARROW'S EDGE MC

5

LISSIE

I ROLL OVER, reaching for my sidearm on the nightstand.

Concentrating on the sounds that woke me up, I swing my legs over the side, and on bare feet slip out of the bedroom.

There's that scratching at the door again, but this time it's followed by the sound of the lock turning. I press my body against the narrow stretch of wall between the window and the front door and raise my gun.

"Don't fucking move."

The figure pushing open my door has one foot inside when he freezes in his tracks at the sound of my voice.

"The fuck are you standing there for? Move out of the way."

Yuma's voice startles me.

I haven't seen him since he stood at my door quite unexpectedly a couple of days ago. He'd looked lost and haunted, and I instinctively recognized the precariously faint line separating hard-fought sobriety from the dangerous slip back into a bottle. So I let him in.

"The gun aimed at me says different, brother," the guy at the end of my barrel rumbles casually.

Jesus. I blow out a breath and lower my gun.

"Better."

I take in the man in front of me. Large, dark, and a bit on the husky side, with part of a tattoo snaking out of the top of his leather cut, along his neck, and disappearing in the hairline of his buzz cut behind his ear. *Brother*. One of the Arrow's Edge members.

"Tse, man. Move out of the way." Yuma appears behind him, his eyes locking on me right away. "Shit. Didn't know you were home, Lissie. Your truck isn't here."

I will my heart rate back to an acceptable level as I walk through my apartment to the kitchen, dropping my gun on the counter.

"Dropped it off for an oil change last night," I explain, setting about making a pot of coffee. "I'm off this morning."

Behind me I hear movement. When I turn around, the new guy is standing in the middle of my living room and Yuma is stalking toward me.

"You wanna put some clothes on?" he says in a low voice, his eyes trailing down my body. I'm hardly indecent, wearing men's boxer shorts and an oversized tee.

"Not on my account," Tse comments with a provocative grin.

"Fuck off," Yuma grumbles, blocking the guy's view while crowding me. "Clothes," he repeats impatiently.

"I'm wearing clothes," I snap, annoyed.

"Don't mind me," Tse announces, pulling out a stool and sitting down. "I'll just sit here and enjoy the show."

"Please…"

The plea is reflected in Yuma's eyes and I realize this may be about more than him being a bossy jerk. I nod sharply and without a look at his friend, I slip down the hall and into the bedroom.

When I get back to the kitchen, dressed appropriately and my hair no longer a bird's nest, Yuma is pulling mugs from the cupboard.

"Was hoping to finish up your apartment today," he says, pouring coffee and handing out mugs like he's the one living here.

"That's fine. Once my truck is ready, I have some running around to do anyway. I'll stay out of your way." I turn to the rough-looking biker sitting at my counter and stick out my hand, which he takes in his big paw. "I'm Lissie. Sorry about earlier."

"Tse," he rumbles with that almost lascivious grin. "And don't apologize. Haven't been that turned on in a long time."

Yuma unexpectedly hauls out and slaps the guy upside his head, only making him grin wider.

"Fuckin' drink up and let's get started." Tse winks at me and tosses back his coffee when Yuma turns back to me. "We'll tackle the small window in the bathroom first. Leave the sliding doors last."

"Whatever works."

I pull my laundry basket out of the bathroom so they can move around, which leads to actually doing the laundry. It takes them less time to install that window than it does me to pull my first load from the dryer. My phone rings just as they're starting to pull the trim off the doorframe.

"Truck's ready. We had to put new brake pads on, though."

"What do you mean, you had to put brake pads on? I brought it in for an oil change."

It's not the first time a mechanic's trying to pull a fast one on me, and I won't stand for it. They see what they think is a hapless woman and con them into expenses that aren't necessary.

I notice Yuma walking up, throwing an inquisitive glance my way. I give a brief shake of my head and turn away.

"Standard to check the brakes, ma'am."

"Bullshit. Even if it was, and even if it needed new pads, you had no right to do any work I didn't authorize beforehand."

The patronizing chuckle on the other side works like a red flag on a bull.

"Ma'am, we can't have you driving an unsafe vehicle."

Instead of answering, I end the call and shove my phone in my pocket, moving to the front door. Behind me I hear Yuma saying something to Tse, but I don't know what until I notice him following me out of the apartment.

"Hold up. I'll take you."

I start to tell him he doesn't need to when I realize I have no transportation. I nod instead, but when I see him walk toward his bike I have second thoughts.

"On that?"

"Yup," he states, lifting up the seat and pulling out a helmet. He fits it over my head, fastens the strap under my chin, and swings his leg over the bike before holding out a hand.

"You coming?"

I take his hand and put my foot on a peg he indicates. I'd be lying if I said I wasn't just a little bit excited climbing on behind him. I rest my hands loosely on his shoulders, but he moves them to his stomach, pulling my arms around him so I'm flush against him.

"Hold on," he says over his shoulder, before he starts the engine.

I feel the vibrations under me, which isn't exactly an unpleasant feeling. I'm a bit tense when he first pulls out on the road, but soon relax into the ride. It's not until he pulls up to the auto shop and parks beside my truck that my anger resurfaces.

Inside the open bay, the owner I just talked to on the phone wipes his hands on a cloth as he watches me dismount. I quickly take off the helmet, and hand it to

Yuma.

"Thanks for the ride," I tell him, before turning and walking at a decent clip toward the garage.

I've taken just a few steps when I hear Yuma's footfalls behind me.

YUMA

LIKE HELL I'M going to leave her here and drive off.

I understood enough from her side of the conversation to know that some douche mechanic is trying to pull a fast one on her. She didn't exactly sound like she needed help handling him, but there's a reason I took her here on the bike, wearing my cut. I won't have to say a damn thing. If the guy has half a brain cell, he'll think twice about giving her a hard time.

"Ma'am?"

Even though the smug asshole is probably six two or three, Lissie stretches to her full length and squares her shoulders, making it clear she is not to be intimidated.

"Ma'am me one more time and I'll have you singing soprano in the Durango Choral Society before you can blink." That takes the wind out of his sails. "I would like the keys to my truck."

"You can have them," he snaps back, clearly not down for the count yet. "As soon as you pay for the work done. Fourteen hundred and twenty-seven dollars, including parts, labor, and tax."

"You may want to try that again. I brought the truck in for an oil change. That's what I'll be paying for and not a penny more."

The idiot snorts at her.

"Sorry, darlin', no can do."

Then he throws me a lopsided grin, clearly misreading my silence as weakness. I take an inadvertent step toward him but as if sensing me, Lissie sticks out a hand to hold me back.

"The name is Detective Bucco." I watch with some satisfaction as he flinches at that information. "I'm with the Durango Police Department, and I strongly suggest you fetch my keys. Otherwise, I might be motivated to throw a pile of charges at you, just to see which ones are gonna stick. That should be fun, right, Yuma?" she asks me, but her eyes never leave the bastard.

"I'd be amused."

"Fuck me," he mumbles, turning on his heel. He grabs a set of keys off the tack board on the wall and tosses them at Lissie, who smartly plucks them one-handedly from the air.

"I still have to pay," she announces.

"On the house," he counters; a calculating glint in his eyes, but the woman has more smarts than that.

"I'm paying for my oil change," she insists, walking past him into the small office off to the side and I head back to lean on my bike, waiting there.

A few minutes later she reappears, slipping her credit card in her back pocket.

"All done?" I straighten up when she approaches.

"Yup."

"He didn't give you any more trouble?"

She turns a wide grin on me. "Nah. Nothing I couldn't handle."

"No doubt about that." I swing my leg over the bike and start the engine.

She tilts her head to the side and regards me through narrowed eyes. "Then why didn't you leave?"

"And miss that dressing-down?"

She shakes her head as she makes her way to the truck, but can't quite hide the smile. She opens the driver's door and looks at me.

"Can I bring you back something for lunch?"

"You don't need—" I don't get very far.

"I know. I'm picking up a sub for me. Got a favorite?"

I try to stare her down, but I only last a few seconds when she raises her eyebrows and bulges her eyes, making me laugh. She's cute as fuck.

"Roast beef."

"And your handsome friend?"

"He doesn't eat," I grumble, to her great amusement.

"Two roast beef subs it is."

With a big grin, she climbs behind the wheel of her truck and I watch her drive off before exiting the parking lot.

Not sure what I was looking for from Lissie Bucco when I knocked on her door the other day, but whatever it was, she seemed to sense what I needed. I keep looking for excuses to avoid dealing with my unhealthy interest in her, but then the next moment I'm seeking her out again.

Can't remember the last time I was this hung up on a

woman.

Fuck, who am I kidding?

I can't remember much of anything prior to my stint in Denver. All I know is a lot of the women I encountered wanted something from me. Either my dick, a permanent spot on the back of my bike, or something else they thought I could give them. I never lied—not that it's a redeeming factor—and was always clear on what I was willing to share. Basically my dick and a couple of drinks, tops. Didn't mean some of them didn't try for more.

That's the reason I started partying with couples. No risk there. At least not for me. They had something missing that I could provide, without it being anything more than it was. No messy feelings.

It worked until I got sober, then I lost my appetite for random sex.

Unfortunately, I have a feeling sex with Detective Lissie Bucco would be anything but casual.

Shit.

I find Tse stretched out on Lissie's loveseat—his legs dangling off one end—watching a rerun of *Live PD* on TV.

"What the fuck, man?" I slap his boots. "Get your shit-kickers off her couch."

"Couch? This ain't more than a club chair with an inflated ego." He grudgingly pushes himself up. "Need to get that girl some decent furniture."

"She's not a girl."

"No need to tell me that, I've got eyes." I grab the

remote and aim it at the TV. "Hang on," he says, holding up a hand. "Been checking out this chick." He points at the TV where the camera is pointed at a pretty blonde police officer searching a suspect. "God, that's hot. Seen her take down a guy, then his girlfriend who's twice her size, all the while with their fuckin' dog growling and circling her. She's badass." I turn the thing off. "Bet Lissie can kick some ass too. Shit, I'd volunteer for her to pat me down."

"Yes, she can, and over your dead body," I warn him, looking over at the sliders to the balcony. "Why is that door still in the frame?"

"Brother, even I can't manage that thing on my own. All the trim's down. It'll take the two of us a second."

He's right, it doesn't take long for us to carry it out to the dumpster and haul up the new doors.

Tse is out on the balcony having a smoke and I'm filling the gaps with foam, when Lissie walks in with a couple of bags. He immediately makes his way inside. Asshole.

"I hope water's okay?" she asks, setting the bags on the counter and pulling out a few bottles.

"A beer'd be better," Tse blurts out, peeking into the other bag.

I'm about to ream him a new one when Lissie coolly responds, "Sorry, no alcohol in my apartment."

"Shit," he swears, chuckling. "You're doin' that for him?" He cocks a thumb in my direction.

"No. I'm doing it for me," she says defiantly, looking straight at him.

Tse's eyes dart from her to me and back again.

"Fuck me. Match made in heaven."

"Shut up and eat, asshole," I grumble, as Lissie hands him a sub, before handing me one. "Thanks, Babe."

It slips out and earns me a long hard look, but just when I think she's going to call me on it, she grabs a water bottle, slips it in the bag with her sub, and walks toward the front door.

"Lock up when you leave," she says over her shoulder. "I've gotta go. Just got called into work. See you later."

"Thanks for lunch, gorgeous!" Tse calls after her, drowning out my own more moderate, "See you later."

"Fuckin' A, roast beef," he mumbles around about two inches of the sub in his mouth. "She even knows what I like."

"She got me *my* favorite, you moron," I grouch, taking a bite.

6

LISSIE

WHEN I WALK into the open office—dubbed 'the bullpen'— at the station, I can tell there've been some developments, judging by the tension in the room.

I drop my lunch on my desk and stick my head over the partition separating my desk from Blackfoot's.

"What did I miss?"

He lifts his head from the file he was studying and leans back in his chair.

"You've probably heard about that big case involving a group of nationalist militants we had last year?"

"The FBI raid on the training facility in Moab? That one?"

I'd heard about it when I was still in New Mexico. The case drew quite a bit of airtime, and in the months following lots was written about it. It's actually how I learned about the local MC. One of the articles mentioned a couple of the boys found at the ANL training facility in Moab had found a home in Durango. Specifically with the Arrow's Edge MC. It caused me to dig into the club a little deeper. Get as much background as I could.

Thinking about my ulterior motive for requesting the transfer to Durango a couple of months ago comes with a pang of guilt, but history has taught me to keep things close to my chest, until I have facts to back up my suspicions.

"That's it. Lunatics creating some kind of Aryan nation. Anyway, remember that list of project investors we dug up a few days ago? Ramirez asked Greene, the IT guy from the FBI, to see what he could find out since he has better resources. This morning he sent over some interesting info."

He hands me a copy of an email listing each of the five major investors, followed by some background. I study the list that has two names with little in way of background. One is a company by the name of Red Mesa Holdings, and the other appears to be a private investor, Victor Nowak. The name rings a bell.

"Nowak? Why does his name seem familiar?"

"Probably because he is a media mogul. He owns about seventy-five percent of newspapers, radio, and TV stations in twelve states."

"I remember now. He bought up a local TV station in Albuquerque a few years ago. Didn't go over too well at the time, some outsider taking control of local media."

"Nowak's been doing that for the past fifteen years. Came out of nowhere. Greene is digging hard and ran into a connection between Nowak and the American National League. In the past five years, he has apparently invested millions of dollars into the organization."

"Still, why would a media mogul want to invest money in a subdivision development on the outskirts of Durango?" It doesn't really make sense to me.

"That's the big question. It's what we're trying to figure out."

"Can I keep this copy?" I wave the email.

"It's yours."

"Anything you want me to focus on?"

"Actually, I was hoping you could focus on that Albuquerque acquisition? Put out some feelers? We're looking for anything the ANL might be tied to."

Not what I was hoping for. I get why he's asking, he figures I still have connections there, and I do, but none who'd be thrilled to hear from me.

"Sure," I agree grudgingly and sit down at my desk.

Taking a bite of my lunch, I scan the email and notice the second name that popped out at me.

"What about the other one? Red Mesa Holdings?" I ask around a mouthful of my sub.

"Ramirez is looking into that one," Keith says from behind the partition separating our desks.

"Gotcha."

I fire up my computer and one-handedly type in searches for Nowak, ANL, and Albuquerque, while finishing my sandwich. As I'm scanning my screen, one name pops out at me, turning lunch into a heavy brick in my stomach.

Clive Cole.

Now I know why the acquisition of ABQ News by Nowak popped up in my head. I remember Clive getting some flack from his editor when he wrote an article on the subject that wasn't exactly flattering to either Nowak or to ABQ for selling out.

Clive and I had been dating off and on at the time. It was me who didn't want to move beyond that. Mostly because my father staunchly supported Clive in his pursuit to make ours a permanent arrangement. I was content with the status quo, and—I have to give it to Clive—he hung in for a while. At least until I decided to rock the boat and stand up for myself. That's when, along with my father and brothers, Clive distanced himself.

It had been simmering for months, the innuendos, the 'accidental' touches, the requests for me to stay late to discuss an investigation. Until one night, I was asked to drop off a file at my captain's house. He told me to close the door so his cat couldn't escape, but the moment I did, his pants were around his ankles.

My father's best friend—the man I'd called Uncle Charlie and considered family for most of my life—told me if I didn't suck him off, my career would be over. I still shiver remembering the look on his face as he palmed his erection.

I'd worked so hard to become a good cop, despite the lack of support from my family. I'd studied hard for my detective's exam and passed with flying colors. I'd kept my head low, trying hard to toe the line, but in that moment I was done.

I should've anticipated what happened after I launched an official complaint of sexual harassment against him, but it still came as a blow. Colleagues I'd considered my friends backed away from me, but also my own family. My dad tried to convince me to drop it, that it was all a figment of my imagination. When I wouldn't budge, he made it clear he wouldn't hesitate to use my drinking against me.

I was shocked. I didn't think he knew, living under the illusion that so long as I only drank at home, no one would find out. What was a harder blow was the fact he was willing to use it to throw me under the bus if I didn't retract my complaint.

Two weeks later, my reputation was covered in mud and Uncle Charlie was off on early retirement. Right about the same time I received that unexpected call from my troubled friend, Dani, which ultimately led me to Durango.

A lot has happened in the last eight months, most of which I'd prefer not to revisit. Still, knowing I have a job to do, I call the number I never got around to removing from my phone.

"Elizabeth?"

Clive's annoying habit to call me by my full name instantly grates on me.

"Lissie, but yes," I can't resist saying. "Hi, Clive, I'm actually calling in an official capacity."

I explain I'm working on an investigation, without

giving him too many details, and ask his impression of Nowak. Apparently it was Nowak's politics that hadn't sat well with Clive. He reports his concerns have been validated with the clearly biased turn the news station has taken the past few years. Not unlike the other media outlets Nowak's procured over the years. Their political affiliations have been showing and it's becoming clear how there might well be common ground between Nowak and the ANL.

"Have you heard of the American Nationalist League?"

There's a pregnant pause on the other end of the line before Clive finally responds.

"You don't want to be messing with that group, Elizabeth."

"Lissie," I correct him. "And for the record, I'm not messing with anyone."

"You're asking about a powerful group, *Lissie*," he says with emphasis on my name. "Need I remind you what happened last time you started pointing fingers?"

I bristle at his comment but remind myself nothing can touch me unless I let it. So instead of reacting, I take in a deep breath before speaking.

"I'm simply making some general inquiries around an investigation, Clive. Nothing more, nothing less." Despite my good intentions I can't help the next words from escaping. "And as for my memory, it's perfectly clear, including the way you turned your back on me under pressure." I notice Blackfoot leaning over the partition, listening in with interest. "I have to go. Thanks for talking to me, Clive. It's been helpful."

I hang up before he has the chance to say anything.

"You okay, Bucco?" Keith wants to know, a look of concern on his face.

"Just peachy."

YUMA

"You coming to the clubhouse for a bit?"

I'm tucking away my tools. We just finished installing the new sliding door.

"Not sure."

The plan had been to go see Momma, then pick up something for dinner, and check if Lissie got home okay. I have no idea when that'll be, and I haven't seen my brothers in a while. Maybe it's time to show my face, although I'm willing to bet Nosh won't be happy to see me. Time to get it out with my old man.

"All right. I'll come, just give me a few minutes to clean up."

"No rush. I'll have a smoke outside."

When Tse walks out, I dig a pen and a piece of paper from one of the kitchen drawers and scribble a quick note for Lissie I leave on the counter.

WINDOWS AND DOOR IN. IF YOU NEED ME: 970 510 7892 TTYL

"What are you doing here?"

My father's hands start flying the moment I walk in the door and spot him sitting at the bar.

"My club too."

It's asinine, standing twenty feet away from Nosh and virtually stomping my foot, but fucking hell, the man sets me back about thirty years in emotional development.

"Hey, brother, good to see you." Ouray rounds the bar and claps a hand on the old man's shoulder before heading my way, effectively blocking my view.

"Same," I grunt, taking the hand he offers.

"Yuma!" I look past Ouray to see Ezrah barreling toward me.

"Hey, buddy. What are you up to?"

Ezrah cocks his thumb over his shoulder. "Homework. Wanna come see?"

Luna and Ouray's teenage son, Ahiga, is sitting at the massive harvest table with two younger boys. The younger kids look like brothers but aren't. Both are blond and blue-eyed, as were the three older kids who were rescued from a militant nationalist group last year. The boys were being brainwashed and trained like mini-soldiers. Between Ouray and Trunk, they fought to keep the two younger boys with the club, hoping the exposure to people of all races and backgrounds will be enough to erase the bigoted indoctrination they've been subjected to.

I follow Ezrah, who explains in great detail what apparently is a science project spread out on the table, and spend the next fifteen minutes helping the kids make a start on their solar system. It's a perfect way to avoid my father.

"You staying for dinner?" I look up to find Lisa smiling down at me.

"Have enough?"

"Already cooking for an army, Yuma. One more mouth won't make a difference," she says, shaking her head.

"In that case; what's on the menu?"

"Nana's making tacos!" Ezrah contributes.

"And salad," she adds, to which he rolls his eyes, earning him a cuff to the back of his head. The two younger boys giggle. "Dinner in half an hour, boys. Make sure you have the table cleaned off by then."

I leave the kids to it and make my way to the bar, where Nosh's wide back greets me. He barely looks up when I take the stool next to him.

"How's Momma?" I ask, signing. My father is deaf—Ouray's boy, Ahiga, is as well—and I grew up using sign language. Just about every club member has picked enough up to make themselves understood over the years.

"Nice of you to ask."

"Knock it off. I get you're pissed at me, and you probably have reason, but don't hang Momma's condition on me."

I can tell he's angry by the way he tosses back his beer. No way my father is going to hold back on alcohol on my account and he wants me to know it. Conveying a silent message, I grab the bottle Tse slides in front of me and take a swig of the water. I know I made my point when Nosh grunts.

"She's miserable there."

"She won't be for long. You know it's the right place for her to be."

"Fifty years next month, boy. Other than 'Nam, never more than a couple of nights apart, ever. Now it takes twenty minutes to get to her."

Jesus. I can't even imagine that kind of devotion. Almost five decades they've lived and worked side by side, it's no wonder he's out of sorts. All he has left now is his wayward son.

"Have you thought about moving closer to her?" I ask carefully. *"They have some independent senior housing on the property as well."*

The glare he throws me is scorching. If I were a lesser man, I'd cower, but I know my father and he's more bark than bite. Usually.

"Trying to write me off too?"

"Pointing out options," I correct him, trying hard not to react.

I have my back to the door, but suddenly I notice the atmosphere in the clubhouse change. When I turn on my stool, I'm surprised to see Tony Ramirez walk in, followed by Lissie. Her eyes register surprise as well when she spots me, only to look away quickly.

"What brings the Durango PD here?" Ouray asks friendly enough.

"What do you know about the Wildcat Canyon development off Highway 160?" Ramirez asks Ouray, who looks over at the boys at the table before returning his attention to the detective.

"Let's take this into my office."

I watch as Lissie falls into step behind Ouray and Ramirez, heading toward the back of the clubhouse.

"Yuma!"

"That's you, brother," Tse grumbles, and I slide off my stool and follow the group to Ouray's office.

My eyes immediately find Lissie sitting in one of the visitor chairs, and I hitch a hip on the corner of Ouray's desk across from her.

"I know about the development," Ouray says, tenting his fingers under his chin.

"Good," Ramirez says, holding the other man's eyes as he leans forward. "You know Red Mesa Holdings?"

I'm watching Lissie but at the silence following that question I turn my attention to Ouray. A muscle ticks in his jaw and his eyes flit to me.

"It's clear you already know I do."

I'm out of the loop here, I know the development they're talking about, and I know about the body found there, but I've never heard of Red Mesa Holdings.

"I get the feeling I'm missing something here."

All eyes come to me, but it's Ramirez who answers.

"Red Mesa Holdings is one of the investors in the Wildcat Canyon Development. Jasper Greene did some digging and discovered your friend Red Franklin's club joined forces with Arrow's Edge to form the holding eight months ago."

This is news to me. I raise my eyebrow at Ouray.

"You weren't around much back then, brother," he

says by way of explanation.

"Been around for a couple a months now," I remind him, trying to hold off on losing my temper. Any major investments by the club are decided on by the club. Except apparently in this case.

"Was a behind closed doors decision. Only Kaga and Trunk were in on it. Luna doesn't even know."

"With Greene digging up that info, I don't think she'll be in the dark for long," Ramirez points out.

"Fuck." Ouray rubs a hand over his face. "Red and I got to talking one night. I was frustrated with the lack of progress finding any family members for those two boys out there, and Red didn't trust law enforcement to follow through bringing down the ANL."

"Why?" Lissie, who hasn't said a word so far, but has been intently listening, asks. "Did he have reason for that?"

"Red doesn't have a high opinion of the Moab PD anyway, but in this case, he believes the ANL must've had some power over local cops to have been able to operate under their noses that long."

"Still doesn't explain how you came to invest in the development," Ramirez points out. "Especially since the first phase was already up at that time."

"Nowak."

At that moment, the door swings open and Luna comes marching in, shooting daggers at her husband.

"Oh shit," Ouray mumbles.

I use that as my cue.

ARROW'S EDGE MC

1

LISSIE

I'M TEMPTED TO take off after him, but I came with Ramirez, so I have to wait.

Ouray is trying to calm down Luna, an agent for the FBI, whose short frame doesn't make her any less impressive. This is a woman you don't mess with, as her husband seems to be discovering.

"I can't believe you didn't tell me."

"Lots of shit you can't tell me either."

"That's my job, Ouray."

I watch as the large man leans in, his nose almost touching his wife's.

"Looking after those boys is mine, Sprite. You know that. I wanna find out what happened to their families, and I'm not sure it's at the top of the FBI priority list."

"Don't you think I want that?" she argues.

"All right, guys," Ramirez cuts in there. "I'd still like to know how Nowak ended up on the radar."

For a moment it's like Tony hasn't even spoken, but then both turn their attention to him.

"Coincidence," Ouray replies. "After the raid last year, Red heard rumors floating around that Hinckle had been seen wining and dining some bigwig who was in town trying to buy up the local TV station."

"Nowak," Tony confirms.

Hinckle was the former politician and known white supremacist, who ran the training facility for the ANL on his property in Moab.

"Right. That's what we found out. It wasn't much of a stretch to imagine what the two might've had in common. What was a stretch was to consider what Nowak might get out of an investment we discovered he had in a subdivision in Durango. Especially on land owned by Hinckle."

"So you guys decided to join him?"

Ouray shrugs. "It was a way to keep an eye on things. Red managed to get a couple of guys signed up with one of the contractors on the project, and he has a connection in the developer's office."

IT'S DARK OUTSIDE by the time I leave the police station, my mind swirling with all the information that came pouring in today. It took a while to process and plan next steps for tomorrow.

I managed to stuff my private file in my bag on the way out the door. Each time the Mesa Riders MC was mentioned, my ears perked up. It sounds so familiar. I could swear I've heard that name before and I think it may be somewhere in my notes.

Journaling had become a way for me to escape when I was still living at the ranch with my father and brothers. No longer having Mom to talk to, I resorted to writing things down in notebooks. My friend, Dani, had been my only other outlet.

We were in kindergarten together and stayed joined at the hip ever since. Dani was a bit of a wild child, always pushing boundaries and getting herself in trouble. Ten years ago, she got tired of trying to fit into a mold and took off on the back of a motorcycle, chasing the wind.

She called a few times at first, but then we lost touch. The phone number I had for her was no longer in service and until that surprise call early this year, I hadn't heard from her in many years. Despite her hurried whispers, I had no problem recognizing her voice, but before I could ask any questions the line went dead. The number she called me from was unlisted, so I couldn't even call her back.

I'm in trouble, Lissie. Big trouble. There's someone in Durango who—

I have no idea what she was going to say and she didn't call again, but I pulled every page with reference to Dani from my journals and put them in a file. Hoping to find some clue to her whereabouts.

Pulling into the parking lot, I notice the main light in the office is out, but a faint glow is coming from a window of the small apartment beside it. When I park the truck and get out, I hesitate for a second, wondering if I should go check on him, but then I rush up the stairs to my front door.

The tension between Yuma and Ouray was obvious from their earlier exchange, which I assume is the reason he took off like that. If he wants to talk, I already made it clear my door would be open. I don't want to force myself on him.

I've barely flipped on the lights and dropped my stuff on the island, when a knock sounds at the door. He's standing on the other side; his arms braced high on the doorposts, his head hanging down, long hair flopping in his face. Slowly he lifts his head, those blue eyes burning behind the blunt fringe of his lashes.

"Hi."

That's all I manage to say before his hand shoots out, hooks me behind my neck, and he slams his mouth on mine.

I'm in shock, my body frozen even as his tongue pushes between my lips, but it takes only one possessive sweep of my mouth for me to ignite. The abrasion of his beard is a new sensation, one I like a lot. My hand lands on his chest, curling into his shirt, as he walks me backward inside, kicking the door shut behind him.

A picture frame crashes down beside me when my back bangs into a wall, but I'm already beyond caring. I barely notice when he pulls the elastic from my hair, mostly focused on his other hand sneaking under my shirt, his rough palm rasping against my skin.

I moan in his mouth when he pulls down the cup of my bra, his fingers closing around my breast at the same time he presses a leg between mine. My hands skim restlessly along his back, down to his clenched ass, the muscles hard under my touch.

"*Shit*," he hisses when he lets me up for air.

"Wow," falls from my bruised lips.

I can sense him retreating, even before he says anything, as his hand releases my breast and he takes a step back.

"I'm sorry. I—"

"Some tea?" I cut him off, straightening my clothes as I turn to the kitchen. I don't really give him a chance to answer, pulling down a couple of glasses from the cupboard and getting the jug from the fridge.

I don't look but I can hear his footsteps approaching. Turning around I hand him a glass and take a sip of mine.

"I shouldn't have—"

Again I interrupt. "I was right there, Yuma. Participating. Willingly."

Those eyes meet mine and behind his beard I see one side of his mouth tilt up.

"I noticed."

"Yeah. So, you hungry?" I quickly change the topic, feeling my face get hot. "I haven't had dinner. You?"

YUMA

"NOPE."

I was supposed to have dinner at the club but ended up walking straight out of the clubhouse earlier. I'm not happy something so significant was kept from me. It feels like betrayal, not just by Ouray, but by Trunk, Kaga, and Red too. It fucking burns.

"Pizza?"

"Sure."

I watch as she pulls a takeout menu from a kitchen drawer and orders a large pie. The whole time I'm reliving the feel of the weight of her breast in my hand, the slick taste of her mouth, and the heat of her core burning through the jeans covering my thigh. I quickly adjust myself but not fast enough. Lissie catches me as she hangs up and turns around.

"Meat lovers okay?" she asks, a sparkle in her eyes.

I burst out laughing. A sound I barely recognize anymore. Her soft chuckle joins me.

"You're laughing at me," I admonish her.

"Seemed like a good way to break the tension," she tosses over her shoulder, as she moves to sit on the loveseat.

It's very tempting to sit down next to her, but I'm not so sure that would be wise. The likelihood we'll end up horizontal is great and we have pizza on the way. So instead I pull over a stool and sit on that.

"Keeping your distance?"

"You don't mince words, do you?" I return immediately.

Lissie shrugs. "What's the point?"

"I find it difficult to control myself around you," I admit. "Makes me uneasy not to be in control."

I watch for her reaction, but she doesn't seem offended, just thoughtful.

"Makes sense," she mutters before tilting her head slightly. "Is that why you got so mad? Back at the clubhouse?"

"That was about trust." When she frowns slightly I try to explain. "In an MC, trust is what ties the brothers together. Fuck, it's what makes the club."

"Okay, so it's about you not trusting Ouray? Or because you think he doesn't trust you?"

I grunt, uncomfortable she reads me so easy. It hurts my brothers would think so little of me they cut me out of club business; feels like being cut off from the club altogether.

Luckily the doorbell rings, announcing the arrival of the pizza and I beat Lissie to the front door, pulling my money clip from my pocket before she can fish her credit card from her purse. It earns me a dirty look I ignore. I'm all for equal rights and all that shit, but I draw the line at letting a woman pay for me. I don't much care what that says about me.

We're watching the news while eating when Lissie suddenly turns down the volume on the TV and turns to me.

"Why did you knock on my door?" I turn to look at her. "I'm asking because I almost stopped at yours."

"Not sure," I tell her honestly. "I was restless. Then I heard your truck and wanted to see you."

She nods at that before she asks, "Why did you kiss me?"

I just shoved a bite of pizza in my mouth, which gives me a minute to think about an answer while I chew.

"Wasn't a choice."

She looks surprised first, then annoyed.

"Well, you didn't exactly trip and fall on my face, Yuma." She jerks her gaze back to the TV.

I bite off a grin at her snippy response and slide off the stool, sitting down on the couch beside her. I reach out and, with my fingers lightly on her chin, turn her to face me.

"It was instinct." I lean in and lightly brush her lips. "As natural as breathing."

"Then why did you stop?"

I lift my head up a little and study her face. She'd seemed very matter-of-fact earlier when I pulled away from her, but now I see the confusion in her eyes.

"Because you could easily become my next addiction, Lissie."

"Oh."

I lightly brush my thumb along her jaw, as she appears to process my words.

"Doesn't it worry you?"

She shakes her head. "No, I don't think so. I drank to numb myself from life. It almost cost me everything I worked hard for. Numbing myself is furthest from my mind when it comes to you...to this...whatever it is." She waves her hand between us.

"They advise against relationships the first year of

sobriety."

"I'm aware of that," she acknowledges.

"Especially between two recovering alcoholics," I add.

"I've heard that too."

I'm getting frustrated; it would be easier if she agreed this isn't a good idea. Instead she seems almost flippant, and that annoys me.

"I told you before I'm not a good person, Lissie. Sobriety is new to me. Was hard to get even to this point. I'm scared every day I'll screw it up. I know people around me are waiting for me to screw up. Fucking feels like having to learn to walk all over again, but at every bump in the road, my first thought is a drink. I'm not sure I trust myself."

Don't know why me spilling my guts has her smiling, but it does. She pulls a leg under her and twists her whole body toward me, grabbing my hand.

"And yet tonight you knocked on my door. You didn't go to a bar and stare into a shot glass all night in some kind of dare with yourself. You came here."

"You're a temptation."

That makes her grin wider.

"Perhaps, but I'm not out to hurt you and if I tempt you away from a drink, then what's the harm in that?"

I try to think of something, but nothing comes to mind right now. Hard to be sensible when a gorgeous woman is smiling at you with heat in her eyes.

"Sex and booze always went hand in hand for me. Quick and easy."

She comes willingly when I pull her on my lap, her hand immediately going for my face as she leans in and brushes my mouth with her lips.

"Then we'll take it nice and slow," is her easy response.

LISSIE

"WHERE ARE YOU going?"

Lisa's granddaughter, Kiara, is standing at the top of the stairs; her pink backpack slung over one shoulder.

"To work. Are you going to school?"

"Yes. I'm in kindergarten already," she says proudly.

"That's amazing. Do you like it?"

She nods with a serious face. "Ms. Jonkers is da bestest teacher. She got a guinea pig. I'm gonna look after it for a whole weekend next month."

"Really? That's exciting."

Just then Lisa walks out, almost dragging Ezrah behind her.

"Ezrah is in trouble," Kiara explains, talking in an ineffective stage whisper that is not fooling anyone.

Least of all Ezrah, who glares at his little sister.

"Shu—"

"Do not finish that, boy," Lisa admonishes him sternly. "That would be another strike against you, and trust me, you don't want the consequences of that." It serves to quiet her grandson but doesn't stop him from scowling angrily. Lisa clicks the remote on her old Toyota. "Get in the car, both of you. No lip, Ezrah." She wags a finger in his face. "And no fighting with your sister. I'll be right there."

She waits until the kids are in the car before she turns to me.

"My days are spent in a clubhouse with grunting and swearing men. I come home, I don't appreciate my boy giving me one-syllable responses or tossing around the F-word. Swear that boy's gonna be the death of me."

I swallow a chuckle when she turns a warning look in my direction.

"You're a saint," I mutter quickly, to which she nods appreciatively.

"Bet your booty I am. I can't even remember what it's like to commune with a grown-up anymore. What's with that coffee?"

I feel awful. I haven't forgotten her invitation but between work and Yuma, I haven't really had much time to myself.

"Work's been crazy."

She looks at me with an eyebrow raised.

"That what they call it these days? Guess I've been out of the game longer than I thought," she semi-mumbles to herself. "Yuma been helpin'?"

I look at my toes grinning. Shouldn't surprise me she's caught wind of Yuma spending quite a bit of time here, even though he's gone back to his own place every night.

Apparently he's serious about my suggestion to take things nice and slow. There's been kissing, and some touching over clothes, but I've gone to bed alone and aching these past few days.

"Something like that."

Lisa puts a hand on my arm, taking me in with a solemn look on her face. "Be careful, girl. There's an edge of darkness on that one."

Lisa doesn't know me well, but I'm sure she's trying to look out for me. Sisterhood and all that. If the roles were reversed, who knows, I might've suggested caution too. I'm guessing she's probably seen Yuma at his worst, but she can't know he's been brutally honest with me. Much more honest than I have been with him. I haven't really shared that much about my life before I came here.

"I have that edge of darkness in me too, Lisa," I admit. "I'm just better at hiding it."

She looks at me closely before nodding.

"I see it now." She pats my arm. "Hope I didn't offend."

"Not at all. And we'll work on that coffee."

"Please, because right now living next to a cop is about the only thing keeping me from bloodshed," she grumbles, before jogging down the stairs to where the kids look to be arguing in the car.

I follow at a slower pace and she's already peeling out of the parking lot by the time I climb in my truck. I cast a brief glance at Yuma's apartment but there's no sign of life. His bike is parked out front. Before my mind goes places it shouldn't, I put the car in reverse and back out of my spot.

When I walk into the station, Mike Bolter, the desk sergeant, calls me over.

"The chief called a meeting. They're in the conference room."

"Thanks, Sarge."

Instead of heading right to my cubicle in the bullpen, I take a left. The door to the room is open showing Chief Benedetti, Blackfoot, Ramirez, with the surprising addition of FBI SAC Gomez and Mayor Woodard.

"Going in, Detective Bucco?"

I turn to find the new coroner, Dr. Meredith Carter, standing behind me.

"Yes, of course."

The men look up when we walk in.

"Perfect," Chief Benedetti says. "Take a seat so we can get started." I take an empty seat beside Ramirez while Dr. Carter finds a spot on the other side of the table. "This is a fact-sharing meeting. Mayor Woodard asked to sit in since he has a vested interest in the development." I look over at the mayor, who looks decidedly unhappy. Gomez doesn't appear too pleased either. "In short, the DPD's investigation at Wildcat Canyon development is crossing over into an ongoing FBI case," Benedetti explains.

This should be interesting, jurisdictional scuffles

happen regularly but they can get pretty ugly.

"The FBI has been investigating the American National League for close to two years," Gomez explains. "Last year's raid in Moab was only the tip of the iceberg. Organizations like that grow silently, and widely, spreading tentacles and burrowing deep. The Hinckle compound in Moab was one of the tentacles. Every time we get close, they simply cut off the tentacle and grow another. Each time that happens, we need to start all over again."

As Gomez informs us, Nowak is another tentacle. The FBI apparently has kept a covert eye on him for a while, gathering information to bring them closer to the root of the organization.

Ramirez shifts in his seat. "So what are you asking exactly? You want us to drop the investigation?"

The FBI agent pins him with a hard look. "What I'm proposing is we find a way to work in tandem. We collaborate. Investigate, but leave any digging into ANL connections to us and share information."

"You may wanna talk to Ouray," Tony proposes. "He's been doing some investigating of his own."

"So I hear. We're on it."

"This is all fine and dandy," the mayor pipes up. "But construction has ground to a halt, and every day no work is being done on the project is costing us tens of thousands of dollars."

"Us?"

I didn't mean to ask the question out loud, and it earns me a glare from the mayor, but Blackfoot chuckles.

"Good catch, Bucco," he shares. "Woodard's family owns Pro Concrete, a contractor on the project."

"Forgive me, Mayor," Dr. Carter says with a nod at him before turning to Benedetti. "Don't mean any disrespect, and I certainly don't pretend to be particularly knowledgeable on these issues, but doesn't that potentially constitute a conflict of interest?"

I lower my head to hide the grin on my face. Our new coroner doesn't mince words. I think I like her. The mayor, however, looks pissed.

"Absolutely not," he bites off.

"Sure does," Gomez says at the same time. "Which is why, I suggest we wait until the mayor leaves before we start discussing any further details on this case."

"Need I remind you, as mayor of Durango, I have authority over our police force?"

"I'm well aware," Gomez fires back. "However, you have no jurisdiction over my office. Now, I would prefer to continue working this case side by side with the DPD, but if push comes to shove I won't hesitate to claim jurisdiction, leaving you and your police force out of the loop."

It's a power play if ever I've seen one. Surprisingly, Chief Benedetti seems unfazed, leaning back in his chair and folding his arms over his chest, observing the mayor casually.

"You can't do that."

"Afraid he can," Benedetti answers. "But there's no need to let it get that far, Dan."

Woodard takes a long look around the room before

abruptly getting up and stalking out.

"That was fun," Dr. Carter concludes, eliciting chuckles. "But I have work waiting."

An hour and a half later, it's clear most of the information sharing is on the part of the DPD, but the roles appear to be assigned. We're going to continue our murder investigation for now, while the FBI will continue their quiet pursuit of Nowak and his possible affiliations with the ANL, but we'll communicate findings and share resources.

Gomez suggested it would raise suspicions if the FBI were visibly involved at this point. For now there is nothing concrete suggesting the murder is related to their investigation, despite suspicions in that direction.

I've barely sat down in the office when a new case hits my desk, keeping me occupied for most of the afternoon. I'm on my way to question a witness when my phone rings.

"Where are you?"

"Just heading north on Main," I tell Blackfoot. "Why?"

"I need you to head up to the Arrow's Edge compound. Ouray just called. The Mesa Riders just stopped in on their way home from a run into New Mexico."

We've had trouble over the past days getting a hold of the president, Red Franklin. This explains why.

"You want me to go?"

"Tony's on his way to Monticello to meet with the developer, and I'm stuck in the ER with my kid."

"Aleksander? What's wrong with him?"

"They suspect whooping cough. Anyway, I'll probably be here for a while."

"No worries; take care of your boy. I'll head there now."

YUMA

IT KILLS ME to see her so confused.

Momma sits in her favorite chair—the one we moved from her house here—her eyes bewildered as she looks at me.

"Where's my kitchen, Nosh? I can't find it. I need to get dinner goin'."

This isn't the first time she calls me by my father's name. It's like generations disappear and my father's name is the only one she remembers.

"This is your new place, Momma. You don't have to worry about dinner, someone else is cooking for you for a change."

"But the boys…"

"They're looked after."

I'm ashamed I feel relief when my father walks in, using it as an excuse to escape before he can get on my case again. Unfortunately, I never really got a chance to hash things out with him. It's one of the things I was reminded of in my few visits to the AA meeting: getting sober is not only about staying off the booze. You're also supposed to take ownership for what it's done to your life, as well as the life of others.

I'm not one for blanket apologies—or apologies in

general—and I'm still pissed, but I figure I can at least make the first move. Which means I should probably talk to Ouray too.

Instead of driving home to the apartments, I head up the mountain to the club and am surprised to see more than the usual number of bikes parked out front.

The clubhouse is crowded and I immediately recognize some Mesa Riders. I haven't seen these guys since before I went to Denver and have to wave off offers of booze as I make my way to the bar, where I know I'll find Red.

Not just Red, but Ginger as well, as it turns out. She squeals when she sees me and launches herself at me, planting a wet kiss on my lips before I can avoid it. I untangle her arms from around my neck and try to set her back, glancing over at a grinning Red.

"Brother," he rumbles, clapping me on the shoulder. "I should probably be pissed as fuck my ol' lady is more excited to see you than she gets for me, but you know me—whatever keeps her happy."

"About that," I hook in, determined not to let this get uncomfortable. Or more uncomfortable.

"Get my man a Jack, will ya?" Red orders Wapi, who is manning the bar. The cub darts his eyes at me and give a sharp shake of my head.

"Not drinking, Red," I remind him, trying to ignore Ginger, who is wrapping her arms around my midsection again.

"Fuck," the big man says, slapping the palm of hand to his forehead. "Forgot."

"I'm done partying, my friend."

Once again I unwrap Ginger's arms and turn out of her hold, just in time to see Lissie walking in the door. I'm about to make my way over when I see Ouray beat me to it. He brings her over and I automatically tag her behind the neck and bend down to brush her lips.

"Nice surprise, Babe." I look down in her smiling eyes and it takes me a second to notice a change in the air.

"Really?" Ouray rubs his face with his hands. "A cop? Fuck me. All we need now is a CIA agent."

"I'll get right on that, Chief," Wapi jokes.

Red has pulled his wife to his side when I glance over, a grin on his face. Ginger looks less happy, but she'll deal.

"I'm still on the clock," Lissie whispers, leaning close.

"Red, meet Detective Bucco," Ouray announces. "You can use my office if you like."

I'm a little uneasy as I watch Red lead Lissie down the hall at the back.

"Worried?" Ouray taunts, a grin on his face.

"Fuck off," I grumble as he walks away, chuckling.

"So when did this happen?"

Ginger steps up beside me. Still a stunning woman but no longer as enticing as I once thought her to be.

"Not sure what it is yet," I admit, my eyes still trained down the hall where Lissie and Red just disappeared inside Ouray's office.

"It's clearly something."

"Mmm."

"Does she play?"

My head snaps around at her question. I can see she's partly teasing as she tries to hide a smile, but I can't hold back my knee-jerk reaction.

"No fucking way."

9

YUMA

I'VE RESIGNED MYSELF to the kids' corner.

The beer smell isn't as prevalent here and I'm closer to Ouray's office, where Lissie and Red have been holed up for almost half an hour now.

Kiara is sidled up beside me on the sectional, her head resting against my arm as I'm playing some racing game with the boys. Ezrah, Thomas, and Michael. A couple of the other boys are playing pool with Ouray's son, Ahiga, overseeing.

Not counting Ahiga, or Ezrah and Kiara since they live with their nana, there are currently four kids in the club's care. Some of the boys are reunited with family, or in rare cases are adopted. Some, like Wapi, come in as young boys and stick around. Others yet leave when they turn eighteen.

I'm the only one born into the club. I was just a kid when Nosh brought home the first of the club's lost boys: a rough-looking, lanky teenager my parents baptized Ouray. The man who ultimately started paying it forward when he took the gavel.

Lisa leans over me, checking her granddaughter.

"She sleeping?" she asks softly.

"Almost."

"I'm about to put dinner on the table, can you herd the little ones into the kitchen for dinner in a couple of minutes?"

"Sure."

"Yuma?"

I twist my neck so I can look at her. "Yeah?"

"She's a good woman."

It takes me a second to realize it's not Kiara she's talking about, but Lissie.

"I know that."

She pauses for a moment before nodding and returning to the kitchen.

She *is* a good woman, which is why I'm on pins and needles, because of what Red might be sharing with her. I should be the one to tell her.

Just then I hear footsteps coming down the hall and Lissie walks in first, her face unreadable. Red follows right behind with a blank look on his face. He keeps on walking when Lissie spots me and comes over.

"You havin' dinner with us, Lissie?" Ezrah beats me to the punch.

"I don't think so, Ezrah. I have a little bit of work to finish off."

"Stay."

Her eyes come to me and her face warms with a smile. *Phew*.

"I'm not sure if I can. I'll have to see. Make a few phone calls."

I get up, trying to dislodge Kiara, but she hangs onto me so I swing her up on my arm instead.

"Make the calls. I've gotta get these kids in the kitchen for dinner first anyway. Please?"

Her eyes go soft when she looks at Kiara, who put her head on my shoulder.

"Okay."

"Come on, guys," I call the boys. "Last one in the kitchen is a rotten egg."

Giggling, the three boys scramble to their feet and start running.

"Not hungry," Kiara mumbles.

"Gotta eat, girl. After that Nana can take you home."

She lifts her head and looks at Lissie, who has her phone by her ear but is observing us closely.

"You gonna stay?"

LISSIE

GOOD LORD.

I think my ovaries just spontaneously spit out some eggs. The big rugged man holding that cute little girl, like she's made of glass. Why are men with kids so freaking sexy?

I cover the phone with my hand.

"I'll do my best," I answer Kiara.

"Blackfoot."

"Keith? How's Aleksander?" I watch Yuma head toward the kitchen still holding the little girl.

"On his way home with Autumn and antibiotics for a couple of weeks. Whooping cough, like we suspected."

"Poor baby."

"Did you catch Franklin?" he wants to know.

"Got a few names from him. Two of his guys work for the concrete contractor."

"Seriously?" Blackfoot chuckles. "That's priceless. I wonder what our esteemed mayor would think of that."

"I know. I had to laugh when he told me. Also, he gave me the name and number for his contact in the developer's office."

"Email them to me. We'll deal with it tomorrow. Go home, Bucco. Good work today."

The woman I noticed standing close to Yuma, when I walked in, is studying me when I tuck my phone in my pocket. I'm feeling a little uneasy: hers aren't the only eyes watching me as I walk up to the bar.

"Can I get you something to drink?" Wapi asks.

"Just water is fine."

"Hey, gorgeous," Tse, who was at the other side of the bar talking to a couple of rough-looking guys, comes walking over, throwing an arm around my shoulders. "You hanging around for a bit?"

"She is, and if you like that arm attached, I suggest

you remove it, asshole."

Yuma approaches with a scowl on his face and with a chuckle, Tse drops his arm from around me. It's clear the man is a horrible tease and Yuma seems to be a favorite target.

"Let me introduce you to the brothers before the food comes out," he says, taking my hand in his. Still a little out of my element, I let him take the lead.

I meet Kaga and a guy named Brick, who seems impressed with my choice of vehicle and offers his mechanical services. Then Paco, Honon, and Lusio, who mostly grunts. I'm not sure I'll be able to keep all the names straight; especially when I find out not everyone is here.

An older man, sitting at the end of the bar, looks up when Yuma guides me there. It takes me a second to realize he's using sign language when his hands start moving. To my surprise, Yuma's move just as fast.

"Lissie, this is Nosh," he finally says. "My father."

Yikes. I offer my hand but the man doesn't seem to notice, glaring at his son. I'm about to retract it when he turns his eyes on me, taking me in top to bottom, which doesn't do much to settle the churning in my gut. I feel like I'm being measured and found lacking. Before I can drop my hand, his shoots out and grabs on as he gives me a brusque nod.

"Never mind Nosh," Yuma mumbles. "He's an old coot."

I have so many questions, but I don't get a chance to ask them when Wapi loudly announces, "Grub's on!"

just as Ouray walks in from outside, carrying a massive tray of grilled meat.

There's a sudden cacophony of noise when people start moving all at once, congregating on the massive dining table. A ton of food has been set out, but then there are a good twenty-five or so people here.

"You sit here," Yuma says, guiding me to one of the smaller tables dotting the large space. "I'll grab us something to eat."

I take a seat and watch what looks like an early morning stampede on Black Friday. I'm glad Yuma offered to get me some food, because I don't think I would've been able to get anything on my plate.

"Anyone sitting here?"

The woman who was observing me earlier walks up with a full plate.

"Not that I know of."

"Perfect." She pulls out a chair across from me and sits down. "You not eating?"

"Yuma is getting me a plate."

A bite she was lifting to her mouth stills halfway there.

"That's nice." She almost sounds surprised. "How long have you known Yuma?"

"I moved into the apartments he manages a couple of months ago." I know it's not really an answer, but something makes me a bit careful to share too much with this woman.

"Oh shit." Red Franklin walks up to the table, a scowl on his face. "Ginger, what the fuck are you doing?"

"Having dinner and talking with…Should I just call

you Detective Bucco?" she asks, turning to me.

"It's Lissie."

"...Lissie," she says, turning triumphantly to the still annoyed looking Red.

"Like hell you are." He pulls out a chair and sits down. "Wasn't born yesterday, woman."

I'm not sure what the interaction is about, or the looks the two share, but Yuma is heading this way with two plates loaded with enough food to feed a family of four.

"I'll finish whatever you don't," he announces, sliding one of them in front of me before he sits down beside me. "I got you a little of everything."

No shit. Ribs, sausage, potato salad, mac and cheese, a broccoli salad, and a chunk of garlic bread perched on top of the heaping plate.

Red and Ginger are already digging in with gusto, Yuma eyeing them suspiciously before he turns to me.

"Eat."

At first we eat in silence, with the occasional moan from me when a new set of flavors hits my palate. Simple fare, but so good. When I see Lisa walk by, I call her over.

"You are a goddess in the kitchen. This is incredible." Mumbled words of agreement go up around the table and Lisa, who looks like she's not used to compliments, disappears back into the kitchen with a little smile on her face.

"I'm busting out of my pants," I announce, pushing the plate, which is still half-full away. Yuma, who already finished his, pulls it in front of him and digs in. "Really?

How can you eat more?"

"Our boy has always had an insatiable appetite." Ginger shares with an appreciative glance at him that makes me feel slightly uneasy. "A variety of tastes as well."

"Ginger…" Red growls at her.

"What?" She turns to Red with an innocent look on her face, but doesn't seem genuine. "I'm sure Lissie would want to know what keeps him happy."

"And you're done," Red grunts, shoving his chair back and grabbing her hand to pull her up.

"What was that all about?" I ask Yuma, who stares after them, his jaw clenched.

"Ginger being Ginger," he says, turning back to me.

"They're a couple, right?"

"Yes."

"That's what I thought."

"Don't worry about it. She's an old lady, she's just flexing her muscle, making you feel uncomfortable."

"But you're even not part of the Mesa Riders."

"Makes no difference to Ginger. Ignore her. Trust me."

"Okay."

I still keep my eye on the woman who is back at the bar, Red's arm proprietarily draped over her shoulder, as they appear to be in conversation with Ouray.

"Come on." I turn to Yuma, who managed to empty my plate too. "Let's get out of here." He's already reaching for my hand.

"Wait. I should give Lisa a hand cleaning up."

"Babe…"

"We're not in a restaurant, Yuma. We can't just walk out and leave all this mess for her to clean up."

I don't wait for a reaction and stand up, stacking the four plates. I'm about to head to kitchen with them, when Yuma grabs them from my hands. "I've got it," he mumbles.

I follow him into the kitchen where Wapi is at the sink rinsing dishes, while one of the older kids is loading them into the industrial-sized dishwasher. Lisa is sitting at the table with the younger kids but gets up when we walk in.

"I was gonna offer to help clean up," I tell her.

"No need. I've got plenty of volunteers." The older boy loading the dishwasher snorts loudly, and Lisa throws him a sharp look. "And idle hands that need to be kept busy."

I'm sure there's a story there, as the boy turns all shades of red before focusing back to his task.

Goodbyes take another twenty minutes before we head outside.

"I've got my bike here, I'll follow you home." Yuma follows his words up with a deep kiss that has me forget we're perfectly visible through the big windows of the clubhouse.

I'm not surprised when he's already waiting for me at the base of the steps up to my apartment.

YUMA

Couldn't wait to get her out of there.

Fucking Ginger. She almost managed to shut whatever we've got going here down before we even get started.

I know there are things I need to talk to her about in more detail than I have, and although she's been very accepting so far, I'm not so sure how some of those details are going to go over. I'm not looking forward to that conversation.

Seeing her at the clubhouse was an unexpected but ultimately welcome surprise. She seemed to take the whole thing in stride, even my instinctive kiss, which was more of an announcement than I was ready to make. I may not know how this is going to work out, but I sure as fuck am ready to find out.

"Yuma…" she breathes when I shut the door behind me and crowd her against the hallway closet.

"James," I correct her, my nose almost touching hers. "My name is James Wells. Yuma to the outside, but with you I want to just be me."

Her eyes go soft and her hands come up to frame my face.

"James," she repeats. "Kiss me."

She doesn't have to ask me twice. Her mouth opens under mine willingly, and what starts out as a sweet kiss quickly turns into frantic groping in her entryway. Her tongue in my mouth, her hands tangled in my hair— holding on for dear life—while I pull up her leg and rub myself against her heat. I have to pry my lips from hers before I lose the last frays of my control.

"Don't want to take you up against this fucking closet

our first time, take me to your bed, Lissie."

Her cheeks flushed deep red, her dark eyes even darker, she takes my hand and leads me to her bedroom. Inside, she surprises me when she stops in the middle of the room, and turns around to face me, whipping off her top in the process. With her eyes locked on mine, she reaches behind her and unclips her bra.

Fuck me, she's beautiful.

Not because of her generous tits—they easily fit my palm—but because of the proud tilt of her chin, despite the hint of vulnerability in her eyes. She's challenging me to take her as she is. I almost laugh, because the idea I might have an option in resisting her is ridiculous. Instead I strip my own shirt, kick off my boots and socks, and shove down my jeans.

I hear her sharp inhale, but I'm not sure whether she's reacting to the tattoos covering my chest and stomach or my unencumbered cock pointing straight at her. It doesn't matter either way, because it's my cock she's focused on when she drops to her knees in front of me.

At the first touch of her tongue, I already almost blow my load, so I quickly haul her up under her arms.

"Hey," she protests. "I was enjoying that."

"Me too, Babe. Too fucking much," I grumble, while pulling down her jeans and underwear at once, the scent of her arousal thick and tempting in my nostrils. I can't resist pressing my face against the dark curls at the apex of her legs, inhaling deep.

"James," she whispers, running her fingers through my hair.

The slight scrape of her blunt nails against my scalp sends a charge straight down my spine all the way to my balls.

"Bed, Lissie."

She doesn't argue, just lowers herself on the mattress on the floor. First fucking thing on the agenda, after I fuck her, is getting a goddamn proper bed. I snag my jeans and fish out the hopeful condom I've had in my pocket this past week or so, rolling it on.

I hover over her, lowering my mouth to hers as I drop my hips in the cradle of hers. Immediately her legs wrap around my hips.

"Please, James."

"Fuuuck, Lissie," I groan when I feel the heat of her, as I slide inside her body. "I planned on taking my time."

Her legs tighten around me and her hands slide down to my ass as she chuckles with her face tucked in my neck.

"I'm not going anywhere."

10

LISSIE

OH MY GOD.

I don't even recognize myself.

The moment Yuma rolls off me to get rid of the condom, after a sweet brush of his lips on mine, I turn the opposite way.

I've never been one to be forward—or particularly adventurous—sexually. I don't even think I particularly enjoyed sex, which makes it even more mind-boggling that I would initiate it like some dyed in the wool seductress. Okay, technically he did when he told me to take him to bed, but I'm the one who ripped off her clothes and went down on her knees in front of him.

I can't believe I did that.

My only excuse is I may have known he was fit and

good-looking, but I wasn't really prepared for the full effect of him standing naked in front of me. The man is so gorgeous it should be illegal, and with his rugged looks and those tattoos giving him an aura of danger, he made my bad boy fantasy come true.

"I'd pay a fuckofalot more than a penny to know what's going on in that head of yours," he says, climbing in bed behind me, still a bit breathless from his release minutes ago. I'm not so sure I can even speak. I think I screamed.

Oh my God. What if someone heard me?

"That's enough," he grumbles, propping up on one arm and rolling me on my back with the other. The inhibition I was lacking earlier is back as I quickly pull up the sheet to cover myself. Something that doesn't go unnoticed. "Whatever you're thinking…stop it." He grabs my chin and turns me to face him. "Not doing much for my ego here, Babe."

I roll my eyes. "Nothing wrong with your ego."

"Talk," he urges.

There's no avoiding his penetrating blue eyes and after a few moments I give in.

"I don't do this. This isn't me." I can see I've confused him. "The whole sexy vixen thing, I'm not like that."

"Bullshit."

"It isn't."

He cups my face with a hand. "Babe, you're the most effortlessly sexy woman I know." His fingers drift down my neck and over my chest, pulling down the sheet until he has my breasts uncovered. "These…" He cups one, bending down to flick the tip with his tongue. "…are perfect." Sliding his hand down my belly, he presses a kiss on the slight swell. "Soft," he mumbles as he slowly slides down my body, pushing the covers out of his way.

I force myself to lie still while he briefly plays his fingers through the neatly trimmed patch of curls before leisurely exploring every bump and dimple of my generous thighs. As a lights out kind of girl, this kind of close scrutiny should have me running for the hills, but his quiet, almost reverent, attention to every part of me is addictive.

My breath halts when he spreads my legs, fitting the width of his shoulders between them.

"Beautiful," he whispers, almost to himself before he blows lightly. The touch of his breath on parts of me still sensitive has me inhale sharply and I reach for his head. His eyes shoot up to mine. "Lift your arms above your head, Lissie."

I slowly do as he asks, bracing my hands against the wall.

Holding my gaze, he spreads me with his thumbs and licks along my crease, flicking the tip of his tongue over my clit, his beard lightly abrasive against my skin. I hiss at the electric charge it sends through my body. So sensitive.

"Effortlessly sexy," he rumbles, and I can feel the vibration of his voice against me.

Not many men have gone down there, and fewer still left an impression, but even with Yuma's barely-there touches, he's able to pull me out of my head and place me squarely back in my body.

My mouth drops open when he licks again, paying more attention to that bundle of nerves as he inserts a finger. His other hand presses down on my belly, keeping me anchored to the bed when my body wants to buck against his mouth.

It's sweet torture as he brings me to the edge with firm flicks, only to ease off when he feels my body tense.

"Please…" I finally plead, when I can't control the trembling of my legs any longer.

I lift my head slightly to find his eyes still on me, satisfaction on his face as he penetrates me with a second digit. I close my eyes at the delicious stretch.

"Look at me," he growls and I snap them open. "Sweetest pussy I've ever tasted."

I don't have a chance to react to his words because the next moment his lips close over my clit, sucking hard, and this time my own ears ring when I scream my release.

I'm still catching my breath when he climbs up my body, brushing his nose and lips over my skin before he covers my mouth with his. I taste myself on him as he kisses me deeply, feeling the rasp of his beard on my skin.

"No more thinking," he says firmly before rolling onto his back, this time keeping me firmly in his arms.

I don't even have the presence of mind to offer a return of favors before I feel myself drift off to sleep.

THE SMELL OF coffee wakes me.

Even before I open my eyes, I know I'm alone in bed.

I woke up once during the night to use the bathroom and had a hard time escaping Yuma's hold with half his body covering me, an arm wrapped around me. and one of his legs inserted between mine. I finally managed, though, Yuma grunting his complaint as I tiptoed to the bathroom. By the time I'd come back he was sprawled on his back on the mattress, snoring lightly, but the moment I got in beside him, he was all over me again. Like some heat-seeking octopus.

I blink open my eyes to find one of my mugs sitting on the floor beside me, a piece of paper tucked underneath.

MORNING. PLUMBING EMERGENCY UNIT 3.
CUTE WHEN YOU SLEEP. CUL

I can feel the dopey smile on my face, even as I check my mouth for dried drool. It doesn't escape me, I've graduated from 'talk to you later' to 'see you later' in his sign off.

A quick look at my alarm shows six forty-five, and judging from the steam still coming off my coffee, he hasn't been gone that long.

Mmm. I could get used to good coffee served in bed.

As I carefully sip, my mind wakes up and immediately starts analyzing last night. Determined not to let anything—not even my own thoughts—spoil an amazing time, I direct them to work and the things I want to cover today.

First of all, I need to catch up with that witness I was supposed to interview yesterday, and then I have those names Red Franklin gave me to run down. I quickly realize I have a busy day ahead and scramble out from under the covers, bringing my mug into the bathroom.

I rush out of the apartment half an hour later, a travel mug and half-eaten bagel in my hands. I'm juggling both, trying to get my truck open, when a familiar hand appears from behind me and opens the door.

"Hop in, Babe," Yuma's deep rumble fills my ear.

When I'm seated, my mug in the cupholder, I turn to where he's leaning into the cab, his face inches from mine.

"Thank you for the coffee."

The small tug at a corner of his mouth is barely visible behind the facial hair, but it's there.

"You're welcome."

"How's the leak?" I ask.

"More like a plug than a leak," he informs me, wincing.

"Yikes."

"One of the less pleasant jobs managing a bunch of apartments." He shrugs it off.

"What are the more pleasant jobs?" I fish and his smirk is back.

"Making sure certain tenants get a good night's sleep."

"Certain tenants?"

"One," he quickly corrects. "One certain tenant."

I find myself grinning back.

"Good save."

"I thought so," he mumbles, leaning in farther for an all-too-brief kiss. "Busy day ahead?"

"Looks like it might be."

"Shoot me a message if you're going to be home for dinner."

"You planning to cook for me?"

Now I get a full-on grin. "I might." Another brush of lips. "Get started on your day. I'll see you later."

With a rap of his knuckles on my roof, he backs away, shuts my door, and watches me back out of my spot.

I'm still smiling when I walk into the station.

YUMA

NOTHING LIKE A plugged up toilet to start the day.

Not even the plunger could dislodge whatever was caught down the pipes, and I had to call in a plumber. While waiting for him to arrive, I make a quick stop in my apartment to grab a shower. It pisses me off that the scent of Lissie clinging to my skin is now covered by the smell of sewage.

She'd been dead to the world when I set the coffee on the floor beside the mattress. She was on her stomach; her face turned my way, cheeks slightly squished, forcing her lush lips open. What I wouldn't have given to crawl in beside her, but unfortunately with a tenant panicking with an overflowing toilet, I didn't have time. I did, however, take a minute to pull away the sheet bunched up at her waist to take in her generous, very naked ass underneath. Made up my mind right then, next time I'd take her from behind.

The memory of her taste and those lush curves has me palm my reawakened cock and seek some relief. It's not the same as the real thing, but it'll tide me over until she gets home.

I'm just in time to meet the plumber outside unit three and let him in, glad to hand off that problem. Tse is just pulling in when I walk back to the office. I'd almost forgotten we have a couple more units to outfit with new windows.

"You draw the short end again?" I ask when he gets off his bike.

"Nah, Wapi's better with the kids than I am. I volunteered." I already know what's coming next and brace myself. "Besides, wouldn't turn down an opportunity to check out that sweet ass again."

Tse isn't much older than me and has been a brother for over twenty years. That doesn't mean I don't want to plant my fist in his face at his taunting. I know that's what he's doing and he's fucking good at it. Always poking. So instead of giving him the reaction he wants, I force a smile on my face.

"Sweet doesn't do that ass justice. You have no idea."

I immediately turn and walk toward the small storage unit where I keep my tools. I hear his boots follow.

"Lucky fucker," I hear him grumble behind me, and I don't make any effort to hide the smug grin on my face when I turn.

"Yes, I am."

Without interruptions—other than the plumber letting

me know he fixed the problem in three—we get all three windows installed before the tenant comes home. The door will have to wait until tomorrow, so with one more unit to go after this, we'll need two days to get this job done.

Tse offers to come back both days, which is fine by me; we work well together. Always have.

When he's gone I store the tools, quickly wash up in my bathroom, and put on clean clothes before heading out to the seniors' home. I take my truck, because after seeing Momma I plan to grab a few things at the City Market, and getting groceries on a bike is a pain in the ass.

With Momma being the amazing cook she was, I never really had the motivation to expand on the few convenient dishes she taught me to make. One is bacon-wrapped meatloaf and roasted vegetables, so that's what I'm cooking for Lissie. Seems like a safe choice since discovering she likes her meat as much as I do.

Nosh is sitting at the small table in Momma's room when I walk in. Momma isn't here.

"Where is she?"

"Fucking dance classes. Can you believe it? Momma? Never wanted to set foot on a dance floor, and now she's fucking twinkle-toes."

I bust out laughing at his disgruntled face.

"She any good?"

"Fuck no. Couldn't stand to watch for more than five seconds. If she had any sense she'd be mortified."

I get it. It's a tough pill to swallow when not only does

your loved one not recognize you, but you also no longer recognize them either. It's a loss. A goodbye when they haven't even left yet.

"Was she smiling?" I ask, and his eyes narrow on me. *"Yes."*

I don't say anything else but hold my father's gaze until he finally looks away.

"Fuck." It's rare he uses his voice. He never was able to enunciate words well, so he doesn't bother. This one I understood clearly.

I sink down in Momma's chair.

"What's with the piece?" he asks, and I tamp down my irritation at his choice of words. Nosh is old-school, and other than Momma, and maybe Luna, he's never shown a particularly high regard for women. Something I'm ashamed to admit I haven't done much of either.

"She's got a name, and I like her."

"She's a pig."

Oh, yeah. The old man is trying to get a rise out of me, using his preferred slang for cops.

"She's a cop, yes."

"She know you're a boozer?" He takes great care spelling out the last word and I nod my response. *"Can't be very smart then."*

Christ, he gets on my last nerve. You'd think I'd be relieved he's no longer on about my shortcomings, but that would be preferable to listening to him coming down on Lissie.

"She's sharp as a tack. Why don't you go back to picking on me?"

Surprisingly that shuts him up. At least for a beat or two.

"You like her."

I drop my head back and raise my eyes to the ceiling, but my hands sign. *"Yes. I like her."*

He draws my attention with a knock on the table.

"Never fucking thought I'd see the day."

I have to dig deep, but there's a compliment hidden in that statement.

When Momma walks back in the room a few minutes later, she's all smiles. Even when she looks at me.

"Who are you?"

11

LISSIE

"JEFF LANSING."

I look up from my computer screen when Ramirez walks in, a smug grin on his face.

"Who's that?"

He tosses a sheet of paper on my table. The name he mentioned is printed at the top, with a picture depicting a guy—probably in his forties—underneath, along with a physical description.

"Professional engineer. I was finally able to get a hold of with that contact of Red's in the developer's office, Phil Becker. The guy insisted on meeting in Cortez."

"Isn't Arches Homes' office in Monticello?"

"Yup. Turns out, he had a good reason not wanting to chance being seen with law enforcement."

Immediately my interest is piqued. "Oh?"

"He's nervous. He says he cautiously approached Lansing a couple of months back and discovered the man had his own misgivings about the project, but wasn't ready to go into too many details. Then four weeks ago, he asked Becker to meet him at the site one night but never showed up. The company line was Lansing had received an unexpected opportunity he couldn't pass up on a project in the United Arab Emirates. He tried getting information from the office but was shut down. Then he tried to do some digging on his own, only to discover Lansing seems to have vanished. He's a little jumpy. Swears someone's been following him and his work computer has been accessed. He spent the entire time looking over his shoulder."

"He thinks Lansing is our victim?" I ask, almost eagerly. We've been struggling to get ahead on this case and I'm ready to sink my teeth into a good lead. Identifying the victim would go a long way in opening up this investigation.

"He does and we need to find a way to prove it."

I turn to my computer and throw his name into the system. Half an hour later we have an address, a two-year-old Ford pickup truck registered to him, and the name of a sister in Las Vegas. Ten minutes after that we're in Chief Benedetti's office and have him caught up on the new information.

"Fancy a trip to Vegas?" He's looking straight at me.

"Me? Not particularly."

"Someone's gotta go talk to the sister," he responds

with a shrug. "I have a contact in the police department, let me give him a call and see what they can do."

I listen in on the conversation, mentally crossing my fingers. I have no desire to go to Vegas just now, life is getting exciting here in Durango.

The past two days have been crazy busy. I solved my first solo case—the assault. I finally got around to interviewing that witness, and her information helped ultimately catch the guy last night.

Unfortunately, my crazy hours also meant I didn't get see a whole lot of Yuma. He wanted to cook me dinner—even went shopping—but there hasn't been an opportunity yet. I have my mind set on tonight, so I really don't want to be sent to Vegas.

"You're in luck," Benedetti says to me. "My buddy says he'll swing by her address tonight and see if she's home. He'll bring a DNA swab, just in case." I let out a relieved breath. "Now where are we on the concrete guys?"

"With the site still shut down, the crew's been disbursed on other jobs," Blackfoot informs him. "I'll head out tomorrow."

"Good." Chief points his finger at Tony and me. "Tomorrow, one of you connect with our colleagues in Monticello. Get them up-to-date and let them know we'll want to get into Lansing's apartment. We won't be able to do much until we confirm he's the victim, but as soon as we get the word, I want to get moving."

Blackfoot heads home right after the meeting; while Ramirez follows me back to the bullpen.

"Aren't you heading home?" he asks behind me.

"Just grabbing my bag and then I'm out of here."

"I meant to tell you; good catch yesterday," he says when I bend down to grab my purse from the bottom drawer of my desk.

"Thanks," I mumble, pleased with the easy compliment. I'm not used to praise.

"We may have gotten off on a bit of a rocky start, but I just wanted to let you know I'm glad you're here. You've been a real asset."

"The rocky start was on me," I admit. I had a lot of preconceived ideas when I first arrived and hadn't been particularly friendly. Mostly out of self-preservation, given I'd just left a very hostile environment, but it hadn't taken me long to see things are different here. "And I really enjoy working here."

"Glad to hear it. Hey, I was gonna head over to The Irish for a quick drink. You wanna come with?"

I'm not sure what drives me—maybe it's because in a few words he accepted me as one of the team—but I suddenly feel the need to come clean about something.

"I actually have dinner plans, but also; bars are a bit of a challenge for me," I admit, watching him carefully for a reaction. "I'm an alcoholic."

It costs me to say it. The only person who knew was Joe Benedetti. Apparently it was marked in my personnel file from Albuquerque. He'd called me and asked me straight up if I was dry. We had a long talk on the phone and I ended up with the job. It shocked the hell out of me, but he said my record was otherwise impeccable and he would give me the benefit of the doubt.

"Really?" Tony seems genuinely surprised.

"I should probably have said recovering alcoholic, but I'm told that's a misnomer. I haven't had a drink in almost a year."

"Good for you."

"And I never drank on the job," I quickly add. It feels important he know that.

He just nods in response, turns off his computer, and shrugs on his jacket as he starts walking out of the office. I'm still standing by my desk, wondering if I've made a mistake telling him, when he turns his head.

"Let's go, we'll grab a coffee at Durango Joe's instead."

IT SMELLS INCREDIBLE when I walk into my apartment.

My stomach immediately starts grumbling after sitting at the coffee shop, trying to ignore the sweet bakery smells. I didn't want to spoil dinner, so instead of indulging there, I got some pastries to bring home for dessert.

Tony was a surprise. He shared a little about himself before asking about me, and I found myself telling him a bit about my background. Not much, but enough to give him some insight. By the time we walked out of Durango Joe's, Tony had shifted from being a colleague to being a friend.

I fired off a quick text to let Yuma know when I was

on my way home as agreed, and from what my nose registers, he didn't waste any time.

"What are you cooking?" I ask, dropping my purse on the couch on my way to the kitchen. Yuma is chopping vegetables in big chunks.

He snakes out an arm and pulls me to his side, bending his head down for a thorough kiss. I don't hesitate dropping the bag from Durango Joe's on the counter and wrapping my arms around his neck. I realize I missed this—him—the past couple of days. Unreal how quickly I've become addicted to his touch. Just for a moment, I wonder if I should be worried, but his kiss quickly erases any misgivings.

"Bacon-wrapped meatloaf and roasted veggies," he says when he finally lets me up for air. "What in there?" He indicates the paper bag with pastries.

"Dessert."

"Already had plans for dessert," he mumbles, pulling the elastic from my hair as he shoves his face in my neck. "You smell good." His beard tickles and I pull up my shoulder.

"This food smells amazing. When's dinner?"

"Unfortunately, just twenty minutes. Not enough time to do what I want to. Why don't you get into something more comfortable," he suggests before following it up with an eyebrow wiggle. "Something with easy access."

"You're incorrigible," I admonish him, but do it grinning wide. "I'll be right back."

My head is still in the clouds when I walk into my bedroom and it takes me a second to register what I'm looking at.

Yuma

I LISTEN FOR a reaction, but when the silence stretches for more than just a few minutes, I quickly finish up the veggies, dump them on an oiled baking sheet, and shove them in the oven.

Cautiously I follow her into the bedroom, where I find her sitting on the edge of the bed, and I'm not sure how to interpret the expression on her face. It's either she's pissed and she's trying really hard not to blow up, or she's shocked and struggling with another emotion. I'm leaning toward pissed, since I took that into consideration when I went shopping for a bed today.

I'm not an idiot, I got advice from Lisa, who was more than willing to give me a woman's perspective on what kind of bed to get. Good thing too, because if up to me, I would've picked the first, sturdiest bed I bumped into. Lisa had given me the thumbs-up when I sent her a picture of the solid frame I chose.

"You bought me a bed."

I lean a shoulder against the doorpost and shrug.

"Told ya I would."

"I thought you were joking."

"Do you like it?"

She reaches out and runs her hand along the metal, geometric pattern on the headboard.

"It's beautiful. You got new covers too."

"I did."

I'm still not sure what reaction this is because her mouth is tight, but her eyes look wet. Pushing away from the post, I move to sit beside her on the bed. The moment I reach for her though, she takes off like a shot, only to return with her purse a moment later.

"How much?" she asks, digging through the bag and coming up with a checkbook.

"What are you talking about?"

"The bed, how much was it?"

"Put that shit away," I tell her, getting annoyed.

"I can tell it wasn't cheap, Yuma. Let me pay you back."

"Put it away, Lissie."

"Look…" She puts a hand on my arm. "I really appreciate it, it's beautiful, but I can't expect you to pay for it."

"Why the fuck not?"

"Because it wouldn't be right. I'm sure building management doesn't pay that well."

As pissed as I was starting to get minutes ago, I burst out laughing at her comment. She looks on in shock.

"You're cute. You know that?" I finally manage, pulling her down beside me. "The Riverside is only one of the club's businesses. Each brother gets a cut of club revenue, Babe. All of the revenue. Appreciate your concern, but I'm not hurtin' for money."

"So…you choose to live in that small apartment?" She seems genuinely perplexed.

"I have a house," I confess. "Haven't been able to bring myself to go there in months."

"Why?"

I look into her earnest eyes and don't hesitate

answering. "It probably still reeks like a brewery. Before I hit rock bottom, I'd holed up there for months. Fuck, I didn't exactly leave the place in a good state."

"I get that."

"I know you do."

"It still doesn't explain why you need to buy me a bed," she persists and I chuckle as I stand, pulling her up with me.

"Plan to spend a lot of time there." I wrap my arms around her. "Call it self-interest."

Of course when I bend down to kiss her, the oven beeps.

"Saved by the bell," she teases, and I press my lips to her smiling mouth.

"Get changed. I'll get food ready and I'll have dessert in bed after."

I reluctantly let go of her and head for the kitchen when she calls out.

"Thanks for the bed, Yuma."

"You're welcome, Lissie."

Five minutes later, when I have places set and the food out on the island, she walks into the kitchen, wearing soft, flowy lounge pants and a T-shirt of the same material. I do note the lack of bra and try to stay focused on dinner.

That turns out to be not so easy, since Lissie moans her appreciation with every bite.

"I'm stuffed," she complains when she shoves her empty plate away from her. "That was so good. You may be in trouble, I could get used to being fed like this."

I get up to take our plates to the sink when there's a

knock at the door.

"I've got it," Lissie says, already moving.

"I'm so sorry to interrupt," I hear Lisa say from the front door. "I didn't know where to bring her."

I turn to find her and Kiara standing in the doorway, the little girl is crying and Lisa looks rattled.

"What's wrong?" I ask, joining them.

"I have to take Ezrah to the hospital." She steps aside to show Ezrah sitting on the steps cradling his head in his hands. "We just got home and he tripped running up the steps. Busted his head. Can you keep an eye on—"

"Come here, sweetheart." Lissie pulls the little girl in her arms. To Lisa she says, "Go. We've got things here."

"I'm driving you," I announce.

"I'm okay," Lisa starts protesting but is quickly shut down.

"He's driving."

I bite off a grin at the bossy tone in Lissie's voice. Her neighbor doesn't argue more and nods once before heading back outside.

"I'll be back," I promise Lissie, dropping a quick kiss on her mouth.

Ezrah is surprisingly stoic, given the deep gash over his eyebrow, which is bleeding profusely.

"You okay, bud?"

"I'm good," he grits out bravely, sitting between his nana and me up front in my truck.

"Almost there. Gonna take a few stitches," I caution him.

"Ain't the first time."

I catch Lisa's eyes over his head. She's carefully blanked her face, but her eyes show concern. It occurs to me she has spent many years looking after those kids under horrible circumstances with no one at her back. That's changed. She's part of Arrow's Edge now.

At the hospital I drive straight to the emergency room entrance and let them out. Then I go find a parking spot. Before going in, I quickly call the clubhouse. Brick answers.

"I'm at the hospital with Lisa and Ezrah"

"What the fuck for?" he barks.

"Kid took a tumble and busted his head on the stairs. May only need stitches, but who the fuck knows. You wanna let Ouray know?"

"On it."

I hear the line go dead and head inside after them.

They're in the waiting room, which is luckily not that busy, and I sit down on the other side of the boy. The wait is not that long, maybe twenty minutes, when Ezrah's name is called.

"I'll wait here," I tell Lisa.

The nurse leads them down the hall. When they pass the desk, the person behind it calls Lisa over. Ezrah disappears through the door at the end.

I can't hear what is being said, but I recognize distress on Lisa's face. I make my way over.

"What's going on?"

Lisa keeps her eyes on the desk and mumbles under her breath.

"I don't have insurance, so they want a credit card."

I'm already reaching for my wallet when she takes a shaky breath in and adds, "I don't have one of those either."

"Go with your boy, I've got this."

A hand lands on my shoulder and Brick steps up.

"I'll take it from here," he rumbles, slapping a credit card on the desk before turning to Lisa. "Go to the boy. I'll wait for ya out here."

12

YUMA

LISSIE TURNS HER head when I walk into the apartment and immediately puts a finger to her lips. When I move closer I can see Kiara snuggled up to her on the loveseat, fast asleep.

"How's Ezrah?" she whispers.

"Still at the hospital."

When Kiara stirs, I bend down and pick her up, carrying her straight to the bedroom. She curls up on her side as soon as I pull the covers over her. Not exactly what I had in mind for that bed tonight, but it is what it is. There's no extra bed in the other bedroom.

"She okay?"

Lissie is in the kitchen, pulling her ever-present tea from the fridge.

"Still sleeping. Left the door open a crack, in case she wakes up."

"Good. She cried herself to sleep and I was afraid to move." She hands me a glass of tea. "So how come you're back? Does Ezrah have to stay?"

"Not sure yet. I called the club to let them know and Brick showed up. He all but kicked my ass out of the hospital."

"Brick?" She looks surprised.

"Yup. Came in and waved me off. He'll call when he knows more."

"I hope Ezrah's okay. Be tough on Lisa if she has a kid in the hospital or sick at home. It's just her with those two kids."

I got the sense Lisa is not nearly as alone as she may think she is, but I keep it to myself.

It's about ten when my phone finally rings. I'm almost relieved. I've had Lissie snuggled up to me, but every time I tried to cop a feel she shut me down because of Kiara sleeping down the hall. The movie playing on TV was some chick flick so that was hardly enough to distract me.

"Brick," I answer after checking the screen on my phone.

"It's Lisa, actually."

"Hey, Lisa. How's he doing?"

"Stitched up and pissed he doesn't get to go home tonight. Swelling's pretty bad and they wanna keep an eye on him for a bit."

"He'll get over it."

She chuckles. "Right. How's my girl doing?"

"Zonked out in Lissie's bed. Don't worry 'bout her. We've got her." I look over at Lissie as I'm talking and she nods.

"You sure?"

"Positive. Brick looking after you?" I chuckle when her answer is a displeased grunt.

"Can I talk to her?" Lissie asks, holding her hand out and I give her the phone.

As she settles back with the phone to her ear, I head to the kitchen. Listening with half an ear to her side of the conversation, I get myself a late-night snack of leftover meatloaf, which is even better cold.

Lissie joins me in the kitchen, putting my phone on the counter.

"You're eating that cold?"

"It's good. Try." I break off a chunk and feed it to her.

A mistake. I know it when she closes her eyes and makes those little moan sounds, which make me think of her naked and spread out in bed while I taste my favorite type of late-night snack. Unfortunately, with a five-year-old currently occupying the bed I had big plans for tonight, there will be none of that.

"I should head down," I announce when she tries to stifle a yawn as I pull her into my arms.

"You don't have to." Her little pout is cute. "The bed is big enough."

"Babe, not gonna share a bed with a five-year-old."

"Probably wise," she reluctantly agrees.

"Had plans for that bed."

"Figured as much." She grins, wrapping her arms around my neck. "I'm sorry your plans are spoiled once again."

I shrug. "They say abstinence is good for the soul. Fuckin' hope it's true 'cause I can tell ya—it's hell on the body."

LISSIE

"HELLO?"

I quickly slip out of the room, leaving the little girl asleep in bed.

"Bucco." All I hear are sirens in the background until Ramirez speaks. "We've got a situation and it's all hands on deck. Need you here."

I'd gone to bed after Yuma left last night and when I couldn't fall asleep, took my file on Dani out of the nightstand and started flipping through it. I'd been meaning to do that for a while now. Aside from a few old snapshots, it holds three postcards she sent me, and an impressive stack of journal notes I'd made over the years pertaining to my old friend. I was so sure somewhere in those notes was a reference to the Mesa Riders, but I couldn't find it.

Less than ten minutes later, Yuma answers the door of his apartment, looking rumpled, sleepy, and all kinds of delicious in a pair of barely buttoned jeans and naked torso. I'm instantly distracted by the gorgeously tattooed chest with sparse hair filling in as it narrows down to the V of his fly.

His low growl snaps me out of my fascination and my eyes pop up to meet his tortured ones.

"Not making this easy on me, Babe," he complains, shamelessly adjusting himself.

"Sorry," I mumble, before giving him the reason for appearing on his doorstep at three in the morning. "I hate to do this to you, but I have to get to a scene and—"

"Kiara," he finishes, walking back in his apartment. "Give me a sec."

Seconds later he comes back in view, and I almost groan as he covers that yummy chest with a T-shirt.

"Go," he says, while putting a hand along the side of my neck as he leans in for a brush of lips. "I've got this."

"I owe you."

There's only a twitch behind his facial hair, but his blue eyes twinkle.

"Like the sound of that, Lissie."

My grin only lasts as long as it takes for the reason for my middle of the night excursion to resurface.

Ramirez is waiting for me at a murder scene on Florida Road. The victim happens to be one of the guys on our witness list. Scott Clarkson was a laborer for Pro Concrete and one of the two club members Red Franklin put in place on the Wildcat Canyon project. This is not going to go over well. Blackfoot immediately took off to check on the welfare of the second Mesa Rider, Marty Spengler, who is renting a trailer in Hesperus.

A neighbor in the apartment building had come home after a late shift, and noticed Clarkson's front door open. When he stuck his head inside and called the guy's name, the first thing he saw was someone at the far end of the hallway running to the back of the apartment. Then he noticed a boot sticking out of the kitchen. When he went to check it out, he found Clarkson dead. Whoever else had been there took off through the sliding doors to the small patio.

This apartment building is lower budget than most of the places in and around Durango. Some of the exterior is in poor repair and I notice garbage piling out of a large bin on the far side of the building.

I'm stopped by a uniformed officer I don't recognize as I pull into the parking lot and have to flash my badge to get through.

It's not hard to find Ramirez, who is standing in the door opening of a main floor apartment.

"Bucco. Good. Doc Carter's on her way, but I want to do a quick walk-through with you before she gets here."

One of the crime techs hands me a pair of gloves and some hospital booties so I don't contaminate the crime scene. I take a deep breath in through my nose, which isn't too smart, because I can already smell the sweet, metallic scent of blood. Mouth breathing it is, I remind myself as I follow Ramirez down the narrow hallway to where he steps over a stretched leg jutting out of the doorway.

I thought our first victim at the construction site was bad, but this one is infinitely worse. The amount of blood is unreal, the thick, cloying smell triggering my easy gag reflex.

What is left of the once clearly fit man on the floor

isn't pretty.

Other than his legs—one sticking out in the hallway and the other bent at the knee—the rest of his body is covered in blood.

"First impression?" Ramirez asks, and I purse my lips, blowing out the breath I've held since walking in.

"He was tortured," I force out, trying to focus on individual parts instead of the whole. "Hands look crushed. Superficial cuts up his forearms, shallow stab wounds in the abdomen. Severe beating around the face. His neck, it looks like it was cut twice."

"You're good," Meredith Carter's voice sounds behind me. "The top cut was a threat, the bottom one did the real damage."

She steps around me and bends down beside the body, but the moment she starts manipulating the victim; I'm done. With my hand covering my mouth, I stumble out of the apartment and don't stop until I get to the safe haven of my truck in the parking lot, puking out my guts as I hang onto the gate. Thank God I backed it in against the foliage bordering the lot.

"You okay?"

Shit.

I wipe my mouth with the back of my hand and straighten up to find Tony looking at me with concern.

"Lissie?"

"I'm good. Gets to me every so often, but I'll be fine."

"Sure?"

"Positive. Let's get back in there." I start walking back to the building without waiting for an answer. "He was looking for something," I suggest, as Tony falls into step beside me. "Or someone."

"Until the neighbor showed up."

"Right. So given the guy beelined it out of here, it's possible he may not have found what he was looking for."

"Maybe we can. Let's go look."

We spend a few hours going over every inch of that apartment after Doc Carter takes the body to the morgue. The only things we find of any interest are the pieces of a smashed cell phone on the floor in the corner of the kitchen.

"Still no SIM card?" Ramirez wants to know and I shake my head. It's the only part of the phone we haven't been able to recover, and the one that contains the information.

"Maybe the guy took it with him?"

"Let's make absolutely sure and move the fridge," he says.

The two of us pull it away from the wall and I squeeze into the narrow space we create.

"Give the man a cigar." I hold out the SIM card to Ramirez.

"Want an evidence envelope?" one of the crime scene techs asks him.

"Yeah, but we're sending this to the FBI lab."

The sun is up when we walk out of the building.

"I'm gonna take this to the station and sign it into evidence." Tony holds up the plastic tub with evidence bags. "Do you want to stop at home and freshen up while

I do that?"

"Sure you don't mind? I'll be half an hour ,tops."

"Go. You'll feel better."

Growing up, all I heard was girls don't have the stomach for real police work. At my first murder scene, I'd upchucked my dinner to great hilarity of my brothers and father, who took every opportunity to remind me of my 'weak stomach.' So I made sure I never showed any weakness again in public. I just dealt with the aftermath at home, usually by drinking myself numb.

In the few months I've been here, I've been shown more kindness and thoughtfulness than all my years in Albuquerque. Tony's suggestion alone is proof of that.

The first thing I notice when I walk into my apartment is Yuma's feet hanging over the armrest of my loveseat, and I immediately feel guilty. Easing my shoes off, I tiptoe straight down the hallway to the bedroom, where Kiara is also still asleep, her little body starfished in my new bed. I quietly collect clean clothes and take them with me into the bathroom.

Under the hot stream of water in the shower I let go of the inevitable flood of tears I so carefully guard.

Yuma

I HEARD HER come in and sneak by me into the bedroom.

Assuming she's going back to bed to catch a few more hours of sleep, I close my eyes trying to do the same. Then I hear the shower turn on and a minute or two later the distinct sound of muffled sobs.

I'm off the couch in a flash and first check the bedroom to make sure it's not Kiara who woke up scared, but the little girl is still asleep. Then I turn to the bathroom.

She's sitting on the floor behind the enclosure, her hunched silhouette visible through the frosted glass. I'm stripped in seconds and open the door, step in, and crouch down in front of her. She doesn't even look up, so I sit my ass on the tile floor and pull her huddled body on my lap. She lifts her head just long enough to shove her face in my neck.

"I'm sorry," she finally mumbles against my skin. "I didn't mean to wake you."

"I was awake. What happened?" I brush the wet streaks of hair out of her face.

"Bad scene. I…I don't do well with…bodies."

I almost suggest she might be better off in a different profession but catch myself.

"Does this happen every time?" I ask instead.

"Pretty much," she mumbles, getting to her feet. "You'd think I'd be used to it by now."

She turns off the water and steps out of the shower, and I try not to get distracted by the water dripping down the globes of her full ass. She hands me a towel when I climb out of the shower. I take it and grab her hand to pull her close.

"I've gotta go back to the station," she says, bracing her hands against my chest. "I just came home to clean up."

I kiss her anyway.

"You get ready, Babe. I'll go make some coffee."

I shrug into my clothes and try to sneak out through the bedroom when Kiara suddenly sits up in bed.

"Where's Ezrah?"

"Your nana is still at the hospital with Ezrah, but they should be home today." I cross my fingers that doesn't turn out to be a lie. I walk over to the bed and lift her on my hip. "How come you don't like pancakes?"

"I like pancakes," she corrects me right away, as I carry her down the hallway to the kitchen, where I set her on a stool.

"Are you sure? I could swear you didn't like them. I was going to make you oatmeal for breakfast instead"

"Yuck. Oatmeal tastes like cardboard." She demonstratively makes a face and sticks out her tongue.

"You haven't tasted my oatmeal yet, it's the best. Better than chocolate cake."

"I like chocolate cake."

By the time Lissie walks into the kitchen, I have a travel mug waiting and am pouring batter in the pan.

"Mr. Yuma is making pancakes!"

"That sounds delicious." Lissie smiles at her. "But I am late for work, do you think you could save me one or two for later?"

The little girl nods her head. "I will."

13

YUMA

IF I NEVER see another episode of *Dora the Explorer* again it'll be too soon.

By the time Lisa comes to pick Kiara up, I've sat through at least half a dozen of them.

"Nana!" The little girl jumps up from the couch and comes running. "Where's Ezrah?"

"He's at home." Lisa gives the girl a quick hug before turning to me. "Thank you."

"No problem. Lissie was called in on a new case, so Kiara and I hung out this morning."

"Appreciate it." She turns to the little girl. "What do you say, girl?"

"Thank you, Mr. Yuma," Kiara politely says. "I like your pancakes." Then she darts out the door.

"The boy okay?"

"Crankier than normal but he'll survive, even if I don't," she grumbles before setting out after her granddaughter.

I close the door and pull out my phone to shoot Lissie a quick message.

Me: Ezrah's home. He's fine.

I immediately get a response.

Lissie: Excellent. Thank you for jumping in.

Me: No problem. C U later.

It takes me a few minutes to straighten up her apartment. As I make my way downstairs to my own place, I can't help notice Brick's truck parked in front of the building. Looks like Lisa and the kids are in good hands.

"RALLY IN SANTA Fe this weekend. You gonna ride? We're leaving tomorrow at noon."

I stopped by the club, hoping I could have a word with Trunk, but he's busy with one of the boys. Ouray finds me sitting in the kitchen, having a coffee by myself while I wait. He walks over to the coffeepot and pours himself one before he sits across from me.

The question is not as easy to answer and Ouray knows it. I haven't been out to a rally since last year. Talk about temptation. I used to love them, mainly because it meant partying and pussy, which is exactly why I've been avoiding them.

I knew eventually this question was coming. I'm supposed to be the MC's sergeant at arms, but that's been in name only. Paco has carried out my responsibilities for years, and all I did was ride in the spot he should've had all along.

"You wanted to see me?" Trunk comes lumbering into the kitchen.

"Do you have a few minutes?"

"Sure. Let me grab a coffee."

While Trunk sees to that, I turn my attention back on Ouray. "Can I get back to you on the ride?"

"Sure." His voice is even, but I can read disappointment on his face.

I follow Trunk to his office and sit down across from him.

"You doing okay?" he asks, right off the bat.

"Not bad."

"Keeping up with AA meetings?" Trunk isn't known for mincing words. He's a child psychologist but even with the boys he's a straight shooter.

It's on my tongue to spout excuses, but I don't really have any.

"No," I tell him honestly.

"I get it's not your thing, but there's a purpose to those meetings."

"I've been seeing someone."

"Brother…I *know*. No one missed that lip-lock you put her in out there in the clubhouse. Surprised the fuck out of me; let me tell you. Unless we're not talking about Detective Bucco?"

"Yes, we're fucking talking about her," I bristle, annoyed at his implication, which he apparently finds funny.

"Keep your shorts on. I'm just trying to get the lay of the land here." He sits back and tents his fingers. "And I'm trying to figure out what seeing someone has to do with you *not* hitting up regular meetings."

"She's easy to talk to," I explain. "Not judgmental."

"I'm glad, but you know as well as I do that probably only lasts as long as things keep going well. Can't expect her to understand the dark sides of addiction. The cravings, the stumbles, the pitfalls."

"She fuckin' understands better than you."

Trunk's eyebrows shoot up. "Yeah? How's that?"

"She's been sober for close to a year."

"Shee-it. Really, brother?" He rubs his hands over his bald head. "Big risk. She trips up, she could take you right with her."

"She's not gonna trip."

"You don't know that."

"She's not gonna fucking trip," I reiterate. "She's much stronger than I am."

Even as the words are still forming, I know it's the truth. This morning proved it. Would've been easy for her to numb the effects of a grisly case with a drink, but she didn't. Instead she took the impact on the chin and went right back to work. I don't know if I'd have that strength.

Trunk seems to think on that for a bit.

"Then what brings you here?" he finally asks.

"Two things." If I didn't believe this talk would be completely confidential I wouldn't dream of sharing what I know about Lissie, but I trust Trunk. I tell him what I know about her.

"She's a complex woman and I don't wanna fuck this up," I come clean.

"Why do you think you will?" he doesn't hesitate asking.

"Jesus, Trunk. Have you met me?" I scoff. "Don't think there's anything I haven't fucked up in my life."

"Little hard on yourself, aren't you?"

"Isn't that the point? Accountability?"

"Accountability is. Self-flagellation is not, it's more destructive than the addiction itself."

It takes me a minute to take that in.

He's right; there's a difference between taking responsibility and cutting yourself down at the knees. Which is something that's become second nature. Not sure how the fuck to change that.

"Look, I hear you, man. When I met Jaimie, I had the same kinda fucked-up ideas. She was too good for me...I didn't deserve her..."

"So what changed?"

He grins at me. Used to Trunk's normally gruff expression, the grin looks almost menacing.

"Nothing," he says, his face turning serious. "I'm still nowhere near good enough for her, and I sure as fuck still don't deserve her, but I've discovered it doesn't matter. Jaimie fell for me warts and all. Only difference is, I've learned not to question it."

"Really fucking helpful," I grumble.

"You want advice? Here it is: be whoever the fuck you are. If she's willing to spend time with you, she clearly already thinks you're worth it. Now, what was the second thing?"

"The club," I tell him.

By the time I walk out of his office, Trunk has provided me with the perspective I was looking for. Bolstered, I head straight across the hallway where I find Ouray in his office.

"Yes," I finally answer him, as I walk in the door. "I'll ride with you, but not at your flank." It's customary for the VP and sergeant in arms to ride on either side of the president's rear wheel.

"Why the fuck not?" he barks.

"Because…" I take off my cut and with the letter opener I grab off his desk, rip the stitches attaching the patch to my vest.

"What the hell are you doing?"

"I'm riding behind, with my brothers. This…" I wave the patch in front of him. "…belongs to Paco. Always has and you know it."

LISSIE

IT'S ALMOST MIDNIGHT by the time I finally walk in my door.

We've been going nonstop since I got to the office at seven thirty this morning, starting with a sit-down with the FBI in our offices. Those guys took the SIM card to work on, see what information they could pull off. They would also send an agent to the Mesa Riders' compound in Moab for notifications.

We were able to get a positive ID on Clarkson through his tattoos. Thankfully Ramirez volunteered to attend the autopsy while I headed out to the offices of Pro Concrete with Blackfoot.

Keith had struck out at the other man's trailer and found it empty. Red Franklin's second man, Marty Spengler, was missing and we were keeping our fingers crossed the guy would show up at his club instead of dead somewhere.

The manager we spoke to at the contractor's office was able to tell us that Clarkson and Spengler had been working on a job near Farmington since the Durango site was shut down, but work there had been completed earlier in the week. Right now the crew was waiting at home for the next contract.

We left with a list of names we started going down right away, since most of them appeared to be local. The only guy we weren't able to talk to was the foreman. His neighbor informed us he had a family emergency, and he and his wife had left for Nebraska the day before.

The last few hours I spent back at the office until I fell asleep at my desk and Ramirez, who stayed as well, sent me home.

I don't even bother turning lights on and head straight for the bedroom, where I barely manage to set my alarm and plug my phone in to charge before I fall face-first on my new bed.

I'M STILL GROGGY, and in a rush to get out of the door, when I spot the piece of paper on the floor by the front door.

CALL ME WHEN YOU GET IN.

Shit.

Last time I had contact with Yuma was around dinnertime when I sent him a message, letting him know it would be a late night.

I pull the door shut behind me, and head down the stairs, but instead of going for my truck, I stop in front of Yuma's apartment. I feel bad I missed his note last night, and I really want to see him before work swallows me up again, but at the same time I don't want to wake him up.

Before I have a chance to make a decision, his door opens. Much like the last time, his chest is bare and his jeans barely done up.

"Hey…" I manage, when he grabs my hand, pulls me inside, and holds me tight while kissing me silent.

"You didn't call," he rumbles when he lets me up for air.

"I missed your note last night. I was so tired."

He brushes a strand of hair behind my ear as his eyes roam my face.

"Are you takin' care of yourself?"

"I am." When he raises a questioning eyebrow I add, "The best I can. The guy who was killed? He's connected to the Wildcat Canyon site as well. This case is breaking wide open. It's going to be crazy busy for a while."

"Too bad. Was hoping you could come to Santa Fe with me for a rally this weekend."

"A rally? Like a bike rally? As in me on the back of your bike?"

He chuckles at my excited rambling. "Yeah, Babe, on the back of my bike."

"It kills me, but I can't. Any other time I would've jumped at the chance, but—"

His mouth descends—cutting me off mid-sentence—and my insides melt when he kisses me sweetly.

"No need to explain. That spot on the back of my bike is yours. We'll get you on there sometime soon."

I grin big. Never knew I could get excited about the prospect, I always considered riding on the back of a motorcycle Dani's thing. Thinking of Dani, I should probably talk to Yuma about her. See if he knows anything.

"I wish I had time—there are a few things I'd like to talk to you about—but I'm gonna be late for my meeting if I don't hustle."

"Got a few things to discuss with you myself, but it can wait until after I'm back and you've caught your guy. I'm not in a hurry."

There's a host of emotions, behind those gorgeous eyes of his, I wish I had time to explore. Instead I lift up on my toes and press my lips to his.

"Have fun and ride safe, okay?"

"I will."

"And let me know when you get there?"

"Sure thing."

"I may not be able to message you back right away, but I will as soon as I can."

"Babe, you're gonna be late."

"I know."

I lift my lips for another kiss, this one deep and delicious, giving me time to explore his chest with my hands. When I brush my thumbs over his nipples, he growls deep in his throat and pulls back.

"Killing me here."

I grin up at him and mouth *"Sorry."*

"Sure you are," he teases, grinning back.

"I'm glad I stopped by, James."

His eyes darken when I use his real name.

"As am I, Beautiful. As am I."

I can't remember the last time I drove to work in the middle of a murder investigation wearing a smile that wouldn't go away.

Probably never.

14

YUMA

IT FEELS GOOD, riding with the guys again.

I would've preferred having Lissie sitting behind me, her arms around my waist, but I'm hoping that day will come.

It's been a long time since I've been part of the pack, now that Paco has taken my former spot in front of me.

After my announcement yesterday, Ouray immediately called all the guys into his office. There was protest—in particular from Nosh who handed me the patch over a decade ago—but after Ouray yelled for order, I had a chance to explain myself to my brothers. Paco was voted in as sergeant at arms unanimously.

Next item on the agenda had been Wapi, who's had a rocky road as a prospect, but has done everything he could to make up for earlier mistakes. He proved himself to be a loyal brother and Ouray put his name forward to be patched in. That was another unanimous vote and Wapi was brought in under the cheers of all his brothers.

He's riding beside me at the front of the pack, proud as punch and smiling wide.

"Stop grinning, you moron," I call out to him. "You're chewing bugs."

I shake my head when he turns his head to me, and opens even wider, sticking out his tongue. I can't help grin at the guy's excitement. It's a miracle he's even sitting up straight. The guys partied hard last night. I left early, maybe half an hour into the raucous celebration, but he'd already been three sheets to the wind. I remember when I was patched in. I'd been a few years younger than Wapi, and I got so hammered I was sick for three days straight.

Not my new brother, though, he has to have a stomach of steel.

It only takes us about four hours to get to the hotel-casino just north of Santa Fe, where we usually book a block of rooms. The parking lot is already half-full with motorcycles. Looks like some of the other MCs have arrived.

Manny, president of the Amontinados MC, walks up to Ouray the moment he parks his bike. Even though the Amontinados are firmly on the wrong side of the law, the ties with Manny go back many years, since he was a brother with the Arrow's Edge. He didn't like the turn Ouray was taking the club in after he took the gavel and took the optional patch out given at the time.

Only two other guys chose to opt out. There definitely was animosity, and I don't have a clue where those two ended up, but over the years things have settled some with Manny Salinas.

"Red ain't coming," he announces.

"Why the fuck not?"

"Heat showed up late yesterday. One of his guys was found dead. Remember Scottie? Had that restored '48 Panhead?"

"Crash?" Ouray wants to know.

Manny shakes his head. "No, man. Someone offed him ugly."

"Fuck!"

He pulls out his phone and starts walking toward the edge of the parking lot, where he starts pacing back and forth.

I turn to Manny.

"What happened?"

"Red couldn't get hold of any of y'all so he called me. All I know is Scotty was found filleted in an apartment in Durango, and he needed to talk to Ouray. Red sounded wrecked."

My mind immediately goes to Lissie. With the limited number of murder cases we have in Durango, I have no doubt this is the case she is working on. She never said anything other than it had been a bad scene, and from what Manny described it must've been.

"Let's get the fuck checked in," Ouray barks as he approaches. "I want all my guys in my room in twenty minutes."

No one argues as he stalks right by us into the lobby.

Twenty minutes later, we're all crammed into Ouray's room. Standing room only. Between checking in and getting my gear in the room I'm gonna be sharing with Paco, I'd barely had time to shoot Lissie a quick message to let her know we got here in one piece.

"Okay, everyone shut the fuck up. This is gonna be short and sweet, and I don't feel like yelling or repeating myself." Ouray's deep voice carries, even when he's not trying, and a hush falls over the room. "Scottie Clarkson, one of Red's guys, was found dead early yesterday morning. He'd been tortured, beaten, stabbed, and had his throat slashed."

Immediately a rumble of shocked voices goes up in the room.

"Shut it!" Kaga barks.

"Scottie was working on something for Red and me. We think that may be what go him killed."

He goes on to explain how they formed Red Mesa Holdings and invested in the Wildcat Canyon Development because of the ANL's connections to the project. I can tell some of the guys are as pissed as I was, like Paco, whose glare is aimed at him.

"That's bullshit."

Ouray's head snaps around. "I'd fucking do it again. We're in the business of looking out for kids and that was the objective here. The less people knew what we were up to, the better, and the fact Scottie's dead only proves that. However," he adds looking around the room. "It's possible there'll be more violence, so I need you all to be on alert. Also keep an eye out for another one of Red's guys, Sparky Spengler, he's missing."

We disperse after that, but I notice Paco and Kaga hanging back. I almost go back in, but realize I'm no longer part of the chief's counsel. By my own design.

"Hungry?" I turn to find Trunk waiting for me. "Some of the guys are hitting up the buffet in the casino."

"Sure."

The casino is loud; the sound penetrates the segregated restaurant. Buffet food is mediocre at best, and this one is no exception. I mostly listen as my brothers talk, and sip water while they toss back beer.

"You're quiet," Trunk says beside me. "Any regrets?"

I shrug. "Nah, it's an adjustment, that's all. I was just thinking this kind of thing used to be a lot more fun before."

"You mean before sobriety," he aptly concludes. "Having trouble?"

"No," I answer, holding back the 'not yet' that was on the tip of my tongue.

Half an hour later in the casino bar, those words come back to me when the third person gives me a hard time for not taking the drink they offer. Not my brothers, they know better. It's the guys I've shared many a bottle with over the years, and sometimes more than that.

"What the fuck is wrong with ya?" Bones, a guy from one of the clubs we used to ride with, taunts me after I refuse his offer of a drink for the second time.

The Moab Reds. That relationship had iced over after their vice president shot me last year. A particularly dark time for me. That episode skidded me right to rock bottom. Fuck, I can barely remember a single conscious moment in the months that followed.

"Piss off, Bones," Ouray, who just joined us in the bar, snarls.

"It's like that, is it?" Bones, who doesn't know the meaning of no, also doesn't have sufficient functioning brain cells to realize he's messing with the wrong guy. "Your president holds ya dick when ya piss too? Pussy."

Should've walked away but I can't let the insult stand, so instead I haul out and land my fist under his fat chin. Already good and wasted, he stumbles back, trips over a barstool, and goes down like a brick wall. Immediately stools scrape as his compatriots shoot to their feet, guns in hand. I don't have to look behind me to know my brothers are at my back, probably weapons at the ready as well.

"Walk away."

The voice belongs to Rooster, Moab Reds' new president. He calmly walks in the middle of the standoff, his back to us. I have to give it to the guy; he's got balls with at least half a dozen guns pointed at his back.

"Put the fucking weapons away and walk. *Now!*" he barks.

"Stand down, boys," Ouray says calmly from behind me. "I'm sure security is on its way, and none of us will have a fucking bed tonight if you don't break this shit up."

Five minutes later, Rooster's guys—including Bones—are back at the other end of the bar, doing shots, and occasionally throwing me dirty looks. Security came and went, leaving us with a warning.

"Calling it a night," I announce, more than done with this scene.

My fist is throbbing, which only makes me want a drink more.

LISSIE

"YOU SURE YOU don't want to take some home?"

I'm standing on the gallery outside Lisa's door. I only wanted to pop in to see how Ezrah was doing, when Lisa insisted I stay for dinner. Apparently she can only cook in huge quantities. There was enough to feed a block party; between the four of us we'd barely made a dent.

Ezrah seems to be doing all right. Ticked off his nana wouldn't let him go show off his scar at the club. Lisa mentioned Brick insisted he could take care of the other boys and get them fed at the club for a couple of nights. Seems the whole club, minus Brick and Tse, were out on this run.

"I'm afraid it might go to waste in my fridge, Lisa. We're in the middle of what is turning out to be a major investigation, and it's sheer luck that got me home at a decent hour tonight."

It's true. The murder of Scott Clarkson had ramped up the FBI involvement in the case. Especially since the other plant with Pro Concrete—Marty Spengler—was in the wind. Like yesterday, a lot of today was spent knocking on doors in the neighborhood of Clarkson's apartment. Taking down statements, looking for security footage, trying to pin down times.

It's tedious and exhausting and after an entire day of it, Chief Benedetti sent us home to get a good night's rest.

"Fair enough," Lisa says. "It'll be in my fridge if you change your mind."

My apartment is quiet in comparison. Dinner was a lively event with Kiara's nonstop chattering. Such a sweet child. Ezrah didn't say much, but I would occasionally catch him watching his sister with the hint of a smile on his face. Ornery as he may be, it's clear he loves his sister and nana.

I head straight for the bedroom and change into a pair of lounge pants, heavy socks, and a sweater. Then I pour myself a tea, stuff my phone in my pocket, grab my laptop, and my notes on Dani, and head out my new sliding doors to the balcony. It's a beautiful night, getting cooler, but the air is crisp and fresh.

I set my glass on the small table and sink down in the one purchase I made since moving in—my comfy Adirondack chair. I prop my laptop and phone on the wide armrest and open my file folder.

I've gone over this file many times in the past few months, and although I'm pretty well convinced Dani hasn't holed up in Durango somewhere, I'm still hopeful I can find some answers here.

Between the last postcard she sent me and that single, much too short and alarming phone call early this year, there is a long eight-year gap. Eight years without any kind of communication.

I take out the three postcards she sent. The first one has a picture of the Grand Canyon and all it said on the back is, *'Wish you were here.'* The second card was sent from Vegas and says, *'Having the time of my life.'* She called a few times during that period with wild stories of parties and sleeping under the stars. I remember her trying to convince me to join her in Vegas.

I loved Dani and missed her like crazy but unlike her, the thought of not knowing where my next meal would come from, or where I'd put my head at night was never that appealing. My focus had been trying to fit into the family mold by being the best cop I could be, hoping one day I'd get the respect from my family I craved. Of course that day never came.

The last card was sent from Canyonlands National Park. On the back she had scribbled the words: *'Found my destiny.'*

Then eight years of silence until the thirty-second conversation that had me concerned.

Of course I'd tried to trace the call, and since then put her name in any search engine I've been able to access, but it's like Danielle Gorman disappeared off the face of the earth. Her driver's license was never renewed since she left Albuquerque, and has long since expired. I haven't been able to find any record of her.

The only things I have are the old journal entries I made whenever I would hear from her. Maybe it's time I started putting some feelers out. I've been hesitant before, unsure whether asking around would perhaps do more harm than good. For all I know, the call had been a bump in the road for her, which she'd resolved on her own, but the fact I haven't found any trace of her continues to nag at me. Especially lately.

That feeling I'm missing something has me flip through my notes again, paying closer attention to the last entries where she talked about an awesome rally in Vegas, and a 'big teddy bear from the north woods' sweeping her off her feet. I never did get more information, just the card a week or so after, saying she'd found her destiny.

Big teddy bear is not a lot to go on.

I put the file down when my phone rings. Yuma's number pops on the screen.

"Hey."

"You answered." The sound of his voice immediately sends ripples of anticipation down my back.

"You caught me home. How was the ride?"

"The ride was great." It almost sounds like there's more he wants to say but he holds back.

"Am I hearing a hesitation in there?" I probe and am rewarded with a deep sigh.

"It's tougher than I thought it would be," he admits. "Fuckin' guys giving me a hard time at the bar. Almost ended up in a brawl."

"Yikes. Don't let them get to you."

It's silent for a few moments before he says, "Talking to you helps."

I look up at the mountains, a silly grin on my face.

We spend some time talking about the rally, and a little about the investigation, until the cool night air starts getting to me.

"I'm sitting out on the balcony, but it's getting a little chilly out here. I should get my stuff inside."

"It's getting late, I'm gonna let you go and grab some sleep."

I don't particularly want to end the call but I have another 7:00 a.m. meeting scheduled for tomorrow.

"Okay."

"We're heading back on Sunday."

"Are you gonna be okay?"

"Yeah. I'll be fine."

A silence stretches, as apparently neither of us want to end the call, until I have to stifle a yawn.

"Night, James."

"Night, Lissie."

I'm already lowering the phone when I hear him saying something.

"What was that?"

His deep chuckle settles warm in my belly, but not as much as his words do.

"I miss you, Babe."

15

LISSIE

"DNA CAME BACK on the first body. It is Jeff Lansing."

It's not exactly a surprise, but Gomez's confirmation is another thing off our list and will help us get a warrant for access to Lansing's office and his house in Monticello. Although you'd have to wonder if anything worth finding would still be there at this time. We'll find out soon enough.

We've congregated in the conference room once again—despite being a Sunday—sharing the previous day's findings and coordinating next steps. This investigation is like a ball of twisted wire and no one knows which end is attached and which one isn't, but I don't think there is a single person in this room who doesn't suspect a single source at the core of it.

"We also got some good info from the SIM card you recovered," Gomez continues as he passes around handouts. "List of contacts and three months' worth of account printouts. We need to cross reference those, and then compare them with the list of names from everyone associated with the development, as well as anyone we know has connections with the ANL. Now that we have Lansing's identity confirmed, we'll get telephone records for him as well."

"Anyone have any luck getting any intel on Marty Spengler?" Joe Benedetti asks, looking at Gomez.

"None. The agent who went to the Mesa Riders' compound asked around, but no one's seen or heard from him."

"So they say," Ramirez mumbles. "That crew doesn't exactly put a lot of faith in law enforcement. I'm not sure they'd hand one of their own over."

"Good point, which is why we're keeping an eye on the compound."

"Franklin finds out, he's not going to be happy," Keith concludes.

"Can't be helped." Just then Gomez's phone starts buzzing on the table in front of him. "It's the office," he explains, answering the call.

I listen with half an ear while flipping through the handout, when I hear Gomez say, "Bones?" and my eyes shoot up. So do everyone else's. "Send it over," he tells whoever it is on the other side before hanging up.

He looks around the table.

"Not sure what it means, but it can't be good. Greene

did some creative online digging into Clarkson's financials, and found a monthly charge from Dropbox."

"Isn't that an online storage? Like the cloud?"

The FBI agent's eyes come to me. "Similar idea, yes. Anyway, he managed to break into the account. Found a bunch of images. He's sending them now."

One by one our phones start pinging.

I check the incoming email and open the five attachments. All photos from what looks to be a freshly dug hole in the dirt. The last three show the formwork holding back the soil, and concrete being poured.

"Son of a bitch," I hear Ramirez say. "Zoom in. You'll see it."

"We need to get Doc Carter in here," the chief announces. "Is there any way we can get this enlarged?"

"I can hook my phone up to the projector," Tony suggests, getting up, while Benedetti is already calling the coroner's office.

On my screen I clearly see what look like rib bones sticking out of the dirt at the bottom of the hole.

"THOUGHTS?"

I turn to look at Blackfoot who is behind the wheel. We're just driving away from the Pro Concrete office, where we had the dubious pleasure meeting with the mayor's cousin and owner of the company.

"He's a pompous ass."

Keith chuckles. "That apparently runs in the family.

But other than that, what's your take on him?"

"I don't believe he's clueless. He strikes me as someone who controls every single aspect of his business. And how convenient his foreman—the one person who'd be able to answer our questions on the Durango development—is incommunicado."

"Agreed. At least we were able to confirm they were pouring concrete at the site that day. Good catch on the picture's date signature, Bucco."

We discovered they'd poured the foundation for what is supposed to become a community center on that day.

"So now what?"

"I'm guessing GPR—ground penetrating radar—to confirm there is a body buried there."

Meredith Carter joined us in the conference room this morning and agreed we were likely looking at human bones. She suggested the body had been buried for at least eight or so years to have deteriorated to a skeleton. Gomez was looking into who would've owned the property back then.

"We have that technology?"

"We don't, but the FBI does, as does the Colorado Bureau of Investigation."

It's been a long, crazy week, but at least we're getting some traction on this case. Even though getting it by way of yet another body is not ideal. The problem is, the people who might be able to tell us more are nowhere to be found.

Pro Concrete's foreman is on vacation somewhere in Central America, we still don't have a bead on Spengler, and now Phil Becker from Arches Homes is not showing up at work or answering calls.

On the plus side, we're not short muscle on this case, which is why I don't balk when told it's my turn to take the day off tomorrow. I need to get some groceries, I'm running out of clean clothes, and I have some sleep to catch up on.

Of course there's also the fact Yuma is supposed to get back today, which might mess with my plans of catching up on sleep, but I'm willing to sacrifice.

Me: On my way home.

I figure he's probably still on the road when I don't get an immediate response, so instead of heading straight home, I stop at the City Market. Might as well get groceries over with, so I don't have to leave the house tomorrow if I don't want to.

I pile enough in my shopping cart to last me a few weeks. I'm not sure when I'll next have a chance to hit up the grocery store. With the back of my truck loaded up, I head home.

Butterflies hit my stomach when I see Yuma's motorcycle in the parking lot. I barely have a chance to turn off the engine when my door is yanked open and I'm hauled out of my seat.

"Fuck, baby…" Yuma growls down my throat.

Just like that my legs are around his hips, his hands on my ass, and my back pressed up against the side of my truck. My fingers tangle in the strands of hair brushing his collar when his tongue plunges into my mouth.

I completely forget where I am when he rolls his hips, rubbing the significant bulge in his jeans against the heat between my legs.

"Get a room!"

Ezrah's voice is like a bucket of ice water and I'm suddenly scrambling to get my feet on the ground. Yuma chuckles as he reluctantly lets go of me, grabbing my hand, and pulling me toward the building where the boy is sitting on the stairs, shaking his head.

"Good plan, kid," Yuma mutters as we pass him.

It's not until he kicks my door shut and pulls me straight to the bedroom, I remember my bags in the truck.

"I've got groceries—"

"Later." He yanks off my top and his hands immediately go to the clasp of my bra.

"Some of it needs to go—"

"Later, Lissie," he mumbles, bending low to close his mouth over a nipple the moment my breasts are exposed.

"But…ahh."

I can't do more than moan when he shoves one hand down the back of my pants, presses the other in the middle of my back, and pulls my breast deep into the heat of his mouth.

Suddenly I need to feel his skin under my hands. I claw at his clothes and he gets the message, yanking his shirt over his head. My fingers fumble with the buttons on his jeans until he brushes them away, doing the honors himself.

In seconds we're naked. I'm tumbled back on the

bed, his body landing heavy on top of me, as his mouth catches mine. Then he rolls, taking me with him so I end up on top. He arranges me so I'm straddling his hips. Sliding his hands into my hair hanging down on either side of my face, he gently lifts my face.

His softly muttered, "Ride me, baby," sends a full-body tingle over my skin. I'd love to ride him, but I have something else in mind first.

I slowly slide down his body, my tongue trailing over his skin. A growl sounds deep from his chest when I stop to tease his bellybutton. My lips draw into a smile when I reach the salty tip of his cock and he whispers, "Mercy."

YUMA

I'M PRETTY SURE she killed me.

My heart is hammering in my chest as I gasp for air.

Lissie is sprawled on my chest, her hair spread over my face and neck.

"I'm too heavy," she mumbles, trying to push up but I tighten my grip on her lush ass, holding her right where she is.

"Don't move."

I love the feel of our slick skin pressed together as her body still pulses around my cock. I inhale deeply, enjoying the heavy scent of sex mixed with the sweet smell of her hair.

"Are you sniffing me?"

I chuckle as she lifts her head.

"Smells a fuck of a lot better than the exhaust I've

been breathing in most of today."

She props her chin on her fist, her dark eyes on me.

"How was the rally?"

I'm tempted to brush off her question with a simple 'good,' but I force myself to be honest.

"The rides were great. The parties hard. I'd show my face and eventually hide out in my room. Not sure if you've noticed, but bikers don't often take no for an answer."

She snorts and fails to hide a smile. "I wouldn't know." She leans forward to brush a kiss on my lips before lifting off me. "Need to go to the bathroom."

Reluctantly I let her go but the moment I slip out of her body, I freeze. I can't miss the jiggle of her ass as she disappears into the bathroom, but it's not enough to heat the sudden chill in my bones.

I hear the toilet flush and then the faucet run, before she comes back in the room, a wet washcloth in her hands. Sitting beside me on the mattress, she gently wipes me clean.

"Shit, Lissie," I groan, regret lacing my voice.

"I know. That wasn't smart, but it's done. If it helps, as of my last check up I'm clean."

"Fuck, baby. Wasn't you I was worried about. I'm the one with the history."

She pelts the washcloth in the direction of the bathroom and stretches out, tucking herself against my side.

"I was considering that, but I'm sure you were given a full physical when you went into the treatment center, am I right?"

I've tried hard to forget what little I remember, especially of that first week in Denver. Now that I think about it, though, I remember my blood being taken.

"I think so."

"Okay. If it makes you feel better, we can both get tested and be sure. For all you know I had a similarly crazy sex life before you too."

"Did you?" flies out of my mouth before I can harness the accusation clear in my tone.

Fucking hypocrite.

She laughs in my face, and I deserve it.

"No. At least I don't think so."

I'm well aware it's a double standard and all, but I breathe out a sigh of relief anyway. If there was ever a good opening...

"About that," I start and her eyebrow lifts. "I think I mentioned booze and sex were an escape that used to go hand in hand?"

"I recall you mentioning something, yes."

"Not proud of it. Not proud of the parade of nameless, faceless people I was with."

"Doesn't matter, I'm not really looking for a blow-by-blow," she says with a wince. Smartass.

"What I wouldn't give to pretend that was never part of my life, but I can't because I know it's gonna come back and bite me in the ass sooner than later."

"Is it that bad?" She scrunches her eyebrows together.

I don't like seeing worry on her face and with my thumb brush at the frown on her forehead.

"Depends what you consider bad. I wasn't particularly discriminate, Lissie. One partner, two, sometimes more, whoever was in, I was game." I try not react to the expression on her face and forge on. Might as let it all fly now. "Was never looking to get attached, and despite being clear about that, not everyone had the same idea." I have to grab her when she moves to the edge of the mattress. I roll partially on top of her so she can't take off. "Not the same with you," I assure her, but I see doubt creeping in anyway. "Different place in my life, baby. I was drunk mostly and didn't mind sharing."

"Sharing?" Her voice comes out like a squeak.

"Partners."

"You mean take turns?"

Shit.

"Well…I guess sometimes, but it doesn't really work like that. More like an all for one and one for all. Mostly I was a third to a couple."

She pushes herself up in bed, resting her back against the headboard as she pulls the sheet up to her chin.

"A couple as in a woman *and* a man?" Her eyes almost bulge out of her face.

"Sometimes it happened," I admit.

She stares straight ahead at the door of her closet, and I try to decipher the thoughts playing out on her face.

"Say something, Lissie," I finally urge her when the tension gets to me.

"I…I don't know what to say. Is that…" She turns her tearful eyes on me. "…what you want? What you need? I'm not sure if I can—"

Realizing where her head is going, I stop her. "No. It's not what I want." I scoot up on the bed as well, and pull her tense body in my arms. "Not in the least. *Fuck.* I was wild, Lissie. Didn't give a fuck about anyone or anything, but that's different now. I've never cared before. Now I do."

"But what if..." She doesn't need to finish that sentence because I can read her well.

"Not gonna happen."

"How do you know?"

"Beautiful, look at me." She resists at first but finally tilts her head back to look me in the eye. "I'm not drunk, I'm not numb, and I've never felt what I feel when I'm inside you. Not ever."

Despite my words, she pulls away and this time I let her go. She grabs some clothes off the foot of the bed and heads for the bathroom.

I swing my legs out of bed and pick my jeans off the floor shrugging them on. My shirt is next.

"Where are you going?"

I yank the shirt over my head and look at Lissie, who walks in, dressed. I almost tell her I'm heading to my place, but take a chance at the last minute.

"Grabbing your groceries from the truck."

She blows out a breath. "Thank you."

"Lissie? You okay?"

The smile she throws me is weak, but I'll take it.

"I'm not gonna run, Yuma. What would that say about me? Running when you trust me enough to show me the edge of your darkness?" I start moving toward her but she holds up a hand. "You're gonna have to give me some time to process, though."

I can give her that and then some.

"All the time you need."

ARROW'S EDGE MC

16

LISSIE

HOLY SHIT.

I never considered myself a prude, but that confession shook me more than a little. Especially on top of the realization we'd had unprotected sex. That was monumentally stupid. I had my Depo shot, but that was right before I left Albuquerque. I'm probably due soon; I'd better start looking around for a new GP.

Other than once when I was young and not thinking clear, I've always insisted on a condom. It's a little scary, after twenty or so years of practicing safety; this man can make me forget my own basic rules. Hell, he doesn't just make me forget, he makes me lose my mind with those blue eyes looking straight into my soul.

I watch him walk into my apartment carrying all eight

grocery bags at once. He sets them on the counter and starts unpacking them while I fish out the perishables and put them in the fridge.

"Are you hungry?"

Yuma looks up. "I could eat," he says, and I hate the caution in his eyes. I hate the tension in the room.

"I want to cook for you."

A faint smile plays over his lips. "What's for dinner?"

"Beef Stroganoff?"

"Won't say no to that, Babe. Need me to do anything?"

"Pour us some tea?" I busy myself with dinner, while he gets drinks and sits down at the island. "How is your mother?" I ask, anxious to break the silence building.

"Taking freakin' dance lessons."

I let out a snort at his disgruntled answer. "Is she having fun, though?"

"I guess."

Silence stretches again while I slice strips of beef and mushrooms, tossing them in the hot butter.

"What was it you wanted to talk about? The morning I left, you mentioned having a few things to discuss with me."

Yikes. I did say that. I wish I knew where to start.

"A friend of mine is missing." A deep frown appears on Yuma's face and I quickly add, "Well, I'm not technically sure she's missing, but I'm worried about her."

I proceed to tell him about Dani while I work on dinner. How close we were when we were younger, how she took off on the back of a motorcycle—I glance over to see that piqued Yuma's interest—how we lost touch after a few years, and finally I recount the very brief final conversation I had with her.

"She said Durango?"

"It's the reason I jumped on it when I saw an opening with the DPD," I confess. "I know we hadn't talked in years, but that's why that last, unexpected phone call left me shaken."

I put the lid on the pan to let it simmer and turn to Yuma, who seems to be deep in thought, staring down at his hands. Then he raises his eyes to me.

"That why you're here?"

I flinch at his voice—rough and full of accusation—but it's not entirely unexpected. He's a smart man; I can see why his mind would go there.

"I'm here because I needed a better place than the trailer I was renting. The fact the building is owned by the only biker club in town was an added bonus."

"And me? Am I an added bonus too?"

"No." I'm being truthful, but I can see he's not buying it.

"Seems pretty convenient. You're in Durango looking for a friend who likes to hang with bikers, and you've gotta admit, you latched on to me pretty fast. Who better than the biggest man-whore in the club?"

My mouth falls open in disbelief.

"Are you for real? You honestly think…?"

He stands up and leans forward with his hands on the counter. "What do you expect me to think?" He abruptly turns his back; both hands go to his head and pull on his hair. I can just hear him mutter to himself, "Knew it was too fucking good to be true."

The moment I see him start moving, I dart out of the kitchen and slip in front of him. I block the exit with my back against door and my arms spread wide. I meet his glare head on.

"Move."

"No."

"*Fucking move.*"

"No. I'm not gonna let you walk away. I didn't. I asked for space, yes, but I didn't walk out like you're about to. If you recall, I was as hesitant as you were to start anything. Do you honestly believe I'm that good of an actor I can fake being into you? You'd have to be delusional." I'm working up a good head of steam here, but I'm not done. "Life isn't perfect, James Wells." His nostrils flare and he takes a step closer when I use the name he was born with. "But to have you dismiss what's happening between us as fantasy, when it's the most agonizingly beautiful reality I've ever known, is inexcusable."

Even as I utter the last syllable, he crowds me against the door, his arms braced on either side of my head, and his mouth slamming on mine in a punishing kiss.

I take it. I take all of it and give it back in equal measure. It's angry and bruising at first—and goes a long way to burning out our tempers—until lips turn soft and the brush of tongues gentle.

When he ends the kiss, he leans his forehead to mine, his eyes full of remorse. I cover his lips with the tips of my fingers to stop him from saying the words he's clearly struggling with.

"Come have some dinner first."

I take his hand and lead him back to the kitchen.

Yuma

"One latte no sugar and one Americano."

I grab the coffees I've already paid for and head outside where Lissie is siting at the small table, her face turned up to the sun.

Won't be long until the temperatures will really start dropping, and before you know it we'll be up to our armpits in snow. That means I'll have to stable the bike until the damn stuff melts again. I should try and get Lissie out for a nice ride next time she's got a day off.

She smiles at me when I hand over her coffee.

"Beautiful day."

"Yes, it is," I agree.

To think I almost walked out on this—on *her*—last night. Almost stepped over that edge I know would've been straight into the darkness, but she held me back. She didn't bow down. Outshouted those demons feeding my self-defeating thoughts.

I was right when I told Trunk this woman is so much stronger than I am. She's strong enough for both of us.

Last night we wound up in her bed, and we ended up falling asleep simply holding each other. Another new experience for me.

"Tell me about Dani." She looks at me over the rim

of her coffee cup, surprised. "Maybe I can help?" It's my version of an apology, one she hasn't allowed me to verbalize any other way.

"You sure?" she asks with barely concealed hope, and I feel like an ass when I nod. "I have notes at home—pages I pulled out of my journals—with some recaps of conversations I had with her. I also have a few pictures and some postcards. Not a lot, and I've gone over them time and time again without finding anything, but I keep thinking there's something there. Something I'm missing."

"Want me to have a look at them?"

"Would you? I can show you later. They're at the apartment."

I grab my cup and get up.

"Then let's go."

I LOOK AT the pictures first. In one of them a much younger Lissie, maybe sixteen or so, has her arms wrapped around a blonde girl with pigtails sticking out all over her head, wearing some kind of corset. She looks familiar.

"That's Dani. She had a thing for Gwen Stefani."

That's who she reminds me of. I had a thing for Gwen Stefani myself.

"I can see that. How old were you?"

"We were seventeen. The summer before our senior year high school."

I flip over the next picture. This one is the girl by

herself, a little older, sitting by a campfire, a tent and mountains behind her. She has a bandana covering her hair, wearing a big smile, and is holding up a bottle of beer.

"Cibola National Forest. Our last hurrah after I graduated college, just before heading to the police academy."

"What did you major in?"

"Criminal justice," she says with a shrug. "My father thought it was a waste of time, neither he nor either of my brothers got their degree before joining the force."

"So why did you?"

She looks at me with a little smile pulling at the corner of her mouth.

"Because I wanted to prove I could."

Yeah. Stronger than I am for sure. I lived down to expectations, but Lissie...she exceeded them.

The last picture is the most recent one. Once again with the bandana, twin braids sticking out the side, and all decked out in leathers. The woman is straddling a Harley Softail.

"Don't know exactly where or when that was taken. She sent it to me not long after she left."

I can't tell much from the background. It's on the side of a road somewhere. Could be anywhere.

Lissie jumps up off the couch when her phone starts ringing in the kitchen. As she answers the call, I reach for the postcards.

The Vegas one was the last one she says she received, so I flip it around to look at the date stamp. September

30, 2012. If I'm not mistaken, that's around the same time as the Vegas Bikefest, which would make sense, I guess. Fuck, it's possible we were there at the time. We haven't made that run to Vegas in recent years, but we used to.

"I have to go." I turn my head to the kitchen. "It's the Wildcat Canyon case. Something's come up. I'm so sorry."

"That's fine. Do what you gotta do. I've got some reading here and may drop in to see Momma later."

She walks up to the loveseat and bends over the backrest. I lean my head back and curve my hand around her neck, drawing her close for a kiss.

"I should get changed," she mumbles against my lips. "I don't wanna keep them waiting."

A few minutes later, she's back for another kiss before she heads for the door.

"See you later."

"Later, Babe."

The moment the door shuts behind her, I grab the stack of journal pages she has neatly marked by date in the top right-hand corners. I start with the earliest date, making my way forward in time.

I get to know a little more about Lissie while I'm reading as well. Each page she pulled from her journal has bits and pieces of her life, in addition to Dani's calls, as well. There are a few entries I could've done without; describing a couple of dates she went on. I'm also gaining a little insight in her relationship with her family. Pieces of work her brothers and father are. Belittling her every chance they get.

I'm not gleaning much on Dani, other than she sounds like a wild thing who likes to party hard. So not what I would've expected from a best friend to Lissie.

The first time Vegas is mentioned is in a journal entry dated September fourteenth.

DANI SAYS SHE'S CAREFUL, BUT I DON'T KNOW HOW SAFE SHE REALLY IS. SOUNDS LIKE SHE'S ON TO GUY FIVE BY NOW. EVERY NEW GUY IS THE ONE FOR HER, OR SO SHE SAYS. NOW SHE'S GOING TO VEGAS, A TRIP WE ALWAYS WANTED TO MAKE TOGETHER, ON THE BACK OF THE NEXT GUY'S BIKE. FOR HOWEVER LONG THAT LASTS. SHE DENIES IT, BUT I GET THE FEELING SHE'S LOOKING FOR LOVE IN HER OWN WAY. I JUST HOPE SHE FINDS IT.

The next entry is dated September twenty-seventh. Just three days before she sent the card.

I WAS SURPRISED TO HEAR FROM DANI SO SOON. AT LEAST SHE MADE IT TO VEGAS IN ONE PIECE, BUT IT DOESN'T SOUND LIKE THE GUY SHE WENT WITH IS WORKING OUT. BUT, IN TRUE DANI FASHION, SHE'S GOT HER EYE ON SOMEONE NEW ALREADY. I WORRY ABOUT HER, BUT WHEN I TOLD HER AS MUCH SHE GOT PISSY. SAID SOMETHING ABOUT KNOWING IN HER BONES HE'S A GOOD GUY. WE'LL SEE.

I turn over the last page when my phone rings. I look at the screen and quickly answer the call.

"Hello."

"Mr. Wells?"

"Speaking."

"This is Janine, I'm Mrs. Wells's nurse. I think it's best if you come in."

17

Lissie

"So how come this was started already?"

I look at the community center, which so far is just a concrete slab. Nothing else.

Blackfoot, Benedetti, Gomez, and the project manager from Arches Homes Development are bent over the site plans spread out on the hood of a patrol car.

"That was a miscommunication," the project manager says. "This whole project has been changed around so much, the contractors don't know whether they're coming or going. Heck, I'm the third manager on this project because it's such a headache."

My eyes are drawn to the guy pushing around what looks like an oversized lawnmower, but in fact is the ground penetrating radar. A large grid pattern has been marked off on the concrete, stretching about five feet around the perimeter. He's walking around the slab first, but it's slow going.

Ramirez comes to stand beside me.

"Sorry to interrupt your day off," he says. "But I thought you'd wanna be here for this."

"Absolutely. Appreciate the call. Did I miss anything this morning?"

"Just Stan Woodard throwing a fit. Gomez was digging into the history of the land and discovered Theo Woodard, Stan's uncle and the founder of Pro Concrete, bought this land in 1992. When Theo died in 2014, his son, John, inherited the company and the land, but sold the property two years later to the developer. Stan came storming into the meeting this morning, flexing his muscle. His cousin probably called him to let him know the FBI had come sniffing."

"That's interesting," I muse. "You think he knows something?"

"Who knows? Woodard is also the kind of guy who would protect the family name at all cost. He wouldn't even need to know why."

Blackfoot joins us.

"Did you tell her about the property?"

"He did," I answer for Ramirez, who the question was directed at. "And thinking about what Doc Carter said about the minimum age of those bones in the pictures, it would mean they ended up in the ground here when the land was still owned by old man Woodard. I'm new in town, but you guys have been around long enough; what do you know about Theo?"

"I don't know much, other than some of the stories that have been floating around town since Stan got elected," Tony volunteers.

"Like what?"

"Rumors he was not so much elected as shoehorned into office by some of Theo's buddies. Other established businesses in town, which would be well-served having someone looking out for their best interests in city hall."

"The man called himself a patriot, but he was nothing other than a glorified bigot," Keith contributes. "He—"

"Got something!" The agent pushing the GPR yells, waving Gomez over. The rest of us follow and crowd around the small screen mounted on the push bar of the equipment to get a glimpse.

All I see is a lot of gray with a few distortions.

"Here." The agent points at what looks like a little ripple. "And here." He points at another spot on the screen.

I can't make heads or tails of it, but he apparently can.

"What are we looking at?" Tony asks.

"These could be shallow graves."

"Graves, as in plural?" I want to know. He turns in my direction and nods somberly.

Jesus.

An hour later a few guys are jackhammering the concrete foundation to manageable chunks to be removed. They'll have to manually dig through the dirt underneath, so as not to disrupt whatever or whoever is buried below in the shallow graves.

I offered to go grab some coffees and a couple of pizzas in town, since it looks like we'll be here a while. I tried calling Yuma in the truck, but he wasn't answering, so I sent a message it would likely be a late night. It's already late afternoon now and they still have to break ground.

When I get back, I see the crime scene unit got here and is setting up a large tent covering the dig site and installing floodlights. There are a few more patrol cars to keep the curious onlookers at bay, who started showing up a little while ago. Doc Carter is leaning against her van, wearing her signature Doc Martens, and watching the procedures.

Before I can get out of my truck, Ramirez has the passenger door open and starts pulling out the pizza boxes.

"Hey! Leave a pie and a couple of coffees for me," I grumble, when he threatens to take off with my entire haul.

Grabbing the pizza and the coffees he leaves behind, I walk over to Meredith.

"Looks like you hit the floor running since you got here," I comment as I hand her a coffee.

"Thanks. Yeah, you're not kidding. I was told this would be only a moderately busy office. Yet new bodies seem to pop up every week."

I flip open the box, offer her a slice, and the two of us put a good dent in the pizza while we chat a little, watch, and wait.

It's dark outside when they uncover the first of the

bodies. There's not much more than a skeleton left, and Meredith jumps into the hole to examine it closer. There's hardly any smell, and I can handle bones a lot better than I do corpses so I stick close, wanting to hear everything she reports.

"What've we got, Doc?" Ramirez asks.

"Light me up here and I'll tell ya," she mutters.

Tony walks over and aims a flashlight.

"Female, mostly intact skeleton. Point that light down here, will ya?" She bends over the pelvic bones and Tony crouches beside her. "She delivered a baby at some point. I don't think she's been down here any more than eight years, maybe nine, but we'll need to do some tests to confirm. Can I get a backboard and a couple of body bags down here?"

A couple?

Two hours later, we close the door on the third body in the back of Doc Carter's van. Three bodies, so far. The only thing we know for sure is all are women.

The hole that was dug up is covered with tarp and will have guards overnight. The crime scene techs should be back tomorrow morning when they have daylight to work by.

"We're hitting the floor running tomorrow, folks," Joe Benedetti says. "We need identities on these bodies, and we need to bring in John Woodard. Gomez is going to have a talk with the big guy at Arches Homes at the FBI office in Moab. Everyone get some sleep. We regroup at seven tomorrow."

The clock in my truck shows ten to eleven, and I pull

out my phone to see if I've missed any messages.

Nothing.

YUMA

OURAY ANSWERS ON the third ring as I peel out of the parking lot.

"What's up?"

"Need you to bring Nosh to the nursing home right now."

"Momma?"

"It's not good, brother. Hurry."

I think it's best for you to come in. Your mother is not doing well.

I shake my head and forcefully empty my thoughts. It doesn't stop the massive fist squeezing my chest, though. I'm on automatic pilot as I drive to the nursing home, and park in the first open spot I see out front.

"Excuse me..." I barely slow my stride. "Sir, you can't park there."

I look at the gray-haired lady, who is jogging to keep up with me as I aim for the stairwell.

"Don't care."

She doesn't follow me up the stairs and I'm sure my truck'll be towed by the time I get back, but I can't bring myself to care about that either.

"What happened?" I ask when I walk into her room and find Momma in bed; her face slack but I can hear her breath rasping. The nurse attending to her turns to me.

"Mr. Wells, I'm Janine. We suspect your mother had

a massive stroke."

"Jesus." I sink down on a chair beside her bed and take her limp hand in mine. "Isn't there something you can do?"

"Sir, I'm sorry, but your mother has a DNR form in her file," she says with a sad smile on her face.

I knew that. She'd filled one out last year after she was shot, and it had been cause for an argument when I found out. I've wondered many times since then whether she'd been aware her mind was going.

"How long?" I croak.

"No way to tell for sure, but we don't expect her to last the night. I can tell you she's not suffering, we made sure of that. Can I get you something?"

I shake my head.

"Can you tell me what happened?" I ask again, but this time it's barely more than a whisper.

"She was dancing in the common room—she really seemed to love dancing—then she suddenly stopped and crumpled to the floor. We brought her here."

I drop my forehead to the mattress and I listen to the nurse's footsteps leaving the room.

Fuck. I'd hoped there would be time…but I guess it was already too late.

I thought she'd have a chance to see me sober—see me change my life around—but she never even recognized me after I came home. She'll never know now.

A grunt sounds from the door and when I lift my head, I see Nosh sagging against the doorway.

I shoot out of my seat and rush to his side. I wrap an

arm around him and help him to the chair I just vacated.

"They think she had a stroke," I sign, moving to stand on the other side of her bed. He nods and grabs her hand, much like I'd just done.

"Yuma," Ouray says from behind me, clapping me on the shoulder.

I softly repeat what I know for his benefit.

"The brothers are on their way. Luna and the boy too."

I nod. For a moment I wish Lissie were here, but that wouldn't change a thing. Momma would still be dying.

Over the next hour the room fills with bodies. Chairs are brought in, Trunk shows up with trays of coffee, and at some point someone starts telling anecdotes.

"Shit." Ouray grins at his wife. "Remember the first time Momma tested your abilities in the kitchen?

"How could I forget? She dared me to cook the Brussels sprouts she'd tried to get you to eat for thirty years." Luna chuckles at the memory. "I'll never forget her face when you asked for seconds."

"She never stopped bugging me about wearing a damn helmet," Wapi shares with a sniffle.

"Did that to me my whole life," I speak up. "That's how you knew she cared."

Nosh, who'd started following the conversation reading lips suddenly signs, *"She loved every one of you like her own."*

Collective nods and hums go up around the room.

She did. She may not have been warm and cuddly, but she was the fiercest momma bear to all her cubs. For all the run-ins I've had with my mother over the years—and there've been plenty—I never once doubted she loved me. She just had an unconventional way of showing it. A tough woman, even hard at times, but always with the best of intentions.

Momma hangs on until the early hours of the morning, when her breathing starts to falter. Pauses between breaths suspend longer and longer, until finally she releases the slightest of puffs and doesn't inhale again.

She's gone.

One by one my brothers, then Luna and Ahiga, and finally Ouray step up to the bed to kiss her goodbye. Then it's just my father and me. I walk around the bed and when I put my hand on his shoulder, he turns and buries his face in my chest. I awkwardly hug him as his frail shoulders start shaking.

A few minutes later he pulls away and wipes his face with his sleeve. Then he looks up at me.

"I'd like some time alone with her, Son."

I can't remember the last time he's called me that and my throat closes.

"Of course."

I lean over the bed and press my lips to my mother's surprisingly smooth forehead, take one last look at her, and leave the room.

Ouray is waiting outside in the hallway and embraces me, his strong arms holding me tight.

That's when I lose it.

Ouray doesn't say a word, but when I finally straighten up I notice his eyes aren't dry either.

"Everyone but Trunk and Paco has gone back to the

clubhouse. Paco went to grab us all some coffee and Trunk is down the hall."

I follow him into the waiting room where we find Trunk talking on his phone.

"Gotta go, Little Mama," he says when his eyes come to me. "I will." He tucks the phone in his back pocket and hooks and arm around my neck. "So sorry, man, she was an institution. Jaimie sends her condolences and love."

"Thanks."

"Where's Lissie?" he wants to know.

Guilt immediately surfaces when I think about the message I never answered.

"Haven't talked to her yet."

"Brother…" I hear the admonishment in his voice.

"She messaged earlier she'd be working late. She's probably in bed by now."

Excuses, I know. Already the woman is like a drug, but I don't want to be leaning on her like a crutch every time I hit a rough spot like I use to do with Jack Daniels.

"Not smart, my friend," Trunk observes.

He may well be right, but it's already too late now.

"I'll call in a couple of hours when she gets up."

Paco walks in with a tray of coffee and hands it off to Trunk, before putting his hands on the side of my neck. "Gonna miss that woman hard, brother. Loved Momma like she was my own," he says gruffly before letting me go.

"We all did," Ouray rumbles behind me.

All I can do is nod.

"We'll check with Nosh, but I'm thinking; quiet funeral with just her club, but a big celebration of her life after at the clubhouse."

Fuck, I can't believe we're even talking about this.

"Sure," I mumble, looking at Ouray who nods.

A few minutes later my father walks in, looking a hundred years old, followed by Janine, the nurse who stayed close all night.

"The doctor is with your mother, filling out a death certificate. Then we'll get her ready for the funeral home to come pick her up. Do you have a preference?"

She looks at me, but it's Nosh who answers.

"Tell her Hook," he signs.

"Hook Funeral Home."

"No problem. We can give them a call, and they'll be in touch with you sometime tomorrow when they've collected your mother."

She gives my father a gentle smile and slips out the door.

I watch as each of the men pay their respects to my father, something he allows only briefly before straightening his shoulders.

"Get me out of here."

To my surprise my truck is still parked in the spot reserved for the physician when we walk outside.

"Some woman was taking down your number when we got here. I had to discourage her to call a tow."

"Appreciate it."

To my surprise, my father gets in my passenger seat instead of Ouray's, and I end up driving him up the mountain. When I pass through the gate at the compound and want to pull in front of the clubhouse, he grabs my arm.

"Home," he insists in his gravelly voice.

I continue past the main buildings to my parents'

cabin. When I park the truck and turn to him, I see the silent plea in his red-rimmed eyes.

For the first time in over twenty-five years, I spend the night under my parents' roof in my old bedroom.

It still smells like home.

18

LISSIE

I'LL ONLY CHASE for so long.

It was two days ago Yuma basically disappeared off the face of the earth, leaving nothing more than my journal notes he'd marked up with pencil spread over my loveseat.

By now I'm pissed at his lack of response. I draw the line at five messages. I will not send more.

If he had second thoughts about pursuing something with me, all he had to do was tell me. Or message me for chrissake. How long does that take? Two seconds to say 'I'm done.'

I've barely been home since we unearthed the three unknown bodies. We have five bodies in total, two identified males, three unknown women, and two potential witnesses vanished off the face of the earth. In addition, we have a complex interdepartmental investigation, political pressure, and a shortening of tempers as we're trying to get answers from people unwilling to talk.

This morning's meeting was evidence of the latter. A brief face-off between Gomez and Blackfoot—who as I understand have been friends since forever—over a different interpretation of what is within the rules of law, had to be called to a halt by Chief Benedetti. The FBI agent's take on the law is pretty rigid, whereas Keith Blackfoot has a more relaxed view.

On the plus side, though, the crime scene techs were done literally sifting through the massive amounts of dirt at the job site and recovered a few things they think may be related to the bodies.

Tony and I are heading over to the lab now to have a look.

"Any luck on missing person's cases?"

I snort. "Statewide we have fourteen who fit the profile. Neighboring states I pulled up another thirty-three. All women between eighteen and forty and all known to have given birth at least once. It's going to take some work to sort through all of them."

The FBI had flown in a forensic anthropologist to help Doc Carter determine the approximate age of the victims. They were also able to get DNA samples from all three victims, which are being analyzed and will hopefully help to eventually identify the women. Time of death differed between the victims, who had clearly not all been killed at the same time, but what they did have in common was all three women had a child or children.

Before we received that information, there'd been moments I had this far-fetched thought: what the odds would be if Dani turned out to be one of the victims, but she never mentioned any children and I'm sure she would've.

"Maybe we'll find something in the evidence collected to help narrow the options down," Tony suggests when he pulls up in front of the lab.

"Ramirez, good to see you."

A rotund man I peg to be in his early fifties approaches the moment we walk into the building.

"Parnak. This is Detective Bucco. Lissie, I don't think you've had the pleasure, meet Investigator Boris Parnak. He runs the lab."

"Nice to meet you," I mumble, shaking the man's hand.

"Like your new partner better than your old one."

"Ignore him," Tony instructs me. "He and Keith have never seen eye to eye." Then he turns to the older man. "You had stuff to show us?"

"Yes. Follow me."

He leads the way into a room with end-to-end stainless steel counters filled with microscopes and other odds and ends of equipment. A woman working at one of the stations lifts up her head when we come in.

Parnak hands us each a pair of gloves.

"We're still examining some of the evidence, so handle it carefully. Lydia is trying to see if she can get any biological material off some of the items that could tell us which victim it might belong to."

He points at a tray next to the woman who is looking at something under the microscope. On the tray is a collection of teeth, a couple of rings, a belt buckle, what looks like an earring, a watch, and a necklace.

I pull out my phone and start snapping some pictures of the items on the tray.

"We'll have pictures which we'll include in our report," Parnak volunteers.

"I know, but this way I'll have them on hand. You don't mind, do you?"

He shakes his head. "Be my guest."

I make sure I have isolated shots of each piece of jewelry before I tuck my phone back in my pocket.

"Don't forget this," Lydia says, pulling a small pendant from under the microscope.

I bend over for a closer look and suck in a sharp breath.

"The chain was no longer attached," Lydia continues, oblivious to my shock. "Just this pendant. Looks like a bean or something with a couple of stones set in."

"Two peas in a pod," I whisper, trying to control the shaking of my voice. "Peridot and topaz."

"You okay, Bucco?"

I plaster on a smile I hope doesn't look too deranged. "Just peachy."

He leaves it alone until we get back in his truck.

"Now you wanna tell me what that was all about?"

No, I don't. Putting it into words makes it real and I'm not ready for that. True, the possibility has always been there something happened to Dani, but I always had hope this was perhaps all a big misunderstanding.

I take in a deep breath, force down the lump in my throat, and dive right in.

"Topaz is my birthstone, my birthday is November. Peridot represents August, which was my best friend's birth month. I had that pendant made at Sunwest Silver Co on Lomas Boulevard in Albuquerque, in June or July of 2005."

"What the hell?"

"It was for my best friend Dani's twenty-fifth birthday. As far as I know, she always wore it."

"I'm gonna need more than that," Tony says sternly. "You don't even wanna know what I think the odds are at this point, your transfer from Albuquerque to Durango was just a change of scenery."

"I have my file at my apartment." At his raised eyebrow I clarify, "The file on Dani's disappearance."

I leave Ramirez sitting on the loveseat to read through my notes and move to the kitchen to make a pot of coffee. I need it. I'm pretty sure my tea isn't going to cut it this afternoon.

He'd listened attentively while I gave him the history on Dani, leading up to the last phone call. Then I handed him my file. While he reads I try to keep my hands busy, so my mind doesn't wander to places I'm not ready to face yet. It's always possible she gave that pendant to someone else, or maybe she had it stolen. I also can't imagine her having a baby without letting me know. It's too early to jump to conclusions, despite what my gut is telling me.

I kill time puttering around the apartment, tidying up, throwing in a load of laundry, and washing this morning's dishes. I'm just putting the last of them back in the cupboard when Tony walks up, dropping the folder on the island.

"Do you have a few Ziplock baggies?"

I dig in my drawer and pull a few out, handing them over. I'm not sure what he wants them for until he slips each of the postcards in a separate baggie.

"DNA."

He looks up at me. "The stamps, yeah. One of the most overlooked sources of DNA."

"I can't even wrap my head around this. If it's her, how did she end up in a grave with two other bodies? And she never once mentioned a child."

To my horror, the tears start rolling. I whip around and grab a tea towel, pressing it to my face while I hear a mumbled, *"Fuck,"* behind me. "I'm sorry, Lissie." I feel his hand between my shoulder blades.

"I'm fine," I quickly mutter, stepping out of his reach and moving to the coffeemaker. "Want a cup?"

"Sure, but make it to go. I want to drop these off at the lab and then we need to go talk to Joe."

Shit. I'm pretty sure the chief is going to sideline me on this case. It doesn't sit well, but I get it. Especially, a case of this magnitude involving several levels of law enforcement, but one that is also politically sensitive.

I'm grateful when Tony takes the lead when we sit down in Benedetti's office, and force myself to look the chief straight in the eye when his gaze snaps to me.

"Tell me you didn't know there was any connection to this case," he grinds out.

"I had no idea," I tell him honestly.

"Jesus Christ..." He agitatedly runs a hand through his hair and I wait for him to speak. "You know I can't have you on this case, Bucco. Can't take that chance."

"I hear you, Sir."

"It's Joe, and I'm not gonna tell you again. Okay. Here's what we're going to do. I'm teaming you up with Jay VanDyken, he's a good man and you're gonna need the extra hands, because I need Ramirez and Blackfoot to focus on the Wildcat Canyon case. You're gonna catch anything else coming in."

"Yes, Sir...I mean, Joe."

"Good. Now get out of here. I'll tell Mike Bolter you're back on regular rotation."

It's dark out when I finally get back to my apartment. As I'm getting out of my truck, Lisa pulls up beside me.

"How are ya? Haven't seen you around much," she says, climbing out of her car.

"Hi, Lisa. Yeah, work's been busy."

Kiara comes running around the car and slams in my midsection. She tilts her head back and smiles up at me.

"Hi, Ms. Lissie."

I can't help smile back. "Hey, sweetheart."

"Guess what?"

"I give up."

"I got a new pretty dress."

"Oh yeah? How come?"

"Nana says we have a party Saturday."

"That's exciting."

"Not a party, stupid," her brother jumps in.

"Is so. Nana said lotsa people gonna be there and she's cooking a lot of food."

"Don't call your sister stupid, Ezrah. And, Kiara, we don't call it a party when somebody died. We call it a funeral."

"Oh, no." I put my hand on Lisa's arm. "I'm so sorry."

She looks at me funny, tilting her head to the side.

"You don't know, do ya?"

I shake my head. "I'm not sure what I'm supposed to know."

"Momma passed away earlier this week." I guess my face is blank because she repeats, "Momma? Yuma's Momma?"

YUMA

"MORE?"

Wapi comes walking up from the clubhouse just as I toss another garbage bag in the back of my truck, which is already close to overflowing.

I shrug in response.

My father has been on a rampage these past couple of days. After making funeral arrangements for Momma, he'd thrown himself on the house. Her closet was first;

my mother rarely ever threw anything out.

Nosh touched every piece of clothing, and occasionally would tell me what he remembered about it. Jeans, the flannel shirts she liked to wear, the occasional dressy pants or skirt. Shoes, nighties, underwear, he touched them for moment as if he was locking in the memories associated with the items, before tossing them into a garbage bag. He was determined every last stitch would go to Goodwill—even stuff well beyond their expiration date—because that's what Momma would've wanted.

Heck, even Momma's old leathers, she hadn't worn since I was in my early twenties, were packed in a box on the top shelf in her closet. Pop had wanted to give those away too, but somehow that felt wrong to me, so I fished the box out of the garbage bag and tossed it in the passenger seat of my truck.

"He's working on the kitchen now," I tell Wapi. "I'm having him toss what he doesn't want in a plastic tote. Why don't you take that over to the clubhouse so Lisa has a chance to go through it first."

"She already left. Was coming to tell you dinner's gettin' cold."

"Just leave it in the kitchen for her then."

Wapi follows me inside, where Nosh is sitting on a chair in Momma's pantry. I tap him on the shoulder.

"Come on. Let's go grab some dinner," I sign when he looks up. *"Wapi is gonna let Lisa have a look at that. Okay?"*

Nosh shrugs, struggling to get to his feet, so I grab his arm to help him up but he brushes me off, determined to do things on his own. He's an ornery old bastard, but for the past three nights I've been lying awake in the small twin bed in my old room, listening to him cry on the other side of the thin wall separating us. I've never seen or heard my father cry before. Not ever.

When we walk into the clubhouse, Ouray walks up to Nosh, inviting him to sit at the large table where Luna and Ahiga are eating dinner.

"Hey, brother," Tse, who is standing at the sink in the kitchen, says when I walk in. "He still at it?"

"Yup. Ouray already took a load to town in his truck yesterday, and I took a bunch of furniture this morning. I'm almost fully loaded up again."

"Jesus. Got anything left in the house?"

I shake my head. "Barely. It's like he's eradicating her from his life."

"Maybe it's just too hard to have her stuff around."

"Maybe." I grab a bowl and ladle some chili from the large pot on the stove, adding a few pieces of cornbread on top.

"What about you, brother? How are you holdin' up?"

"Fuck if I know. One foot in front of the other, I guess." I surprise myself with the truth of my answer. It's all I've been doing, shuffling along, focusing on menial stuff, just to keep my mind occupied so I don't slip and slide downhill. Fuck those demons telling me I don't have to feel this raw.

"Fair enough. You need an ear, you know where to find me," Tse says, clapping a hand on my shoulder.

"Yeah."

I'm about to take the bowl to Nosh, when a familiar voice sounds from inside.

"I need to speak to Yuma."

19

LISSIE

ALL EYES TURN my way.

Most of them don't look too happy.

Maybe this wasn't such a good idea, but when Lisa mentioned Momma had died, I climbed right back in my truck and came here. I was immediately concerned for Yuma, but as I was driving up the mountain, I started getting pissed as well. Why wouldn't he have told me?

Still, it probably wasn't smart to walk into his clubhouse with attitude. In fact, judging from the looks aimed my way; I didn't make any friends just now.

"Look." I raise my hands defensively as I scan around the room. "I'm really sorry to intrude. I—"

"Lissie." My head swings around. Yuma walks out of the kitchen with a steaming bowl in his hand. "One sec."

He takes the bowl over his father sitting at the table, before turning to face me. With a nudge of his head, he indicates for me to follow him.

"Lissie," Ouray mumbles in greeting when I pass the table.

I throw a little smile in that direction before rushing to follow Yuma down the hallway. He waits for me by the office and shuts the door behind us. When I turn to face him, I notice how haggard he looks and any anger I feel disappears.

"I'm so sorry about your mother, Yuma. I didn't know. Lisa just told me."

His head drops and I lose sight of his eyes.

"Shoulda called you."

"I would've been here for you."

"I know, it's why I didn't," he mumbles, lifting his head. His blue eyes are dull and his expression worries me.

"I don't understand…"

"Would've leaned on you, Babe. Fuck, I wouldn't even have thought twice about it. Just would've let you prop me up."

"Why is that a bad thing?"

As his face softens and he reaches for me, I feel something twist in my chest even as he pulls me into his hold. I feel the vibration of his voice in my chest as he starts talking.

"Because you deserve better. Someone who can handle his shit and be there for you when you need him." I freeze up in his arms and pull back, but his grip on me tightens. "I want you, but I can't be that man if I let you carry the weight every time things get rough."

That aching twist in my chest becomes a painful crater when I realize he's ending this—us—before we've even had a chance.

"Don't do this," I plead on a whisper, pushing firmly against his chest until he's forced to let me go. "Please don't." My voice cracks and my nose stings with tears I struggle to hold onto.

His arms drop to his side.

"Baby, I spent the last couple of days watching my father disintegrate before my eyes. I always knew Momma was a force all on her own, but I never realized she was what kept him standing. It scares me."

"That doesn't have to be us," I try, even as I hear the resolve in his voice.

His beautiful blue eyes look pained when he says, "Last thing I want to do is hurt you."

"Then don't!" I yell, but he just shakes his head.

"I need to learn to stop myself from letting that darkness pull me under, without you there shining your light to guide my way. I have to find my own strength, Lissie."

I lose the battle and tears stream down my face as I dart out of the office and run through the clubhouse, keeping my head low. I have to dig in my purse for my keys only to drop them from my trembling hands.

"I've got it, gorgeous." Tse bends down and grabs my keys, hitting the remote lock before straightening up. "But I don't think you should be driving."

"I'm fine." I wipe my sleeve over my eyes.

"Sweetheart, normally I'd agree with that, and I ain't sure what that knucklehead said to you, but it's clear you're not okay. Hop in. I'm driving."

Last thing I want is to stand here arguing in full view of the clubhouse, so I climb in and scoot over to the passenger side. I'm thankful Tse is silent when he starts my truck and backs out.

I look out the side window when tears well up again, and this time I let them fall. I didn't expect I would hurt this much. Didn't realize how deeply invested I already was.

The worst thing is; I understand his point. I'm gutted, even though I get what he's saying: without a steady foundation there's no way you can build something solid. After the day I had today, it's a hard blow.

One that leaves me with nothing to hold on to.

"How are you getting back?" I ask when Tse pulls up outside my apartment.

"One of the guys will come get me."

"I'm sorry about this."

"Got nothin' to be sorry about, sweetheart."

He turns off the engine and jumps out of the truck. I do the same on my side and hear the lock click. He comes up the stairs behind me and reaches around to unlock my door before handing me the keys and heading back to the stairs.

"You can wait inside, if you like," I offer, even though my heart isn't in it. All I want to do is crawl into bed and forget this day.

"Nah, I'm good out here. You get some rest."

"Thanks, Tse. I…I appreciate it."

"No problem, and for the record; love my brother, but he's a goddamn idiot. Just don't give up on him yet; I'm sure he'll smarten up. Give him some time."

I don't know about that, but I still manage to nod and throw Tse a watery smile before closing the door. I don't even bother turning on the lights and head straight for my bedroom, where I strip and crawl into bed, but sleep doesn't come until the early hours of morning.

YUMA

"YOU FUCKED UP, brother."

I'm sitting on the picnic table outside the clubhouse, trying to get away from the decent crowd inside when Trunk joins me.

The service for Momma this afternoon was simple, just like the woman she was. She didn't much believe in organized religion, so there was no minister or pastor attending, but Ouray gave a eulogy that had a lump sit thick in my throat. My father was stoic, up to the point where we lowered her body in the ground. He broke down then, and it took both Ouray and me to get him back to the truck.

Lisa put on a big spread and some friends—both local and out of town—were already gathering when we got back to the clubhouse. After saying my hellos and making sure Nosh was settled in with some food—and eating a bite myself—I disappeared out here. Inside the booze started flowing and therefore the noise level started rising to the point where it was becoming uncomfortable. As were the meaningful looks Ginger was sending me. The irony doesn't escape me, since not that long ago I probably would've been all over that, looking for an escape.

I haven't really had a chance to talk to Trunk since the night Momma died. I've been holed up in the house with Nosh, only surfacing for a bite to eat. Usually by that time, Trunk would've left for home to have dinner with his family.

I've already been chopped into verbal mincemeat by Tse a couple of nights ago, which almost ended in a brawl had Ouray and Paco not stepped in, so I'm not exactly waiting for another dressing-down. Not fucking today.

"Trunk…"

"Warned you, brother," he continues anyway. "Story goes you had her beelining it out of here in tears."

"For her own good."

"You the expert? On what's good for her? You're full of shit, my friend."

I don't need this now. Moving to get up, I feel his hand on my arm, holding me back.

"Running again?"

I shake my arm loose. "Not fucking running from anything, *brother,*" I sneer.

"Like hell you're not. You're always running and hiding. First in the bottle, then in that little apartment, and now in your father's house. Fuck, you even hide your grief behind your father's."

"Let up, Trunk," I growl in warning.

I'm seething—I came out here for some peace and quiet—but Trunk holds fast when I try to pull away.

"Fuck no. I ain't done yet. You're running from her too. Sobriety is more than not picking up that bottle. It's having your eyes wide open. Hearing, smelling, tasting everything like it's brand-new. It's being stripped raw and every real emotion abrading your soul. It's feeling every fucking thing like it's the first time—good and bad. It's overwhelming."

He lets his hand drop from my arm but I don't move, because what he says resonates. He continues in a calmer voice.

"You got hit with a lot, brother, and I commend you for not grabbing for that drink, but sending that woman packing was not the right move. Nothing but negative feelings left now. Nothing to help balance that scale, for you *or* for her. Don't delude yourself."

With that he gets up and saunters casually back inside.

I don't know how long I stay sitting on that picnic bench, staring unfocused off in the distance, his words slowly burning the message into my bones.

Eventually, Ouray wanders outside; he doesn't even notice me sitting there as he taps a cigarette from his pack.

"Bum one?" I ask and he whips around.

"Shit. Yeah, sure." He walks up and hands me the pack. "Thought you'd left," he says casually, as he lights my smoke for me.

"Nah. How's Nosh doing?"

I'm still bleeding from that earlier lashing, I don't need another one.

"Surprisingly good, actually. He's hanging with the boys at the bar. How are you holdin' up?"

"Don't know," I tell him with brutal honesty. "Can't quite believe she's gone." I take a deep tug on the cigarette, the burn in my lungs a distraction as I blow out circles of smoke. "Was gone for a good while already, but I guess I always stupidly hoped she'd come back. She'd know who I am, could see I'm trying to turn my life around. Instead her last words to me were, 'Who are you?'"

"Shit, Yuma." Ouray's voice reflects the pain I feel. He loved her too.

"Yeah. Kills me, man."

"She loved you, brother. You've gotta know that."

"I know. Woulda been nice if she could be proud'a me too. I never gave her that chance."

He doesn't say anything to that. Nothing *to* say. It's the brutal truth.

We sit here smoking in silence, each lost in our own thoughts, when the clubhouse door opens and Lisa's little girl, Kiara, comes wandering outside.

"Hey, sweetheart. Where are you off to?"

She turns to face me, big tears rolling down her cheeks.

"Boys are stupid," she says, with quite a bit of venom behind that singsong voice.

I hear Ouray stifle a chuckle before he shoves off the table and heads for the door, ruffling the little girl's hair.

"All yours, brother," he says, with a grin in my direction before slipping back inside.

"Come here, honey," I invite the little girl to come sit beside me.

When she's close enough, I lift her on the table beside me. She immediately leans in to me and I leave an arm around her narrow shoulders.

"Tell me about the stupid boys."

"Thomas says Momma ain't a star, but my nana say she is, watching over us. Like my mama. When you're gone you turn into one."

"A star?"

She nods so vigorously; her curls bounce around her face.

"Thomas says it's stupid, but *he's* stupid. Thomas says his mama was put in the ground."

I find it interesting that Thomas—the youngest of the two boys Ouray took in after the ANL raid in Moab last year—would say something like that. From what I understand, neither of the boys has ever talked about their real families. It was assumed because they were too young to remember when they were taken, but maybe the information was just buried too deep. I should mention something to Trunk.

"Well," I start cautiously, wondering how in hell I'm gonna explain this to a five-year-old. "Maybe we can figure this out. Let's have a look." I lie down on my back on the picnic table, and Kiara copies me. Thank God for the clear weather tonight. At this elevation, the stars seem so close and there are plenty out tonight. "See that?

Lots of stars. Which one do you think is Momma's?"

"That one." She points up at a bright one. Then she indicates another one. "And that's my mama."

"Huh, guess you were right. But you know, maybe Thomas is a little right too. We buried my momma in the ground, but now I can see her up in the sky. Maybe you're both right."

"It's magic," Kiara whispers.

Who am I to argue with magic?

I close my eyes and let some of the little girl's magic soothe me. I don't even realize tears are slipping from the corners of my eyes until I feel a little hand on my face. When I open them, I find a very worried Kiara leaning over me.

"Are you sad, Mr. Yuma?"

I smile at her. "I am, but you're making it better."

After I'm done eating a slice of pecan pie—Kiara dragged me inside because, according to her, the best cure for being sad is Nana's pie—I check in on Nosh, who is nodding off on his barstool.

"Ready to go home?"

My answer is a nod, and he slides off the stool. He looks tired, old, and hangs on to my arm like it's a lifeline. We forego doing the rounds, and with a quick thank-you for Lisa and a wave for the rest, I lead him outside.

The fresh air seems to do him good because by the time we get to the cabin, he's walking on his own. The moment we step through the front door he turns.

"Your mother didn't raise a fool," he signs, taking me aback. *"I appreciate you looking after me, but I know*

she'd want me to knock some sense into you. Had fifty or so good years with Momma, but it wasn't nearly enough. Give up anything to have just a few minutes more."

He steps close and clasps a hand around the side of my neck. Something he hasn't done since I was a kid. His watery eyes burn into mine as he says out loud in his raspy voice, "Don't waste time, boy. You'll regret it later."

20

LISSIE

I DIDN'T SLEEP much again, but at least I managed to keep my mind occupied, otherwise I would've spent it thinking about Yuma burying his mother today.

The past few days I hung in there, going through the motions, keeping myself as busy as possible with work. Being teamed up with VanDyken during the day, working on some cold cases and whatever new case comes in, hasn't been bad. It's when it's time to head home to my pathetic loveseat—which I enjoyed so much more before I got used to Yuma's large body lounging on it with me—I have a hard time.

I may no longer be on the Wildcat Canyon case, but that doesn't mean I don't still want to find out what happened to Dani. So the last couple of nights, I've just stopped in at home to change, before heading back out on my own time. It served the dual purpose of avoiding Lisa checking up on me as well. Both made me feel a little guilty, but not enough to stay home and risk looking for other ways to cope.

To be honest, I'm not quite sure where to start, so I had a few larger copies printed of the picture I have of Dani straddling a motorcycle. I've been knocking on doors at phase one of the Wildcat Canyon development, hoping someone perhaps has seen her.

One hundred and seventy-two houses on eleven streets. It'll take more than a couple of days to cover them all, but at least I'm doing something.

Tonight I'm back at the new subdivision, marking off the houses where the owners are home on my little map. I don't even have to identify myself as Durango PD, all I ask if they would mind looking at a picture. They don't even question me with the heavy police presence in the neighborhood. So far no one's seen her. I know it's far-fetched, but all it takes is one person.

After about two hours, my feet are killing me. Every night, I park my car in the small, new strip mall on the road into the development and I do everything on foot. Mainly because, even though I'm technically not doing anything wrong, I don't want to be seen by any of the DPD cruisers regularly patrolling these streets. I've seen them a couple of times, and would duck my head as they drove by, tugging on the bill of my ball cap down to hide my face.

Two more houses to do on this street and then I'll call

it a night. It's getting a bit too late to be knocking on doors anyway.

At the first house a young kid—maybe fourteen—answers the door. His parents aren't home and I don't want to ask him anything without an adult present. I don't mark the house, so I'll remember to revisit.

There's an SUV in the driveway of the last house but all the lights are off inside, so I decide to skip. Last thing I want is to get someone out of bed and have them pissed at me. Having a hard time not to feel defeated, I head back to my truck.

While I walk, I'm starting to wonder if I'm just spinning my wheels. Even if Dani is one of the two more recently deceased found on the construction site, the likelihood is she didn't just happen to hang around this neighborhood: she was brought here. This is stupid.

The only other thing I can think of is taking her picture to any known biker hangouts, but other than the Arrow's Edge MC clubhouse, I don't really know any. Maybe Lisa would know, which would mean answering the questions I'm sure she has for me.

I get an idea when I walk up to the small plaza and step into the convenience store my truck is parked in front of. I've handed out a copy of Dani's picture to two people who asked for it so they could ask their spouse later, and I jotted my cell phone on the back. I still have quite a few left.

Against the far wall of the store I find packing tape, a Sharpie, and scissors hanging from a pegboard. In the corner I spot a display with sheets of poster board and pick a white one. I take all my purchases to the counter.

"Did you find everything?" the middle-aged Asian lady asks, as she starts ringing in my items.

"I did, but I have a favor to ask. A friend of mine is missing and I was wondering if I could put a picture of her up somewhere in your store. Maybe on the window?"

I pull out one of the copies and show her.

"Sure. On the door so people see when they walk in. Fourteen thirty-five, please." She rattles off what I owe her without breaking stride. "Pretty girl. How long she been missing?"

"Last I heard from her was the beginning of this year. So eight months." I count out my bills on the counter.

She hums and shakes her head. "So many bad things happen."

Oh, I know all too well.

She lets me use the counter to cut the poster board in four equal pieces. I turn them into makeshift flyers with Dani's picture taped to the front—the word 'missing' at the top and 'please contact:' with my phone number at the bottom—and attach one to the door.

"Thank you," I call out to the lady before heading outside.

I'm allowed to hang one in the window of the pizza joint a few doors down as well, when I stop in to pick up a small meat lovers for a late dinner. I toss the box with the two remaining posters in the passenger seat of my truck and hop behind the wheel.

Once home, I change into my flannel pj pants and a tee, before sitting down in front of the TV with my pizza and a glass of tea. I've just found an episode of *NCIS* I haven't seen yet, when a knock sounds on my door. Probably Lisa. I may as well get it over with

The last person I expect when I open my door is Yuma. That pisses me off, and I'm about to tell him so when I notice he looks wrecked. Then I remember the man just buried his mother today.

"Can I come in?"

Even his voice sounds tortured, and although I know it's the last thing I should do, I step aside and let him in. He stops in the middle of the room and turns to face me. I close the door, leaning my back against it as we stare at each other.

"How are you doing?"

He shrugs. "Hanging in. Tough day."

I nod my understanding as his eyes bore into mine.

"I don't know what you want," I finally say.

"Not clear myself," he admits in a low voice. "I just know I want you, but I fucked it up, and I don't know how to fix it."

I hate myself for the flicker of hope his words invoke.

"I don't know either."

"What I said at the clubhouse...it's true, you deserve much better, but who the fuck am I to argue if it's me you want? Truth is, I was scared—*am* scared—of this feeling; I can't breathe when I'm not with you."

That hope blooms a little bigger, but then I remember how close I've come these past days to falling off the deep end. It would've been so easy to soothe myself with a bottle, and I had to fight so hard to resist. I'm not sure how strong I'd be if I had to go through that again.

"What do you want me to say? You shut me out, Yuma. You say things you think justify it, but in the end you simply shut the door in my face. It hurt me to a point where I don't even trust myself to be alone."

He takes a step closer. "I'm so sorry."

"I believe you are, but I don't know if I'm strong enough to risk going through that again."

Yuma

It's bitter—the taste of remorse.

"Please…"

Her tear-filled eyes look sad but her chin lifts with determination. I understand it—she's protecting herself—but what kills is that it's me she protecting herself from.

I close the distance and cup her face in my hands, as I pour everything I'm feeling in the kiss I plant on her lips. At first, I feel her need as strong as mine, as her mouth opens to let me in and her hands fist in the shirt at my chest. Fueled by her kiss my resolve builds, until she pulls back and those fisted hands become flat palms, pushing me away. Reluctantly I let her go.

"I can't do this," she whispers, darting by me.

I turn and watch her disappear down the hallway to her bedroom, slamming the door behind her. I have to fight the urge to go after her, but if I push any harder, I'm afraid I'll do more damage than good. I'm not sure what it'll take to win her back, but I sure as fuck plan to do just that. Failure is not an option.

I turn off her TV, grab her glass and the pizza box, and stuff both in the fridge. When I turn, I notice two posters lying on the counter with the picture of her friend, Dani. I throw a quick glance down the hallway before grabbing one to take with me. Then I dig into her junk drawer for the pen and notepad I know she keeps there, leave her a note, and turn off the lights, pulling the door shut behind me.

Tucking the poster in my saddlebag, I head back to the clubhouse.

"BACK ALREADY?"

I look up to find Trunk standing in the shadows of the clubhouse porch, having a smoke.

"Yeah. It's gonna take some time."

He chuckles. "Welcome to the club. Pretty sure every man lucky enough to find a good woman has fucked up once or twice. Hard work to get back in there, but I promise…the payoff will be sweet."

"So noted." I point at his cigarette. "Got another one'a those?"

"Picking it up again?" he inquires, handing me his pack and a lighter.

"Not planning to. I thought you'd quit?"

"Keep a pack at the club, brother. Jaimie'd have my hide if I smoked around the house."

"She still here?" I take a deep drag.

"Left shortly after you did to pick River up from her

mom's. I was just having my last smoke before heading out after her."

"Glad I caught ya. I've got somethin' to show you." I quickly walk back to my bike to grab the poster and hand it to him. "You ever see that woman?"

He looks at it closely and shakes his head. "Not ringing any bells. Who's she?"

"Dani. Friend of Lissie's, who's been missin' for a while."

"No shit, huh? So this is your plan? Winning brownie points by finding the friend?"

"Can't hurt. Besides, the girl's known to hang out with bikers. Figured with some guys from the other clubs here for Momma's funeral, I could ask around."

"True." He takes a last pull on his smoke and grinds it out in the bucket of sand, as he announces, "I should head home."

"Before you go," I stop him, remembering the conversation I had earlier with Lisa's little girl. "I almost forgot, are you still striking out getting background from the two boys? Thomas and Michael?"

"Pretty much. Can't push too hard, they're young kids."

"Right. Don't know if this helps, but Kiara got into it with Thomas, apparently." I relay what the little girl told me. "A bit odd for a small kid to say his mama was put in the ground. I know you guys have been looking for answers."

"It's more than I've been able to get out of him." He drops a hand on my shoulder. "Look, man, I'm sorry you were kept outta the loop, but—"

"It's fine," I cut him off. "I get it. The end justifies and all that."

"Somethin' like that. Later, brother." He starts walking toward his bike.

"Later, Trunk," I call after him, toss my butt in the bucket, and with the poster under my arm, head inside the clubhouse.

The atmosphere has ratcheted up a notch or two since I left to take Nosh home. It's noisier, more like some of the parties of old, now that the old man and the kids are gone. I'm sure most of the guys are tanked up good. A few women—mostly hangers-on—have shown up in the meantime and don't seem too selective or too subtle with their attention. It really is like old times, but what is new is my aversion to it. A quick glance at a half-naked trio on the couch shows a scene I might've been tempted to join just last year. I'm surprised Ouray hasn't put a stop to it. Since he married Luna, he strongly encouraged that kind of partying to take place in one of the rooms at the back of the clubhouse, behind closed doors.

I scan the space and note the largest group is crowded around the bar, but there are a few pockets of people spread around some of the small tables. Ouray is sitting with Wapi at one of them, each staring at the empties in front of them. I aim for them.

"Nosh okay?" I ask Wapi, who was going to keep an eye out, as I pull out a chair.

"Asleep, last time I checked."

"Thanks for checking, brother."

"Thought you'd left for the night?" Ouray asks with an eyebrow raised.

"Yeah. Turns out I mighta been a bit optimistic."

"Takes work, brother."

"So I'm findin' out."

Ouray chuckles until I spread the poster on the table for him to see.

"Who's that?"

"Lissie's friend, Danielle Gorman. She's been missing since January. Girl had a thing for bikers and the last we know she was heading for Durango."

"Can't say I know her."

"Me neither," Wapi offers.

"Guys! Come over here. Yo, Red!" Ouray calls out before turning to me. "He knows more people than the rest of us combined."

I know he does. He's fucked most of them too.

Some of them amble over, Red among them, with Ginger trailing behind.

"Any of you know this girl?" Ouray holds up the poster.

"Nice-lookin' piece." My eyes fly to Manny Salinas, who has some redhead with a sour look on her face draped around him.

"Shut the fuck up, Manny," I bite off. "She's someone's fucking best friend."

The asshole raises his hands in defense and backs away.

"Pretty sure I seen her around," Red says, and my ears perk up. "Can't remember where though."

"Norwood." I throw a look over my shoulder at Ginger.

"Norwood?"

She nods. "She belongs to the Moab Reds."

21

LISSIE

"BUCCO! GOT A minute?"

VanDyken and I just got back from a long day of interviews after a morning robbery call at an elementary school. Some yahoos took off with all of the recently acquired, brand-new computers from the library. They timed it so the alarm went off just as Sunday service let out at the Baptist Church next door, and mass at the Catholic Church on the corner across the road. Like every Sunday morning, the entire block was congested with vehicles and our patrol cars took forever to get to the school. By the time they did, the thieves were long gone, blending in with heavy church traffic.

We're pretty sure there was more than one person involved, in order to carry fifteen new computers out of the building. At least one of them was very familiar with both the school and the neighborhood, seeing as they knew about the recent silent donation of the computers to the school, and they were obviously aware of the gridlock on Sunday mornings in this neighborhood.

There is still a long list of people to talk to.

Joe Benedetti is sticking his head out of the conference room the Wildcat Canyon investigation has taken over. I haven't been in there since I was benched and have to admit I'm a little curious to what is going on.

"Coming."

Inside Ramirez and Blackfoot look up from where they're sitting at the large table. Behind them, one wall of the room is covered with plans of the different phases of the development, headshots of the main suspects, of all evidence gathered, and pictures of the victims. I try not to focus on the latter.

"Have a seat, Lissie," Joe urges from behind me.

I take a chair on the other side of the table beside Tony and lift my eyes to Joe. His face is difficult to read, but he's definitely not giving me good vibes.

"What's going on?"

"We got back the forensic anthropology report earlier this week, and two of the bodies—the more skeletonized ones—have been there in excess of seven or eight years. The third one has only been down there between six and twelve months. They haven't done the full analysis of the soil yet, which will help narrow that timeframe down."

I'm not quite sure what he's leading up to, but it's not giving me a good feeling.

"Okay."

"The DNA labs on the victims just came back this morning," he continues. "The lab was also able to withdraw a sufficient sample from the stamps on those postcards you provided for DNA testing, and those results came back as well." My entire body tenses up in preparation of the news I already know is coming. "I'm sorry, Lissie. The DNA retrieved from the postcards matches the DNA of the third body."

I manage to nod and push myself up from the table.

"Thank you," I mumble, moving stiffly to the door.

"Lissie." I go rigid at Tony's voice right behind me, and almost lose it right there and then when I feel his warm hand on my shoulder. "I'm so sorry."

"Thank you." This time I manage no more than a whisper.

"Go home, Bucco," Joe orders. "See she gets home, Ramirez."

I open my mouth to object but Keith speaks up before I get a chance.

"Take her truck. I was gonna run out to grab some food anyway, I'll swing by to get you."

"Don't wanna see you here tomorrow, Lissie," the chief says sternly.

"But—"

"No arguments. We've got things here."

My eyes start blurring, sitting in the passenger seat of my own truck as Tony drives me home. By the time he pulls into my spot I'm barely hanging on, only nodding when he hands me my keys and says he'll check in with me later.

It's not until I enter my apartment and drop down on my loveseat I allow myself tears.

Pain, guilt, anger—the waves of emotion hit me all at once, making it hard to breathe. The pain I feel sharply—like a deep burning in my chest with every breath. I set aside the guilt. It's useless now, I just lost my chance to make things right. What I focus on instead is anger. At Dani for waiting until it was too late to call for my help. At myself for not trying harder to find her when she disappeared. But mostly I'm angry with the animal who killed her, mutilated her, and put her in that hole.

I shrug off my jacket, toss it over a stool, and snatch the file folder off the counter. First thing I see when I flip it open is the note I slipped in there this morning.

PIZZA IN FRIDGE. NOT GIVING UP.

Yuma's note, which had been waiting for me, when I rolled out of bed, rumpled, groggy, and not in the best of moods. Reading it lifted my spirits. A little. Now I shove it in the kitchen drawer so I can spread out my journal pages.

I notice some of the pencil marks Yuma left, underlining a few references to Vegas and circling the date I'd scribbled at the top of that particular page. I get my laptop from the bedroom and type 'Vegas' and September, 2012, into the search engine. Scrolling through three pages about President Obama visiting, a Justin Bieber show, and a collection of expos and trade shows, before bumping into a reference about Vegas Bikefest on page four.

I lose track of time as I dig up anything I can find on the bike rally: newsletter articles, write-ups, blog entries, and pictures—tons and tons of pictures. I scroll through, hoping to get a glimpse of Dani's face. Something— anything—I can sink my teeth into.

My eyes are gritty from peering at my laptop's small screen when I hit on a group picture taken in front of the fountains at the Bellagio. I spot Dani right away, her smile wide. My breath sticks in my throat. She looks so happy and...*alive*.

Hot tears roll unchecked for my best friend, but I don't stop scanning the image, zooming in on the face of the man next to her with his arm draped around her in a proprietary manner. I take a screenshot before focusing on the other people in the picture. I'm shocked when I see the familiar face of Red Franklin in the crowd, but my heart stops when I spot the couple right beside him, just steps from my best friend. I recognize the woman, her head thrown back, as Red's wife, Ginger. Most of her body is blocked by a man with his face buried in her neck.

But I don't need to see his face to know it's Yuma.

YUMA

"YOU SON OF a bitch!"

I move the phone away from my ear to check the screen. Yup, definitely Lissie calling.

I'm standing in the doorway to my mountain home, looking at the disaster inside.

"What the hell, Babe?"

I managed to get as much information from Ginger as I could about Dani, after she dropped that bombshell last night. She couldn't tell me much; just that she'd seen the girl around with the Moab Reds over the years.

I'd been ready to saddle up and ride up to Norwood to the Reds' compound, but Ouray reminded me, in no uncertain terms, of what happened the last time I did something like that. He said he'd make some calls and dig around. Probably smart, he's a better diplomat and more careful than I am. My style is more of a bull in a china shop, which hasn't played out so well for me in the past.

I spent most of today dealing with Nosh, who woke up this morning announcing he wanted to give the entire house a new coat of paint. Ouray listened to my concern when I brought it up with him, and he suggested maybe it's just my father's way of coping and to let him do what he wants. So this morning, I went and got a few gallons of paint and spent the rest of the day moving furniture out of the way, taping, and we even managed to get the entryway painted.

When one of the boys knocked on the door to let us know dinner was ready, I told Nosh I had plans tonight and would be heading out. I didn't mention those involved Lissie.

Now it sounds like I may have to rethink things since she's apparently already pissed off with me.

"You were there. In Vegas," she snaps, but her voice cracks. "You knew her."

"What? Wait a min—" But she's already hung up.

Fuck.

My plan had been to show Lissie my house. My real house, where I haven't been in about six months. That's why I went there right after dinner to tidy up a little.

It's a great log home with an awesome view down the mountain, but it needs a fuckofalot more work inside than I had bargained for. Empty bottles, garbage, dirty dishes, rotting food. The smell is turning my stomach and I quickly step outside and pull the door shut. I have more urgent things to deal with now.

I make it to the Riverside Apartments in record time. Lissie's truck is parked outside, there is light on inside, but she's not answering the door when I knock. I try again with the same result. Then I slide my master key in the lock and open her door.

Just the kitchen light is on, but I can see her sitting on the couch, her back to the glow and her face in shadows. When I close the door and move closer, she shifts, pulling her knees up defensively.

"What did you mean I knew her?" I ask, stopping a few feet away. "Your friend?"

"Found a picture." Her voice sounds lifeless as she indicates her laptop sitting opened on the kitchen island. "You were with her in Vegas."

"Yeah, I was there, but—"

"Go look," she snaps.

Curiosity moves me to the laptop. The screen is dark

but when I tap my fingers on the trackpad, an image pops up. I recognize where it is, it takes a second before faces start popping out at me. I do a double take when I spot myself with a much younger Ginger. *Jesus.*

The last person I notice is the guy with his arm around the missing woman's shoulders. Fucking Chains. The same man, who a little over a year ago put a bullet in my shoulder, who would've killed me if my brothers hadn't shown up to rescue my ass. The Moab Reds' vice president, who paid for a multitude of sins with a bullet in his brain. He may be dead, but I still feel the rage for him burn in my gut.

"Fucking Chains." This time I say it out loud, turning to face Lissie. "His name is Chains and he's dead. The man with your friend. I was wasted out of my brain in that picture. Fuck, I was wasted out of my brain most of the time. Can't even remember this picture being taken, let alone who was all in it." I can see in the eyes she turns to me, I'm getting through to her. "But I may know where to find your friend."

Immediately her tears well up and spill over as she shakes her head. "I…I already know where she is."

"You do? Where?"

"The Durango morgue."

For a moment I'm frozen, unable to process what she's saying. Then I rush over to her and wedge in beside her, wrapping her in my arms.

"Baby…" I mumble when she does a face-plant in my chest.

We sit like that for a while, her tears soaking straight

through my shirt as I mumble soothing nonsense into her hair.

"Sh-she w-was one of the bodies w-we found at the construction site," she finally says, as she pulls back and immediately hides her face behind her hands. "She must've died not long after that call to me. When I came here looking for her, she was already in the ground just a few miles away."

"Shit, Lissie. I'm so sorry."

"Please don't be nice. It's much easier if I can be mad at you." A chuckle escapes me. "I thought you lied to me," she mumbles.

"I didn't, but I get why you'd think that, seeing that picture. I didn't even know that existed. How did you find it?"

"The markups you made on my journal pages. Vegas and the date. The rest was all Google."

I kiss the top of her head and get up. In the kitchen, I grab a dishtowel and wet part of it under the cold tap before I go to sit back down beside her. I gently pull her hands away and wipe her face before lobbing the towel in the direction of the kitchen sink.

"You're being nice," she grumbles, as I tuck her back against me.

We sit quietly in the dimly lit room, but my mind is going a mile a minute. Fuck, I'd love to blame Chains, but he was killed last year. He couldn't have had anything to do with the reason Dani called her friend in a panic, or with her subsequent death. But someone did, and buried her at the new subdivision.

"Yuma?"

I thought she was dozing off, but Lissie's soft voice tells me otherwise.

"Mmm."

"You looked…cozy with Ginger Franklin in that picture."

Yeah, I'd been afraid that would come up at some point, I just didn't think it would be now. I may have shared some of my history with her, but only in the most general of terms. I didn't want to give out too many details. Didn't think it would serve any purpose but to make things uncomfortable.

They just got uncomfortable.

I tighten my hold on her before I speak.

"About that. Told you I didn't mind sharing if it meant no one getting tempted to lay claim to me." I can feel her stiffen in my arms.

"Ginger?"

"Red and Ginger like to play, and I didn't mind being a third. Served their purposes and it served mine at the time. That stopped last year."

It's quiet for a bit and then she asks, "Last year?"

"Yeah."

"That picture is from eight years ago."

"I know, Babe."

"That's a long time."

"Meant nothing, Lissie," I reassure her.

"That's what you say, but I'm not sure. Ginger's reaction to me at your clubhouse suddenly makes a lot more sense."

"She just likes getting her way and doesn't like when her toys get taken from her," I explain dryly.

Suddenly she pushes away so she can look at me with those liquid brown eyes.

"And you're okay being seen as a toy?"

"Not now, but it worked for me at the time."

She nods, a frown on her face. "Do you miss it?"

"With you sitting next to me? Fuck no, baby. Not even for a second."

22

LISSIE

THE ANGER HAD felt almost comfortable—a shield to hide behind—but his honesty and gentle concern had doused that fire.

Yet currently his mouth and hand between my legs are stoking up a fire of an entirely different kind.

Much earlier he'd followed me into the bedroom, ignoring my protests and announcing there was no way he was leaving. He did nothing other than hold me until he fell asleep.

I didn't. I'd lain awake, tormented by my rambling thoughts, until he mumbled sleepily a few minutes ago, "Can't sleep?" Then at my vague hum, he started sliding down my body, promising to make me forget.

He's doing exactly that. With my fingers curled in his

hair I keep his head right where he's doing wonderful things to me.

"James, honey…"

"Mmmm," he hums, the vibrations against my sensitive core making me suck in a sharp breath.

When he fills me with two fingers and at the same time sucks hard on my clit, I detonate, crying out his name. My thighs are still trembling when he slowly makes his way back up my body, his facial hair lightly scraping my skin, causing me to break out in goosebumps.

I taste myself on his lips when they find mine. The soft stroke of his tongue along mine keeps me suspended in my bubble of mindlessness a little longer.

"Now sleep, Beautiful," he mumbles, ending the gentlest of kisses.

I sigh with the loss of him, but don't argue when he rolls on his back, taking me with him so I end up with my cheek resting on his chest. I snuggle in and promptly fall asleep.

I'M ALONE IN bed when I wake up.

A quick peek at my alarm shows it's already nine thirty. I notice a piece of paper stuck underneath my bedside lamp.

HAD TO CHECK IN WITH MY DAD, DIDN'T WANT TO WAKE YOU. CALL ME WHEN YOU GET UP. AM AT THE CLUBHOUSE.
Y.

I lie back on my pillow, a smile pulling at my mouth, but then I remember yesterday, and sadness threatens to overwhelm me. Crying is not productive so I force myself to get out of bed and in the shower, making quick work of getting ready. The most I can do for Dani now is find out who killed her, and to do that I need to figure out what happened between Vegas in 2012 and her panicked phone call January of this year.

I make a cup of coffee while I call Yuma and not just because he wanted me to. Something he was about to say last night got lost in the shuffle, and I'd like to hear it.

He answers right away.

"Did you sleep okay?"

"I did. How's your father?"

"Off his rocker." I snicker at his deadpan delivery. "Not kidding, Babe. He started this shit right after Momma died. Emptied out half the house, giving shit away to Goodwill. Clothes, furniture, kitchen shit, you name it; he got rid of it. Yesterday he wanted to paint not just one room, but the whole goddamn house. We're not even close to done with that, and he announced half an hour ago he wants to redo all the flooring. Like I said; off his rocker."

"Or maybe…" I suggest cautiously. "…he wants to stay busy. Perhaps he copes by staying active."

"Possible. Thought maybe he couldn't handle the reminders of her every day."

"Have you asked him?" It's silent on the other side. "Worth a try. You might even get a good answer."

Finally he says, "You bein' a smartass?"

"Maybe."

His deep chuckle warms me.

"What are your plans?" he wants to know.

"Actually, that's part of why I'm calling. You said something last night that I'm curious about. You mentioned knowing where Dani could be found—what did you mean?"

"I grabbed one of your posters to show around the clubhouse. We had folks here from out of town for the funeral, and Ginger happened to see the picture and recognized Dani." I try to ignore the tinge of jealousy at the mention of her name. It doesn't sit well that she was there for him and I wasn't. That was all on me, though. Not Yuma, not even her, but me. "She said as far as she knew Dani belonged to the Moab Reds."

I jot down the name.

"So they're in Moab as well?"

"No, that's the Mesa Riders. The Moab Reds are from Norwood. That guy, Chains, with Dani in that picture? He was their vice president."

I write that down too.

"Lissie, do me a favor? Tell me you wanna know so you can pass it on to Ramirez?"

"Yeah, of course."

I will, but that doesn't mean I won't do a little digging of my own. I owe Dani at least that much.

"Good. You wanna come here and help me paint?"

The thought of doing some physical work is actually quite appealing. The fact he's asking me to help out in his parents' house feels significant.

"Now?" I realize the moment it slips from my mouth that it could be interpreted as reluctant, so I quickly add, "I mean, I'd love to, but I wanted to drop in at the station first."

He chuckles. "Love to, huh? You may change your tune after a day of this. Come whenever you're ready, Beautiful."

"Okay. See you soon."

I pour myself a coffee and sit down at the island, firing up my laptop. I dig up what I can about the Moab Reds, which isn't a lot, but it does include a phone number. I hesitate, but only briefly, before punching into my phone.

It keeps ringing and I almost hang up when a woman finally answers.

"Reds' clubhouse."

Shit. What now? I should probably have thought about this a little more before I called. Best thing to do is stick as close to the truth as I can.

"Yes, hi. I'm looking for my friend, Dani? She was supposed to be there."

"Here? Ain't seen Dani around in forever."

Bingo. She'd been there. That was almost too easy.

In the background I hear the mumble of a man's voice, but I can't make out what is said.

"Who'd you say you were?"

Fuck.

"Lissie Bucco. I'm actually pretty new in Colorado and Dani told me if ever I was in the neighborhood to give her a call. But you're saying you haven't seen her in a while? Is there anyone who might know where she is?"

"Hang up." I can suddenly hear the man's voice clearly, followed by a sharp click.

I try to call back, but I already know no one's going to answer.

I email the number, names, and the image to my department email so I can print it off when I get there. I want to hand it over in person.

Oh, who the hell am I kidding, I feel out of the loop and want in.

I dart into the bedroom to grab some old clothes, because after I nose around the station, I plan to head straight to the club.

"THE HELL ARE you doing here, Bucco?"

Mike Bolter, the desk sergeant looks at me sternly. I guess someone must've told him I wasn't in today, because I didn't think to call in.

"Just dropping something off. Are the guys in?"

"Conference room."

"Thanks."

I first head to the bullpen to print off a few copies of the email I sent myself before going across the hall. The door is closed when I walk up and I politely knock.

"Yeah!" I hear called out and I enter.

Tony, Keith, Gomez, and Ouray's wife, Luna Roosberg, are sitting at the far side of the table, looking up when I walk in. Blackfoot is the first to speak.

"Hey, Lissie. Didn't expect you in."

"Hi. I popped in because I have some information you should have. Unless someone already dug it up." I hand out the copies.

"Where'd you get this?" Gomez wants to know and I proceed to tell them how I discovered the image and let them in on the information I got from Yuma.

"You've been poking around?" It's the first thing Tony's said since I walked in, and I can tell he's pissed. "Joe's not gonna be happy hearing that."

"She was my friend. She called *me* when she was in trouble and I wasn't able to help her then, but I may be able to help catch her killer. Tell me you wouldn't do the same thing." I pin him with a glare and I'm surprised when he's the first to turn away.

"I would," Luna says, looking at me with something like respect.

"As much as I appreciate the general sentiment," Gomez intercedes. "And as much as the information you brought in is helpful, we can't forget the fact there are five victims in total—not just one—and a dangerous organization right beyond our reach. We can't afford to lose sight of the bigger picture or everything we've done so far will have been for nothing."

As much as I know he's right, I don't like hearing it. I nod my understanding and turn toward the door, where Joe Benedetti is leaning against the doorpost.

"What are the chances you'll drop this?" he asks.

I wisely keep my mouth shut. I don't want to make promises I can't keep. Behind me, Luna chuckles.

"We may be able to use this to our advantage,"

Blackfoot voices, and the chief nods.

"That's what I'm thinking," he agrees.

"I wish someone would explain it to me," Gomez grumbles.

"To the outside world Detective Bucco is grieving the loss of her friend and is looking for answers on her own time. In reality she's rattling cages, while we wait in the background to catch whatever she shakes loose."

"We need something believable that puts her out there by herself, in the first place."

"That's easy," Joe claims, looking me straight in the eyes. "Detective Bucco has been compromising our investigation by doing some digging on her own. A suspension would not be out of order."

Understanding dawns and I have to bite my lips to hide my smile.

"I can be her relay," Luna pipes up. "The Arrow's Edge clubhouse would provide credible cover."

"Good. If we're all on board, Detective Bucco, I need to see you in private."

I follow him down the hall and into his office, where he closes the door and invites me to sit across from his desk.

"Are you on board?"

"Yes, Sir."

"You realize this might put a target on your back?"

"I'm aware."

"This is far outside of your scope, Lissie. You've just had a hard hit. I need you to think about this carefully. We're gonna need you to lay low for a day or two, so we can put a few safety measures in place. Don't do anything until you hear from Luna."

I appreciate him giving me an out, but I don't need it. "I understand, Sir. I can do it."

He nods curtly.

"All right. This has to be believable so I'm going to ask for your badge and your service gun, do you have your own sidearm?"

"Yes, Sir."

I hand over both, dropping them on his desk. He opens his desk drawer places them in there.

"I'll also have to write up an official report, which will be removed from your record when this is over."

That gives me pause. Other than the sexual harassment fiasco, I've not had a blemish on my record ever. I made sure of that. I get it's necessary but it still stings.

The chief gets up from his chair and I do the same.

"Detective Bucco, you are hereby relieved from duty until further notice," he says in a firm voice, before adding in a softer tone, "And Lissie—my fucking name is Joe."

23

YUMA

"I SEE YOU smartened up."

I follow Nosh's gaze out the front window and notice Lissie walking up, a plastic bag in her hand. Ignoring my father, I open the door and go outside, waiting for her to come up the steps to the porch.

"Hey," she says, a hesitant smile on her face. "Lisa directed me here. Hope that's okay?"

I reach out and tag her behind the neck, pulling close so I can kiss her, which I do soundly.

"More than okay," I mumble, when I reluctantly lift my mouth from hers. "Hope you brought some old clothes." She holds up the plastic bag.

"You can change in the bathroom." I guide her inside and point down the hall but Lissie goes the other way, toward my father who has his roller suspended midair.

"I'm so sorry for your loss," she says, before surprising the shit out of me by giving him a one-armed hug.

Nosh is equally taken aback as his eyes dart to me, a hint of panic visible on his face at the unexpected display of affection. That never was my father's strong suit, or Momma's, for that matter. His free hand awkwardly pats her back and he even manages a rusty smile when she steps back.

"You too," he tells her in his rusty voice.

Clearly moved she gives him a nod, throws a glance my way, and heads off down the hall to the bathroom.

"Can't figure what a girl like that sees in you," he signs, but with a spark of humor on his face.

"Fuck if I know," I answer, grinning.

When Lissie joins us a few minutes later, Nosh has a tray prepped for her and points her to the wall separating the living room from the kitchen. She sets to work right away. My dad and I share a look before we get back to it as well.

There's little conversation over the next hour or so while we finish the first coat in the living room.

"Lunch," Nosh announces.

"Let's go grab a bite," I mention to Lissie, who is rinsing out brushes and rollers at the kitchen sink.

Wapi, my father, and I moved the appliances out on the back porch this morning, along with the handful of pieces of furniture he has left in the living room. Nosh's plan is to get the entire main floor done by the end of today before tackling the upstairs.

I still haven't questioned him about his motivations. The process seems to be cathartic for him—and I have to admit, for me as well—so the why of it isn't all that important.

Lissie is still curious, though, and when we sit down in the clubhouse—after slapping together a couple of sandwiches in the big kitchen—she reaches over and places her hand on top of my father's.

"What made you decide to paint the house?"

His eyes dart to me for translation and I quickly sign her question. He seems to think on that for a moment.

"It's time," he says, before he adds to that with his hands. *"Not the same without Momma. I don't need a family home."* He points at Lisa sitting beside her granddaughter at the big table. *"They do."*

Wow. I didn't see that coming.

"Where are you going to live?" I finally ask him.

"Clubhouse for now. Until the guys get tired of keeping an old man company."

"You sure about this?"

"Been thinking on it for a while. You okay with it?"

I'm surprised I am. Seems almost fitting he ends up where he started, in the clubhouse. But especially that Lisa—who's taken to Momma's role of caretaker like she was born to it—have a permanent place in the club's compound.

"It's a good plan. Have you talked to her?"

"Not yet. Want to get the house done first."

I nod my understanding and Nosh tilts his head slightly in Lissie's direction, who's been following the conversation closely.

"He wants the house to go to Lisa and the kids," I clarify in a low voice, so we're not overheard.

Her mouth falls open as she turns to my father.

"That's perfect," she whispers, but Nosh reads her lips.

He picks up his sandwich and takes a big bite, indicating the end of that conversation, but he looks pretty pleased with himself.

"Ms. Lissie!"

Kiara's high-pitched voice pierces the air as the little girl spots us sitting at the small table and races over.

"Indoor voice, child," Lisa grumbles, following behind her.

"Hey, sweetheart," Lissie greets the little girl with a hug.

I notice Nosh observing the two before he turns to me, raising a challenging eyebrow.

"Be about time."

I lift my eyes to the ceiling. Great, now he has visions of grandkids. So much for moving slowly with this relationship business.

"I wored my new dress, but you wasn't here to see," Kiara tells Lissie accusingly, who darts a guilty look to Nosh and then me.

"I'm so sorry I missed that, honey, but maybe—if it's okay with your nana—I could pop by one day and you can wear it for me?"

"Now?"

I chuckle at the girl's eager expression.

"Not now. One day, Ms. Lissie said," Lisa intervenes, grabbing her granddaughter by the hand. "Leave these people to eat in peace, girl. You were going to help me in the kitchen."

As easily as that, Kiara's attention is diverted and she skips to the kitchen at her nana's hand, babbling something about cookies.

A sharp knock on the table has me look at my father.

"Eat up. We've got shit to paint."

"He says—"

"I got that," Lissie interrupts with a smile for the old man, who looks pleased.

Back at the house he disappears into the kitchen only to come back out moments later, carrying a notebook he hands to Lissie. I read over her shoulder.

WE'RE GOING SHOPPING TOMORROW. NEED A WOMAN'S OPINION.

"Fuck, Nosh," I grumble, signing as I speak. "How do you know she's not working? Or even wants to?"

"I don't mind," she tells me with a smile. Then she adds, "And, uhm, I'm off for an undetermined time, so that won't be an issue either."

A red flag goes up.

"Off for an undetermined time?"

She hesitates, looking a little embarrassed, but finally says, "I got suspended from duty."

"You what?" I'm instantly enraged for her. "What the fuck for?"

"What's going on?" Nosh signs but I ignore him.

"Well," she starts hesitantly. "The chief wasn't too pleased I'd been poking around in a case I was told to stay out of."

"You have gotta be fuckin' kidding me. Benedetti?" I pull my phone from my pocket and am already dialing.

"Benedetti."

"You sonofa—"

"Give me that phone!" Lissie grabs my arm and twists the phone from my hand. "I'm sorry, Chief. Yes. I will. Nosh? Yes, he is. Okay. Sorry again."

I'm fuming by the time she ends the call and shoves it at me. She's just as pissed, stabbing a finger in my chest, making my father chuckle in the background.

"That was out of line."

I grab her hand to stop her finger from poking me.

"You got shafted for doing your damn job, Lissie. *That* is outta line."

LISSIE

IT TAKES ME fifteen minutes to explain things to Yuma, who translates for his father. It does little to calm him down, though. Now he's pissed at Joe for potentially putting me at risk.

I'm lucky my boss is a good guy. I never asked him if I should keep his plan to myself, and wouldn't have said anything to Yuma if Joe hadn't given me the green light to tell him and his father. He said it wasn't a bad idea having someone at my back.

Joe was actually chuckling when I got on the phone

after I wrestled it from Yuma. Thought it was hilarious. I don't see the humor myself. Especially not when Yuma is still glaring at me like I did something wrong.

"I don't like it."

"That's pretty obvious," I return. "But you're just going to have to suck it up because I'm doing this. It gives me a chance to do something meaningful for Dani."

The instant I mention her name the angry expression melts off his face.

"Shit, baby."

"Let's paint." I turn, walk into the kitchen, and grab the trays and rollers from the sink.

I can feel the men watching as I pour some paint in my tray and start rolling the second coat on the wall. After a beat or two, I hear movement behind me and when I sneak a peek, Yuma is getting his own tray ready.

We work in silence for a while until I have to go on my tiptoes to roll as high as I can. I yelp as I'm suddenly lifted off my feet, two strong arms around my middle.

"Keep rolling, baby," Yuma's voice rumbles behind me.

He holds me up long enough for me to finish the top edge, and then he lowers me down the front of his body, before turning me in his arms.

"Are we okay?" he asks softly, his eyes warm on mine.

Not really an apology, but I wasn't expecting one. After having had a chance to cool off, I can appreciate the fact he clearly cares enough to be worried about me. It's the kind of man he is, which isn't necessarily a bad thing. Depending on where this is going, likelihood is this won't be the only time we'll bump heads.

"Yeah. We're good."

"Good." He lowers his head and brushes my lips with his. "Because watching you bend over every time to get paint on your roller has been messing with my head."

"Your head?" I tease, one eyebrow raised.

"Both of them."

His grin is infectious and I'm smiling when I lift up on my toes for another kiss.

We're interrupted by Yuma's father banging on the dinner table in the middle of the room. He starts signing and I look at Yuma for translation.

"He says to get our asses out of here. He's worked up a good appetite and doesn't want us to ruin it." A laugh bursts out of me and when I look over at Nosh, humor twinkles in his eyes. "He wants me to make sure I have you back here at ten to take him shopping."

I give the old man a thumbs-up.

Twenty minutes later, Yuma is following me back to my apartment. That happened without much of a discussion, but I'm not complaining.

Far from it.

I'm still not complaining two hours later when Yuma leaves me boneless and tangled in the sheets to open the door for the pizza delivery. I'm still in the same position when he comes back in carrying the box, two bottles of water and a roll of kitchen towels, all of which he deposits on the bed. But when he strips out of his jeans again, I roll on my side to watch him.

I like watching him; the way the muscles of his arms bunch and flex as they move, the beard he tries to smooth into submission with his hand, the slight puckering of his skin underneath the tattoo on his shoulder. He's not classically handsome, clean-cut, or carefully sculpted, but the sum of his parts makes for a beautiful man.

"Gotta stop lookin' at me like that," he grumbles, climbing in bed beside me. "Fuel first."

I push myself into a sitting position, tucking the sheet under my arms, which he promptly tugs down.

"What?" he says when I roll my eyes. "I like looking at you."

"Not much to look at." I'm referring to my underwhelming boobs as I grab a slice of pizza from the box and take a big bite, moaning at the taste. "Besides," I mutter around my mouthful. "I'm sure you've seen your share. You see one pair, you've seen 'em all."

"Bullshit. Wanna know what the difference is? I can't remember a damn thing about any'a them, but I don't ever wanna forget a single detail about you."

The masticated bite of pizza seems to get stuck in my throat, and I have to swallow hard to make it move.

"You can't say nice things to me when I'm eating," I grumble. "It's hazardous."

He grins and leans over the pizza box between us to brush my mouth with his smiling lips.

"I'll keep it in mind, baby."

"You know what's funny? My whole life I've had an aversion to being called babe or baby. It was usually meant in a derogatory way, like a distracted pat on the head to appease an annoying child."

"Jesus, Lissie, coulda told me that before." Now it's his turn to grumble.

"No, what I'm trying to say is it doesn't feel like the same when you call me that. It feels...I don't know... treasured?"

"Good, 'cause you are."

Like he didn't just say something profound—to me anyway—he shoves another impressive bite in his mouth.

I sit back against the headboard, eating my pizza with a growing sense of well-being. To my father and brothers I'd mostly been an annoyance. I haven't felt this appreciated since my mom died and I like it.

Then Yuma knocks off my rose-colored glasses.

"And it sure don't hurt you've got a thing for meat lovers' pizza."

ARROW'S EDGE MC

24

LISSIE

"GOT A MINUTE?"

I look over my shoulder to find Luna walking into the kitchen.

We just finished dinner in the clubhouse, after another full day of painting, and a whirlwind shopping trip with Nosh this morning. Yuma had decided to tag along so he could translate.

His father had wanted me to pick out paint colors and window coverings for the three bedrooms, and new flooring for the entire house. Don't get me wrong, the house needs it, but he was spending a healthy amount of money. When I voiced my concern to Yuma, he laughed, stating his father probably had more socked away than any normal person would see in a lifetime and that it was high time to put that money to good use.

Not normally a huge fan of shopping, I had a surprisingly good time picking things for someone else's house, with someone else's money.

"Of course, let me just rinse these." I quickly run the plates under the faucet and stack them in the dishwasher.

"We'll grab Ouray's office?"

"Sure."

I wipe my hands and follow her, throwing a little wave at Yuma, who had moved to the bar and was chatting with Tse. I have butterflies in my stomach, guessing this will be the go-ahead sign.

"You up for this?" she asks, when she closes the door behind me.

"Absolutely," I say, with a lot more confidence than is probably warranted and all the excitement I feel.

"Few things first to get you up to speed," she says, sitting down at the large table and indicating for me to do the same. "We've been able to identify another of the victims. Candy Wilson, a thirty-one-year old single mom from Reno. She and her five-year old son, Alex, went missing eight years ago. Her DNA had been uploaded to CODIS at the time."

CODIS is the FBI acronym for Combined DNA Index System, a national DNA database.

Luna opens a file folder and pulls out a photo she hands to me of a pretty woman with an adorable little boy. Then she hands me another picture, this one more like a mugshot of an older boy.

"Is that the same kid?"

"That is Zach, one of the boys found at the ANL training facility in Moab last year. He's in foster care in Denver. They're testing to confirm it's him as we speak. We're testing all the boys against the DNA of our victims."

I shake my head. This is completely beyond the scope of my darkest imagination.

"Wait. Do you think Dani may have—"

"God, I'd hate to think anyone would be so evil they'd methodically harvest kids, killing off their mothers, but I'm afraid that's what it looks like. Both Candy Wilson and your friend—and I'm sorry to say this—seemed to be living less than established lives. Candy was a stripper at a dingy Reno club, and Dani..." She lets her voice trail off but I can fill in the blanks. My best friend wasn't exactly a pillar of society. "Also, we've located Marty Spengler. One of Red Franklin's contacts? He was holed up with one of their hangers-on."

"Hangers-on?"

"Club property. Women looking to be part of the club by whatever means."

"Sounds desperate," I observe.

"Often is. We have a handful here too, but they're not around as much as they used to be."

I must've made a face because she chuckles.

"You wouldn't happen to have something to do with that, would you?"

She pulls up a shoulder. "Maybe. Anyway, Spengler was around when they poured the foundation for the community center and saw the bones. He also saw his

285

buddy, Scott, take pictures. The foreman reminded the crew of the power of the Woodard family in town and warned them they were not people to mess with. Marty freaked and bailed, and has been hiding out ever since. Too scared to even report back to Red."

"And what about the other guy? Becker? Any sign of him?"

"Nothing. Gone to ground." She slides a small Victoria's Secret bag across the table. "Greene got a package together for you. Inside are three dime-sized trackers you should carry on your body at all times. If you're ever in a position where one is discovered, they might look for a second one, but rarely a third one, so be creative. There's also a carbon copy of your iPhone in there. Except this one has a tracker installed."

I pull out the phone and notice my contacts are on this new phone.

"Is it okay if I'm a bit freaked out now?"

Luna snickers. "Understandable. Jasper Greene is good. It's still your own phone number, it just has a few built in safety measures. You will need to set up your facial recognition and password, and I'll hold on to your own phone for the time being. You don't want to confuse the two. And don't worry, you'll be monitored closely."

"Okay." In truth I'm a lot overwhelmed, but a little excited as well. "So now what?"

"Now you do what you were doing before, be yourself and do a little digging. The only thing to be aware of is people need to think you have gone rogue. That's what's going to make them more willing to talk." She gets up.

"We should get back out there."

Feeling a bit more confident, I stand as well and grab the Victoria's Secret bag, when Luna stops by the door.

"Before I forget, there's an emergency alert on your phone. Hit the pound key three times and we'll know you're in trouble."

Just like that the butterflies are back.

"That for me?" Tse comments, waggling his eyebrows as he points to the bag in my hand.

"Oh, I'm sorry." I turn to him batting my eyelids, and his lecherous smile only gets bigger. "Had I known, underneath all that leather and brawn, you had a penchant for lacy underwear, I'd have gotten you some in your size."

Whoops and hollers go up around the bar and Tse's smile drops right off his face as he clutches his chest. Yuma, who'd looked ready to take on his friend just moments earlier, laughs heartily at his expense.

"You'll do, Lissie," Luna mutters behind me. "You'll do just fine."

Yuma reaches for my hand and starts pulling me to the door.

"Wait! Where are we going?"

"Riverside. Plumbing problems," he mumbles, as I trot to keep up with his long strides.

YUMA

OH, THE IRONY.

I'd barely pulled my truck into the empty spot when

Mr. Denby—the retired mailman in unit sixteen—was suddenly standing beside my door. He had water coming down his walls. His upstairs neighbors weren't home, but I got inside their apartment to find water flooding from underneath their dishwasher.

Now, two hours later, I'm soaked to the skin and in the office making calls. The plumber is doing his magic up in the unit after I discovered it was too much for me, probably charging a premium since it's after hours.

I had plans and they involved the enticing Victoria's Secret bag that sparked my imagination. I don't give a shit Lissie wears sensible underwear—she'd be sexy in a burlap sack—but the thought of those perky tits and that lush ass covered in lace had me hard in seconds. Then Tse opened his fucking mouth and I almost lost it on him, but with a smile on her face Lissie had the perfect comeback, which only made me harder.

I'm still hard. The only difference is, I'm damp, uncomfortable, and cursing the insurance company who's had me on hold for the past twenty minutes. I have to get this settled before I go back up.

After another agonizing ten minutes, I'm finally patched through to someone who can take my information and I'm promised a claims adjuster will be here tomorrow to take a report of the damage. I place a brief call to Ouray after to fill him in, then grab a quick shower and put on dry clothes before locking up and heading upstairs.

I hear the raised voices inside the apartment when I walk up to the door. Lissie's and a man's I don't recognize. I don't even bother knocking; I use my own key to open her door.

The first thing I see is her face, her eyes dark in the pale face. I focus on the back of the large man in the middle of her living room.

"What the fuck is going on here?" I bark, and the guy turns, a scowl on his face.

He doesn't have a lot on me size-wise but he has that don't-mess-with-me look.

"Who the fuck are you?"

His booming voice doesn't impress me. Lissie's lips are pressed together and I quickly move to her side, tucking her rigid body against me without ever taking my eyes off the guy. He doesn't look too pleased.

"Yuma, this is my brother, Peter," she says stiffly, before she adds with a hefty dose of sarcasm. "He's traveled all this way to check on me. Haven't heard from him or anyone else in months, but apparently news of my shameful suspension has made its way to Albuquerque."

"Didn't exactly sound like a warm family reunion when I was coming up the stairs, Babe."

"*Babe*?" her brother echoes me with clear disgust. "Jesus, Elizabeth, this is the kind of lowlife you've been associating with? I knew you were desperate but this is sinking really low, even for you."

My blood boils at his disdain for his sister, and I struggle to hold back slugging the bastard's pretty face.

"You're standing in your sister's living room insulting her, you asshole. I think you've outstayed your welcome."

Instead of looking at me he glares at Lissie. "This was

a waste of time. Dad thought maybe you would finally come to your senses and sent me to bring you home, but I see you're still making poor decisions."

"Fuck you, Peter," she hisses pulling from my hold. "And fuck that sanctimonious horse you rode in on. You're so damn blinded by your own righteousness, you can't even recognize a good man when he's standing right in front of you." It feels like a balloon expanding in my chest at her words. But she's not done. "And for the record: the first time I came to my senses was the day I left Albuquerque. Best decision I ever made. Don't pretend you're concerned about me when all you fucking care about is the family reputation I've muddied."

"Nice language. I see your poor choice in friends is rubbing off on you."

That's it. I'm done with this shit. I step in front of Lissie, my hands fisted at my sides.

"Leave," I growl. "Not gonna ask you again."

For a moment I think he's going to put up a fuss, but with a last scowl at me he turns and walks out the front door. I close and lock it behind him before I turn to Lissie, who's still standing in the middle of the room.

"Come here, Beautiful."

She doesn't need more encouragement and rushes into my arms.

"I hate my family," she mumbles into my shirt.

"Not feeling a lot of love for them myself right now, Babe."

She snorts and I'm surprised to hear a chuckle.

"You know, I could really use a drink right now." The

moment the words are out of her mouth she pulls back, her eyes big. "Shit. I'm so—"

I swallow the rest of her words when I kiss her until we're both breathless.

"Don't apologize for being real. Not with me." I rest my forehead against hers.

"Fair enough. But I am sorry for the awful things my brother said about you. None of it's true."

I love how her big brown eyes are so expressive, it's easy to read her feelings in them.

"You already made that quite clear, Babe. Peter is a dick."

She turns out of my hold and walks into the kitchen, taking the always-present jug of iced tea from the fridge. She also starts pulling out the makings of a sandwich.

"And he's the mellow one," she mutters, as she pours us a glass.

"What the hell did he want?"

"What they've always wanted: for me to quit the force. I'm a blemish on the impeccable record of generations of Bucco men joining the department. Especially after what happened in Albuquerque."

"What happened?"

"I reported my captain for sexual harassment. I'd grown up with the man; he was a close friend of my father's and well-loved in the department. He also whipped out his dick and threatened me to suck him off."

"You have got to be fucking kidding me. Let me guess, your family believed him over you."

"To be honest, I don't think the truth even mattered

to my dad or my brothers. My father told me to drop the charges against his friend or he'd make my drinking habit public knowledge. I didn't even know he was aware I was self-medicating with alcohol."

"So you left."

"Got clean, got out of town, and stayed under the radar. Until now. I knew they'd be keeping an eye out through the old boys' network."

She's got eight pieces of bread lined up and is piling slices of cheese on half of them.

"What do they want from you?"

"Come home. Learn to knit. Marry one of their friends and pop out babies like I'm supposed to. Who the hell knows?"

She's agitatedly waving the knife she's holding as she speaks. I grab her hand, take the knife, and finish slapping mustard on the other half of the bread.

"They don't have a single clue who you are, do they?"

"None."

She pulls a large frying pan from a cupboard and sets it on a burner, while I stack the cheese sandwiches.

"Hope we're fucking done with unwanted surprises tonight," I grumble, and she lifts an eyebrow in my direction as she drops the sandwiches in the pan. "Been waiting long enough to see what's inside that pink little bag of yours."

"Afraid you'll be disappointed," she snickers.

I walk over to the bag she dropped on the loveseat and peek inside. She bursts out laughing when I fish out the phone and the small box, lifting the lid.

Over grilled cheese sandwiches, she reminds me she's a trained police officer and this is part of her job. That still doesn't mean I have to like it. The idea a few small disks are supposed to keep her safe isn't nearly enough reassurance.

I'm still grumbling when she drops our dishes in the sink and grabs my hand, dragging me to her bedroom. When she drops to her knees, her eyes on mine, as she deftly unbuttons my fly and frees my cock, I'm already halfway over my snit.

The warmth of her mouth as she takes me deep inside has me forget my own name. She braces herself with a hand on my thigh, while rolling my balls with the other. I only narrowly escape blowing my load down her throat as I abruptly pull out and yank her to her feet. In a scramble both of us are naked in seconds. I topple her back on the mattress and pull her hips to the edge, spreading her legs open.

"James…"

The softly whispered plea and her darkly flushed pussy are all the invitation I need. I wrap a hand around my hard cock, brush her wet folds with the tip and poise it at her entrance.

As I slide inside the hot grip of her body, there's no room in my mind for anything other than her.

25

LISSIE

WHILE YUMA HAS been busy at the apartments dealing with plumbing issues that turned out to be much more involved—apparently parts of the complex have to be retrofitted with new pipes—I have been either helping Nosh with his house, or showing the group picture around to anyone willing to take a look.

I haven't discovered much, other than I need to really start learning some sign language to make communicating with Nosh easier. He doesn't want to be bothered with electronics, so the handy cell phone app I've seen Luna's boy, Ahiga, use is wasted on the old man. He prefers simple pen and paper, but that method is slow.

Paco vaguely recalled seeing Dani with Chains, but that would have been prior to last summer, so not exactly new information. What I need to find out is what happened to her after that man died. Yuma mentioned Ginger had recognized Dani, and told him she was with the Moab Reds. Maybe she has more information.

Although I'm not looking forward to talking to the woman who shared more with Yuma than I care to think about.

"Wapi?"

The young guy lifts his head from where he's stocking the fridge behind the bar.

"Yeah?"

"Do you know where I can find Ginger Franklin's number?"

The silence is immediate, as every head in the clubhouse seems to turn to me. Nosh taps me on the arm and slowly shakes his head before grabbing his notepad.

WHAT DO YOU WANT WITH HER?

"I want to ask her about Dani."

He shrugs and scribbles some more.

YOUR FUNERAL

Ouray ambles over and hands me a scrap of paper with a phone number.

"You can use my office, darlin', but a word of caution: Ginger sometimes shows her teeth."

"Y'all can stop worrying. I already know what she's armed with, and it's not gonna stop me from finding out what happened to my friend."

"Fair enough," he says, lifting his hands.

I bring my phone into Ouray's office and close the door. Taking a deep breath in I dial the number.

Just as she answers with a sharp, "Who's this?" I realize this call will likely be recorded by the FBI. I hope to God she doesn't bring up her past with Yuma.

"Ginger?" I used my perkiest voice. "It's Lissie. We met a while ago at the Arrow's Edge clubhouse?"

"Yes?"

It's not a 'Hey, how are ya' but at least she didn't hang up.

"I understand you knew my friend, Dani?"

"Didn't know her, but I've seen her around at the Reds' clubhouse."

"Can you tell me anything more? When was the last time you saw her? Or who she was with?"

It's quiet on the other side for a few beats before she comes back with a question of her own.

"Whadda you want with her?"

I don't need to fake the emotion that fills my voice as I answer.

"I want to find out what happened to her. Her body was one of the ones found at the Wildcat Canyon construction site."

"She's dead?" I don't bother responding to that and Ginger doesn't seem to expect it. "Damn. Sorry to hear that." She sounds genuine.

"Thanks. We lost touch over the years but she was a good friend, so if there's anything you can tell me, it would be helpful."

"Like I said, I've seen her around, but never paid much attention. We've been at their clubhouse a few times over the years for parties, but not since last year, so any time I've seen her woulda been before then. Some of our guys have friends over there, though. I can ask around."

"That would be great. Thanks, Ginger."

It's quiet for a minute and then she goes there. I'd been bracing for it.

"So...you and Yuma?"

"Me and Yuma," I confirm, not giving her more than what she puts out there.

"He used to be such fun," she taunts, but I'm not biting.

"Alcohol can make it look that way."

"Nothing wrong with a drink," she says defensively.

"Not if you don't need it to forget what you're doing."

The silence on the other side stretches until she finally says, "You're not as prissy as you look, are you?"

I'm not quite sure whether to take it as an insult or a compliment.

"Not nearly."

All I hear is a snort on the other side and then dead air.

I'm thinking I may have won that round. I'm wearing a smirk as I walk back into the clubhouse.

"Not the look I was expecting," Ouray says with a grin. He's sitting with Nosh at the table where we'd been having lunch before.

I shrug. "She struck. I countered. She wasn't prepared

for that. I'd call it a win."

Nosh scribbles on his pad before turning it to show me.

YOU'RE A SURPRISE LISSIE BUCCO.

My smirk spreads into a full-fledged smile as I follow him back to his house.

We spent the morning clearing out what used to be Yuma's room so we could paint it for Ezrah. It had been a bit of insight into Yuma's childhood: pictures, school yearbooks, an old Green Day poster, and even a sports trophy or two. This afternoon we're painting it the light blue-gray I picked out.

Nosh still hasn't told anyone else what we're doing this for, even though a few of the guys have been in to see what we're doing. It's not up to me to share so whenever someone would ask me, I just shrugged.

We've just finished the first coat, and I'm rinsing out the rollers in the bathroom when my phone rings. I quickly wipe my hands on my jeans and pull out my phone.

"Hello?"

"Is this Lissie?" It's a woman but she's keeping her voice low.

"It is." I pull the phone away and quickly check the number. I don't recognize it. "Who's this?"

"You called about Dani last week?"

"Yes," I respond cautiously. If this is the same woman who answered at the Moab Red's clubhouse last week, that conversation ended quite abruptly.

"She left some of her stuff behind. I stuck it in a box. Do you want it?"

She sounds rushed and a little out of breath. I'm scared she'll hang up again so I answer quickly.

"Uh, yeah, absolutely. Where are you? Can I come pick it up at the clubhouse?"

"No! Don't come here. I'll figure something out. I'll text you."

"Hey, what's your name?"

"Tammy, but I gotta go. I'll text."

She hangs up before I get a chance to answer.

Half an hour later I get a text.

TELLURIDE AT CAFEE. 4:30.

It's two o'clock now. I'll have to hustle if I want to make it to Telluride in time.

OKAY.

I barely have a chance to hit send on my response when my phone rings again.

"Hello?"

"FBI Agent Jasper Greene here. Lissie? We need to talk."

YUMA

"Where's Lissie?"

Nosh puts down the roller.

"Got a call and had to leave. Said she'd be back later. Police business."

Damn.

These past few days have been a clusterfuck. Two apartments flooded, tenants up in arms because of the unscheduled repairs to the water pipes, and we've barely even started. Twenty-two units and in the past couple of days only four got done. I had to be there to let the plumbers into the apartments, and then patched up the holes they left behind. The whole thing is requiring far more patience than I have.

When Wapi showed up this afternoon, I told him I needed a break and rode here on my bike, hoping maybe I could take Lissie on a ride.

"When did she leave?"

"Couple of hours ago."

Shit.

"Well, don't stand around. Grab a roller."

"Give me a second."

I shoot Lissie off a quick message.

AT NOSH'S. WHERE ARE YOU?

It's after five by the time we finish painting my old room. I've checked my phone several times to see if Lissie sent me anything back. Looks like she did receive my message, but no response. We clean up, leaving the paint trays and rollers to air-dry and head over to the clubhouse for a bite.

"Mr. Yuma!" Kiara comes running at me and I scoop her up easily, setting her on my arm. "We've gots hot dogs!" She points at the barrel grill where Ouray looks to be cooking a selection of meat. "Nana made tater salad and broccoli salad, and if I eat a bite of both we gets to make s'mores after."

"Tater salad, huh?"

"And broccoli salad," she adds and pulls a face. "I don't like that, but Nana says it's good for me and makes me grow big and strong. Do you like broccoli salad, Mr. Yuma?"

I grin at her. "I do. How do you think I got this big and strong?"

"Kiara!" Lisa comes outside, carrying the little girl's jacket. "Told you not to go outside without your jacket."

"I've got it." Brick walks up to her and grabs the jacket from her hand before walking toward us. "Come here, Princess." He plucks the little girl from my hold and tucks her under his arm, carrying her to a picnic table while she squirms and giggles. "Now you need to listen to your nana," he gently scolds her, as he sets her on top of the picnic table, tugging the jacket over her skinny arms. "Otherwise, you'll catch a cold out here and then there ain't gonna be any s'mores, hear me?"

"Yes, Mr. Brick," she answers in a little voice.

He zips her up and lifts her off the table, setting her on her feet. "There, now you can go play."

She immediately runs off to where her brother and the other young kids are kicking a ball around.

"Another goner," Nosh signs, shaking his head as he

starts inside.

I walk up to Ouray.

"What brought the cookout on?"

"Ahiga got to pick dinner. He picked meat on the grill."

"Where's Luna?"

"Working late. They picked up a couple of suspects today they're questioning. Be good for this case to be over."

"It's probably where Lissie went off to as well. Nosh says she got called out on police business."

"Wouldn't surprise me. Sounds like it's all hands on deck."

Guess I shouldn't expect Lissie back soon either then.

I update him on the progress at the Riverside before I wander off to join Tse and Honon, and bum a smoke.

"Where'd you leave the woman?" Tse asks. "Fucked that up already?"

"Fuck off, asshole. She's working," I grumble.

"So what's with Nosh and his reno all of a sudden?" Honon wants to know. "Can't remember the last time a paintbrush touched that house."

"He'll tell y'all when he's ready. Not mine to share."

"Jesus, that's what your woman's been telling us. We're worried about him, man."

"Trust me, brother. He's okay. It's just his way to work through things, but he's got a purpose. You don't have to worry."

"Soup's on!" Ouray yells, walking inside with a big aluminum pan full of burgers, steak, and hot dogs.

It's instant mayhem. The kids stampeding into the clubhouse, adults filing in. I take one last drag and toss my butt in the can before trailing them inside. Instead of heading for the table where a crowd's already formed, I head over to the bar where Nosh sits.

"Want me to grab you a plate?"

He answers with a nod.

When I get my turn at the table, I load up two plates and go sit next to him at the bar.

"Want to sit at a table?" I know he asks for my sake and I appreciate it, but we're good where we are.

"Here is fine."

Partway through dinner Ouray walks up, and the expression on his face has me immediately on alert.

"What's wrong?"

"Luna just called. It's about Lissie."

26

LISSIE

THE MOUNTAINS ARE beautiful.

I really haven't taken the opportunity to explore beyond the immediate area around Durango. Even though Telluride is not that far as the crow flies, driving there takes two, two and a half hours, because of the mountains. I'd love to take this drive again some time, without the anxiety I'm feeling now.

My conversation with Agent Greene had been brief. Just enough for him to explain the investigation was running hot and everyone on his team was tied up. He'd be calling the marshal's office in Telluride to see if they could spare an officer to keep an eye on the location for backup and wanted to make sure I was aware of that. He also reminded me to be cautious, and use my phone to record any conversation with the woman, just in case.

Nosh just nodded when I told him I had to go and I tore out of there in a hurry. My GPS told me it's over two hours to get to Telluride, which didn't leave me much wiggle room.

So far the drive has been uneventful, but it's not one I'd want to try once the snow season hits. At least not on a timeline.

I left Dolores behind me a while ago, and it's a good thing this road will take me straight to where I need to go, because cell phone reception has been almost nonexistent the last half hour or so.

With the radio tuned to an oldies station and taking in the beautiful scenery around me, it's not a bad drive, if not for the sense of urgency I feel to get there in time.

Tammy had sounded jumpy on the phone and I'm afraid if I don't get there by four thirty, she'll bail on me, and I really want to get my hands on Dani's things.

With just a few minutes to spare, I finally pull into a strip mall on the side of the road. Cafee is the small sandwich shop in the end unit, closest to the road. I note the patrol car parked at the opposite end of the parking lot, which makes me feel a little better.

I peg Tammy the moment I walk in the door and not just because of the shoebox she's clenching on the table in front of her. Her eyes shot up the moment I opened the door. A brunette like me, I'm guessing her age to be close to mine, although she looks well-worn. Part of that may be the stress visible in the tight line of her mouth and the frown between her eyebrows. Her eyes seem to flit around as I approach the table.

"Tammy?"

"Yes." Even as she answers she darts a glance behind me.

I slide into the booth across from her and immediately a waitress appears at the table.

"Can I get you something?"

"I'd love a coffee. What about you, Tammy?" I ask, noticing the empty water glass on the table in front of her.

"Yes, coffee is fine," she tells the waitress but she keeps her attention on me. When the woman walks away she shoves the box across the table at me. "This is it. All of it."

"I really appreciate this." I take the box and set it on the seat beside me. I'd love to examine what's inside, but that can wait until later. First I want to see what information Tammy might have, before she spooks and hightails it out of here.

"She gave it to me. Asked me to keep it safe but she never came back."

"When was this?"

Her eyes do a quick scan of the place again before she answers.

"January. It was the last time I seen her."

"Do you know why she wanted you to keep it for her?"

She seems to be waging an internal struggle when the waitress walks up with two mugs of coffee and a handful of creamers.

"Do you?" I prompt her when we've doctored our coffees.

"She was scared. Asking a lot of questions after her old man—Chains—got himself killed. I always knew there was something wrong with her, but she never told me what until she gave me that box."

"What was it?" I nudge her again when she falls silent.

She leans forward with her elbows on the table and looks at me intently.

"Dani tried to leave him once—Chains—when Jesse had just turned two."

"Jesse?" My heart is pounding so hard I'm afraid she can hear it across the table.

"Their baby boy. She was gonna take him and make her way back to New Mexico she said. I guess Chains found out and went after her. She was gone for three days and when she came back, the baby was gone. In all the years after that she was like the walking dead. Never smiled, rarely spoke, and never shared what happened to the baby. Not until Chains got killed."

"And no one did anything? No one asked?" I hear the accusation in my voice and see her flinch.

"No one dared cross Chains. The man was ruthless. When she gave me the box she said someone was after her. She made me swear not to ask questions or I'd be in trouble too."

"She didn't say who was after her or why?" I probe.

Tammy shakes her head. "I just took it and hid it under my bed. I was too afraid to look inside."

I look over at the box and notice the lid is taped down.

"You don't know what's inside?"

She shakes her head again. "I just wanna get rid of it." Then she looks at me with tears filling her eyes. "Dani's not coming back, is she?"

I'm about to break the news to her when Tammy's eyes go wide, and she suddenly gets out of the booth and starts running for the exit. I don't think and take off after her as she runs to a small silver two-door vehicle.

"Wait!" I yell, but she's already got her keys out and is reaching for the door.

Time slows down when I see her body jerk and a fraction after that I hear the report of a gunshot. She jerks again. Another shot, and I'm still moving toward her when she crumples to the pavement. I stop and reach for my gun, turning in the direction of the road where I heard the shots coming from, but I never quite get my hand on it before I'm spun around and knocked to the ground.

YUMA

"I'M COMING WITH you."

I turn around at my father's rusty voice.

"Go inside."

"Like hell. I'm coming."

"Let's go," Ouray calls out, clicking the locks on his Traverse. He said he was driving and I'm not about to argue.

There'd been a shooting up in Telluride. An officer was found dead beside his patrol car and two women had been rushed to the hospital. According to Luna, Lissie

311

had gone up to Telluride to get some of Dani's stuff from a friend of hers. They hadn't been able to confirm yet, but the assumption was Lissie is one of the victims.

"Luna called from the car. She's on her way up to Telluride," Ouray mentions as he heads toward Durango.

"Why was she up there alone?" My voice sounds as rusty as my father's.

He glances sideways at me before his eyes focus on the road again.

"Brother, I don't know. I didn't get all the details. All I know is they picked up one of Red Franklin's plants, Marty Spengler, and since he started talking, they've been scrambling to keep all the pieces in place. Your woman is a cop. A detective. She's not helpless."

I don't give a flying fuck if she's a certified ninja warrior; she bleeds all the same.

Nosh's heavy hand lands on my shoulder, giving it a light squeeze before letting go. The comforting gesture so alien coming from my father, I almost lose it. Fuck, what I wouldn't give for a shot of something, anything, to dull the fear eating me from the inside out.

We've just left Dolores behind when Ouray's phone rings. He answers it on hands-free.

"You're on speaker, Sprite," he warns his wife.

"Good. I don't have an update on the condition of the victims at this time, but both are being flown into Mercy. I have confirmation one of them was Lissie."

I'm not sure if I was still hoping maybe it wasn't her, but hearing that has the bottom fall from my stomach.

Telluride has a medical center, but it's not really

equipped for major trauma. Those patients are usually helicoptered to Mercy here in Durango, which is a Level III Trauma Center.

Ouray is already turning the truck around, back to Durango.

"They were able to identify her from her driver's license." Luna is still talking. "According to a witness, it was over in seconds. The officer was there for backup, but it looks like he barely had a chance to get out of his cruiser. Two shots for the first victim, but the shooter dropped the second woman and the cop with single shots, all in quick succession. The waitress had a good description of the truck the shots seemed to originate from. It was idling along the side of the road and she was pretty sure there was only one person in the vehicle. Unfortunately it was found a few miles out of town, the shell casings still in the truck but no sign of the shooter."

"Sounds like he was a good shot," Ouray observes.

"Clearly. Anyway, I'm about twenty minutes south of town. Wish I didn't have to continue to Telluride, but law enforcement is waiting for me on the scene, so I have to check in there. I'll let you know if I hear any more."

"Okay, be careful."

"I will. Yuma?"

"I'm here."

"She's tough. Haven't known Lissie long, but she's made of stern stuff. Hang in there."

Ouray ends the call and Nosh taps me on the shoulder. I twist in my seat.

"Lissie is being flow to Mercy hospital. We're heading

back."

He nods and turns his gaze out the window. It occurs to me I'm not the only one for whom this scenario is eerily similar to last summer when Momma was shot. Momma survived, but was never the same.

I reach over the seat and tap his knee to get his attention.

"She'll be okay. She has to be."

He nods, but I see him swallowing hard as he turns back to the dark mountains.

We drive the return trip in silence, until we finally pull into the all-too-familiar parking lot at Mercy. Ouray pulls up outside the emergency department and tells us to go ahead, he'll find us.

We walk straight up to the desk.

"My girlfriend was just flown here from Telluride. She was shot. Where can we find her?"

She averts her eyes. "I'm going to have to ask you to take a seat in the waiting room. We had two patients arrive at the same time and staff is working as hard as they can. As soon as we know something more, we'll come find you."

"I just wanna know how she is," I insist.

"I don't know. I'm sorry. I'll see if I can find something out for you."

I'm about to start arguing when Nosh grabs my arm and pulls me to the waiting area. Shortly after, Ouray comes walking in and sits down across from us without saying anything.

Ten minutes later, I'm up and pacing back and forth,

my father following my every move, when Joe Benedetti comes stalking in. He spots us and comes straight over.

"Any news?"

"Nothing."

"Give me a few minutes."

He heads for the same nurse I talked to and I guess being the chief of police counts for something, because after an intense exchange she disappears through the doors behind her. Five minutes later she reappears, a doctor in her wake who starts talking to Joe, but he points the man our way.

"Elizabeth Bucco's family?"

"Yes."

"Let me apologize for the confusion first. Two gunshot victims were brought in, both ended up in surgery within minutes of arriving, with much different results. Ms. Bucco is still in the OR. She received a gunshot wound to the upper chest, right under the clavicle, but the bullet ricocheted off her scapula. The surgeon is removing some fragments that could become a problem in the future. No major organs were hit and Ms. Bucco was very lucky. Unfortunately, the other victim wasn't so lucky. Margaret..." He indicates the nurse at the desk. "...had heard one of the patients had expired in the OR, but wasn't sure which one, which is why you were asked to wait. As soon as Ms. Bucco is out of surgery, we will let you know."

I sink down on the chair beside my father, and drop my face in my hands as soon as the doctor retreats to the ER. My body suddenly feels like Jell-O when all the tension releases at once.

"I've gotta make some calls," Benedetti announces. "How about I pick up some coffees on my way back?"

"I'll come give you a hand," Ouray announces.

I hear them walk away, when suddenly my father's hand grabs me by the neck and pulls my head to his shoulder, wrapping his other arm around me.

Unable, and even unwilling to hold back, I let it all out—relief, fear, grief, old pain—a lifetime of bottled-up emotions spill over, and my father holds me the entire time.

LISSIE

"LOVE YOU."

My eyes, blinking just seconds ago, shoot wide open.

The bright light blinding, I go straight back to blinking, but zoom in on the shadowed face looming over mine.

"W-what?" I stammer, sure I must've been dreaming.

"You heard me." His voice, deep and rich, holds a hint of humor.

Slowly his features come into focus. His heavy eyebrows frowning over those crystal clear blue eyes, the firm nose with a prominent bump where I'm sure it's been broken before, and those lush lips peeking from behind his beard.

"I heard you," I admit, only now feeling the deep throbbing ache in my left shoulder.

"Good," he whispers, brushing his lips gently over mine. "Was scared I wouldn't get the chance, baby."

My heart melts at the emotion behind his words. I lift my right hand to cup his face, stroking my thumb over his cheek.

"I'm sorry I scared you, honey."

He closes his eyes and presses his face in my palm when a knock sounds at the door.

"Shit, I forgot. My dad's been waiting outside."

"Let him in."

He presses another sweet kiss on my mouth before he straightens up and goes to the door, opening it. Nosh barely acknowledges him but walks right over to me.

"Give an old man a heart attack," he says in his monotone voice, but the missing emotion is visible in his eyes.

I look at Yuma behind him. "How do I say sorry in sign language?" He shows me and I turn back to Nosh, rubbing a fist over my sternum, mouthing 'sorry.'

He signs something and Yuma translates. "He wants to know how you're feeling."

"Sore, a little more damaged than I was before, but I'll be fine."

"Good," the old man says before his hands start moving again and Yuma bursts out laughing.

"What?'

"He says you should use your recovery wisely and learn ASL already."

27

LISSIE

"HOW ARE YOU feeling?"

I step aside to let Ramirez in.

Yuma brought me home this morning before leaving to deal with the ongoing plumbing issues.

I'd been lucky, the surgeon was able to clean out the bullet fragments, and all I was left with was some soft tissue damage that would heal over time. My left arm is immobilized with a sling, strapped around my chest for now, but I'm right-handed so I can still manage pretty well.

Tammy hadn't been so lucky. She didn't make it and apparently neither did the young officer who'd been assigned to keep an eye out. That's all I know. I've been out of the loop, and other than Joe Benedetti sticking his head in the door, I haven't seen anyone who could get me up to speed.

Until Tony knocked on my door.

"Not too bad. You want coffee?"

"Sure. Don't have a whole lotta time, though." He follows me into the kitchen. "You know, you really should invest in some more furniture."

"So I'm told." I get coffee going before turning back to Tony. "Come on. Tell me what's been going on, I feel like I've missed this whole case being unraveled."

"Not quite unraveled yet, there are still a few missing pieces."

"You got Spengler, I know that much," I prompt him.

"Technically the FBI got him, but yes, and he had lots to tell once the FBI assured him they'd keep him safe. He finally admitted John Woodard himself supervised the pour of the foundation for the community center. That foreman we've spent money and resources on finding was nothing but a red herring."

"You're kidding me? The mayor's cousin?"

"None other. Gomez picked him up at the Pro Concrete office, armed with search warrants for his home and business. The mayor went apoplectic when he found out. Now that was a thing of beauty. He stormed into Joe's office, throwing his weight around, and Joe just shrugged his shoulders, claiming his hands were tied since the FBI had jurisdiction over the case."

"You'd think our mayor had some inside knowledge," I observe.

"You have no idea how true that may well be. Not

sure if anything will stick legally, but I can guarantee his reputation is gonna be shot to hell. At first, John wasn't talking, but as bits and pieces of information started coming in from the searches at his house and the office, he could see the writing on the wall."

The coffeemaker beeps to indicate the brew is ready and I quickly pour us a cup, before focusing my full attention back on Tony.

"So what made him talk?"

"Hunting trophies. His home office has several mounts—elk, bear, and even a mountain lion—hanging on the walls. Stuck behind each mount was a dated Polaroid of the fresh kill, always with the same three hunters: John's father, Theo, former Utah senate member, James Hinckle, and none other than Victor Nowak. Apparently the three were tight and had been for quite a few years. Was hard for him to deny knowing those two after that. Combined with Spengler's testimony, he knew he was in a tight spot."

"No wonder the mayor was peeved."

"Understatement of the year," Tony snickers. "John claimed Nowak came to him shortly after he sold the land to Arches Homes. He said the media mogul was livid. There'd been a long-standing arrangement around the land that could leave Nowak, Hinckle and the Woodard family in hot water if discovered."

"The bodies?"

"Got it in one. Wasn't all though, Hinkle also liked to bring his boys out there for field training."

"Boys? You mean those kids?"

He nods. It makes me sick to think of what those poor boys had gone through. I'd seen the two kids who live with the Arrow's Edge a couple of times, and they just look like little boys to me. Field training? I shudder to think what that looked like.

"Nowak invested in the development, got Pro Concrete on board. Woodard swore he didn't know about the bodies until they were excavating for the community center foundation and hit on those bones."

"I don't believe that for a minute," I comment. It all sounds very self-serving to me.

"Neither does anyone else. He says Nowak was there to keep an eye out while he poured. Says he did see Lansing—the project coordinator—arrive but that he and Nowak walked off to the site office. He has no idea what happened after."

"Or so he says."

"Exactly. At least it was enough case for the FBI to talk to Nowak. They're trying to locate him."

"And Dani? Her body was buried there after the development was well underway. Did he say anything about her?"

I already know the answer to that from the regret on Ramirez face. "No mention of her."

"So you figure it was him up in Telluride? Nowak?"

"Doubtful. Not so sure he'd take chances like that. More likely some hired muscle. The man is rich as Croesus." Right. A man like that wouldn't get his hands dirty if he could avoid it. "Anyway," Tony says, standing up. "I should head out. Shit to do. I'll let you know if I find out more. Thanks for the coffee."

"Oh, before I forget, do you know if Luna found a shoebox up in Telluride? I left it on the seat in the coffee shop when I took off after Tammy. It holds some of Dani's things I'd like to have."

"As far as I know she's still up there, but I'll get word to her."

I walk with him to the front door.

"Appreciate you dropping by," I tell him as he opens the door.

"Elizabeth?"

I freeze at the sound of my father's voice.

I see the big hulking shape of my father outside my door when Tony takes a step aside.

"Dad."

"Hear you got yourself shot." My father has a way of looking down his nose at me like I'm something smelly stuck under his shoe.

"I didn't exactly volunteer for it, and hello to you too." I turn to Ramirez, who is observing the interaction closely. "It's all good, Tony. Just my father."

"Sure?"

"Positive."

He nods, gives my dad one more glance, and steps by him.

"Might as well come in." Not much of an invitation, but my father doesn't really need one. He'll do what he wants anyway, and unfortunately for me, today he apparently wants a go at me. "I'm popular these days. Not a peep for months and then suddenly Peter shows up on my doorstep and now you."

It was my father who taught me that offense is the best defense. He knocked me off balance by showing up unannounced, so to balance the scales I make sure I get the first jab in. If I show weakness he'll pounce on it.

"That one another boyfriend? Your brother says the last one looked like he walked straight out of lockup. This guy seems a little too clean cut. Trading up?"

"I'm doing well, Dad, how are you?" I know I'm just pissing him off by not reacting to his digs, but I'll be damned if I let myself be played.

"Well, since I had to find out through the grapevine my daughter got shot, instead of hearing it from her, I'd say not well. I'll have a word with your chief of police as well. I should've been notified immediately."

"Actually, no, you shouldn't. Not calling you was my choice to make."

Behind my father the door swings open, and Yuma comes stalking in. Fucking Ramirez, I'm sure. He doesn't even acknowledge my dad but walks right up to me, putting his hands either side of my face.

"You okay, Babe?"

"I'm fine, honey."

"Want me to put him out?" he asks, and I almost laugh out loud at the disgruntled sound coming from my father.

"It's okay," I assure him before turning to my dad. "So why are you here, Dad? Why was Peter here? What's this sudden interest in my well-being?"

YUMA

IT WASN'T HARD to see the family resemblance. Even from behind, I noticed the similar build. The gray hair gave away this had to be Bucco senior, but I didn't give the man the satisfaction of my attention and instead aimed for Lissie. She looked calm, though, almost resigned at his presence and I was happy to leave her the lead.

When I turn to face him, the glare he had fixed on me turns to his daughter at her question.

"You're my daughter," he says, like that should answer her questions.

"Have been my whole life, Dad, although I haven't always been sure you were aware of that fact."

I have to say, if the man is an actor, he's a damn good one because the surprise at her comment seems genuine.

"Of course I have been. I was worried about you."

"Well, as you can see, I'm doing fine. Or I will be as soon as I get rid of this thing," she says, pointing at her sling.

"You could've died." The words come out gruffly.

They're probably as different as two people can be, but I'm realizing there's a strong similarity between Lissie's father and my own. Men who have a certain view of the world and don't handle anything or anyone veering from that perspective particularly well. Being on the receiving end of their displeasure, it doesn't feel like they care, but as I've discovered since Momma died, my father cares, he just has a piss-poor way of showing it. It may just be Lissie's father cares too.

"I didn't, Dad," she says gently, and I wonder if she's just come to that realization as well.

I feel her leaning into me. Something her father notices as well.

"Take the load off, Babe, before you hit the ground. You're swaying on your feet." She doesn't object when I lead her to the loveseat.

"And who are you?" her father asks sharply.

Lissie opens her mouth, but I give her shoulder a squeeze before holding my hand out to him. My natural instinct would be to make some smartass comment at his arrogant tone, but I didn't miss that glimpse of vulnerability earlier, so instead I step out of my own comfort zone and hold out my hand.

"James Wells."

He hesitates for a moment, but then he grabs it in a firm shake.

"Robert Bucco."

"Coffee, Robert?"

I have to give him credit for checking his daughter before he answers. She forces a little smile for him.

"Sure."

For the next fifteen minutes, conversation is a bit stilted. Lissie asks about her nephews—apparently the older brother has two boys—and her father questions me. I can't fault him for that. If I ever have a daughter like Lissie, I'd be up one end and down the other of any guy looking at her twice. So I answer questions about my work, my club, and my criminal record honestly, albeit with gritted teeth.

Lissie had a positive impact on my relationship with Nosh. The least I can do is try not to mess up hers with her father.

"I have to get back on the road," he announces as he gets up. "Think you could let me know how you're doing every so often?" I notice Lissie going rigid at his sharp tone.

"Absolutely," she snaps back. "I'll make sure to answer when you call." Lobbing the ball right back in his court.

Robert nods at her stiffly, having received her message loud and clear and without sparing me another glance, walks out the door. We watch until he gets in his car and drives off the parking lot. Then she shuts the door and turns to me; the smile on her face soft and her eyes damp.

"Thank you for doing that."

"Dunno what you're talking about," I lie.

Her smile only stretches wider.

"Right. Well, then thanks for being you."

"Don't have to thank me for that." I lower my head and brush her lips. "But I'd better go check on my pipes."

"You make it sound so dirty."

I grin at her snicker.

"Hold that thought until you've recovered. I have every intention of showing you how dirty my mind really is when it comes to you."

"Promise?"

I groan, dropping my forehead to hers. "You're making me hard and I have a plumber waiting."

"Go," she says with a gentle slap on my chest. "Go fix your pipes."

"Okay. You want to stay here tonight or go to the

clubhouse?"

"Stay here tonight, clubhouse tomorrow?"

"Sounds good. I'll cook us dinner."

I kiss her again before opening the door.

"James?"

I glance back over my shoulder.

"Yeah, baby?"

"Love you too."

ARROW'S EDGE MC

28

LISSIE

"CAN I HELP?"

Lisa is working in the large kitchen when I walk in.

"With one hand?" she points out, smiling.

She's got a point. I have use of my right hand, but it's a little difficult to, say, peel potatoes one-handedly. I sit down at the large kitchen table.

I just spent the last hour watching a movie with Kiara, who fell asleep on the couch, and I'm bored.

This morning started early when I woke up, my shoulder throbbing. Yuma offered to get me pain pills, but I don't like taking them. I'm terrified I'll get hooked on them. They say once an addict, always an addict. The last thing I need is replacing one addiction with another. He seemed to understand, and instead of meds found another creative way to distract me from the pain, with his mouth between my legs.

I wanted to return the favor, but he insisted he could wait until I felt better. Then he cuddled up to my good side and we dozed off and on until eight.

After he made me some breakfast, we headed out to the clubhouse, but he took off shortly after with his father and Wapi to pick up new flooring for Nosh's house. Apparently the painting is all done, and ripping out the old carpet is next on his list of things to improve. He's been talking about updating the kitchen and the bathrooms as well. By the time he's done fixing up the house, it'll be virtually new. He hasn't mentioned anything to Lisa yet, though. I'm wondering when he's planning on doing that.

"How are you feeling?"

"Sore, and annoyed I can't do much. I'm not used to sitting still."

"I can imagine. How long are you supposed to wear the sling?"

"I have a checkup in a couple of days, I'm hoping it can come off then."

Lisa turns to me, her face serious.

"You were very lucky," she states solemnly.

"I know."

"Do they have any idea who did this?"

I shrug. "Not as far as I know. I wasn't much help. I was just turning when the round hit me and I went down. There were witnesses, but as far as I know, all they saw was the truck and that turned out to be stolen so it was a dead end."

Lisa is about to say something when Trunk walks in with one of the young boys.

"Can I leave the boy with you?" he asks Lisa after mumbling a greeting. "I've gotta head into town."

"Sure. You hungry, Thomas?"

The kid just nods.

"Use your words, boy," Trunk admonishes him.

"Yes, ma'am," he quickly corrects himself, before sitting down at the table across from me.

Lisa washes her hands as Trunk heads out the door with a distracted flick of his fingers. He clearly has things on his mind.

"Grilled cheese, Thomas?"

"Yes, please," he answers politely.

"Let me do that," I offer, getting up.

"If you don't mind?"

I shake my head, happy for something to do.

"Thomas, have you ever had grilled cheese with mustard?" I look over at him and am surprised when he nods his head. "You have?"

"Yes, ma'am. It's good."

"It's my favorite too. You want one, Lisa?" I dive into the huge fridge to get what I need.

"Sure. I'll give it a try. Never had it before."

"So, Thomas, how come you're not in school like the other kids today?" I ask, putting the sandwiches together while Lisa sets a big frying pan on a burner. When the boy doesn't answer, I turn to look at him. His head is down. "Thomas?"

"I got in trouble this morning." His voice is barely audible.

"Oh, no. What happened?"

His eyes dart to Lisa's back and then return to me. "Called Ezrah a bad word."

Lisa catches my eye and lifts an eyebrow before turning back to the mountain of vegetables she's chopping. She must already know about it.

"That's never a good idea."

"Mr. Trunk said I can't say the n-word no more."

Yikes.

"That's not a good word, Thomas. Calling someone names is never a good idea."

"I know," he whispers, his head down.

I feel for the kid. I know he's been indoctrinated into thinking a certain way and must be confused as all get out with the mixed messages he's getting from grown-ups. I imagine it'll be hard for him to trust anyone. I really hope they're able to find the parents or at least family for these boys. People who can love them and help them recover, although I'm sure for some of them too much damage may have been done already. Thomas is still young, though, so there's hope for him.

I wish I had more experience with children, but other than my nephews on occasion, I haven't had much exposure.

When the grilled cheese sandwiches are done, I slide one in front of Thomas and lightly ruffle his blond hair.

"Want something to drink, kiddo?"

"Milk, please," he says in that soft voice. His eyes

stare up at me slightly bewildered, and I wonder how much affection he's been shown in his life.

"You've got it."

"This is good," Lisa mumbles around a bite.

"Right?"

I end up making half a dozen more when a few of the guys come wandering in. Including Brick, who walks in carrying a sleepy Kiara on his arm. I notice a few looks Lisa is shooting in his direction when he sits down with Kiara slumped on his lap, coaxing her to eat something.

Brick, Tse, the two kids, and I are still sitting at the kitchen table—chatting with Lisa who is busy at the stove—when Yuma comes looking for me half an hour later. He walks straight to my chair and I have to lean my head back to look at him, which he takes as an opportunity to kiss me soundly. Kiara starts giggling as Tse makes loud gagging noises, and Brick complains we should get a room. When Yuma lets me up for air and smacks the back of Tse's head, I glance over at Thomas, who looks on with some curiosity. Again I wonder about what he has missed out on in his young life. He's clearly not familiar, or particularly comfortable, with displays of tenderness.

"Nosh wanted me to come get you. He needs your opinion on something." Yuma's statement is paired with a meaningful look I guess is in warning. So instead of asking any questions, I grab on to his offered hand and let him pull me up.

"Later, guys. See you, Thomas." I pull my hand from Yuma's and ruffle the boy's hair again.

"What was that all about?" Yuma asks when we walk outside.

"I don't think he's had much love in his life."

"Safe to say he hasn't had any. At least not while in the care—and I use that term loosely—of Hinckle and the ANL."

"Have either of the boys talked about how they ended up there?"

"Not much, as far as I know. Only revealing thing Thomas mentioned was that comment to Kiara that mothers end up in the ground."

The thought any of those boys were exposed to such cruelty turns my stomach.

"That's just wrong."

"Everything about it is wrong, baby."

YUMA

"I LIKE THAT one."

Lissie points at the octagonal slate tile and Wapi looks triumphant.

We all agreed on an engineered hardwood for the living areas and the bedrooms, both for durability and clean look, but we apparently had very different ideas about tiling for the bathrooms.

The slate had been Wapi's choice. I'd picked a woodgrain tile and Nosh chose a plain white square. It took Lissie all of one second to pick her favorite.

"Go pick them up," Nosh signs.

"Now?" I get a raised eyebrow in response. *"I'll pick*

them up tomorrow morning. Don't feel like going out again."

He harrumphs and dismisses me with an irritated wave of his hand.

"What's wrong?" Lissie asks quietly.

"My dad's way of stomping his foot. He wants me to go back to the store for the tile right away. I told him I'd go tomorrow. He doesn't like waiting."

She presses her lips together but can barely keep her smile contained. Even with Nosh glaring at us, she steps up to him so he can read her lips.

"First thing tomorrow morning," she promises him. "I can call the store now and have the tiles put aside. Okay?"

I get a glare, he sends over her shoulder, before the old bastard turns a much more benevolent look at Lissie and nods. She's got my old man wrapped around her little finger and she knows it. She prompts him to write down how much he needs and walks into the kitchen to make the call.

"Are we gonna get going ripping this carpet out?" Wapi wants to know.

"Have at it. Bedrooms first, I'll be right up."

As soon as Wapi heads upstairs I turn to Nosh.

"I love her."

"Tell me something I don't know," he shoots back at me. I stop him when he's about to sign something else. I'm pretty sure I know what it is.

"I'm well aware I don't deserve her, and I don't fucking care. I want to ask her to move in with me."

"In that small apartment?"

"No, of course not. My house."

Nosh rolls his eyes.

"About time you get that pigsty cleaned then, isn't it?"

Shit. Yes, it is. I've been meaning to do that.

"I will."

"And for the record: I was about to say I think you're perfect for each other."

It shouldn't matter, but it does. It matters a fuckofalot hearing my father say that.

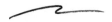

WE'RE JUST FINISHING up dinner at the clubhouse when I notice Lissie yawning for the third time in a row.

"You tired, baby?" I ask her softly.

"A little."

Earlier we ripped out all the upstairs carpet and just made a start on the flooring, when Ahiga came to tell us dinner was on. It took promises to finish up the master after dinner to get Nosh to break for a bite.

"I'll take you home. Let me talk to Nosh."

"You don't have to. Lisa will be heading home soon, I can just hitch a ride with her."

"I can drive you, gorgeous," Tse, who has been shamelessly listening in, pipes up.

"Do you have a death wish?" I ask him sharply, making Lissie snicker beside me.

I know he's looking for a reaction and I'm giving him

exactly what he wants, but I can't seem to help myself. If Lissie wasn't holding on to my hand under the table, I might've been tempted to plant my fist in his widely grinning face. It would've been very fucking satisfying.

"Can I ask you a favor?" she asks Lisa, who comes walking out of the kitchen.

"Sure."

"Are you heading home soon?"

"I'm getting the kids now," Lisa says, indicating the small group of kids crowded on the large sectional watching something on the tube.

"Do you think I could hitch a ride back with you? Tse is gonna help Yuma finish up a floor at Nosh's."

"Of course," she says over her shoulder, as she rounds up the kids.

"Hey," Tse complains. "Who said anything about me helping out?"

"I did," Lissie says. "Least you can do for egging Yuma on every chance you get."

I fucking love this woman and I'm letting her know by leaning in and taking her mouth in a hard kiss.

"Mr. Yuma, why do you kiss Lissie?" Kiara wants to know.

"She his girlfriend, stupid," her brother grumbles, ducking when Lisa threatens to cuff him in the back of the head.

"Call your sister stupid one more time, boy, and there'll be no gamin' for a month, you hear me?"

Poor Thomas, who walked up behind them, stands frozen at the sharp tone in the woman's voice. Lisa is a sweet woman but she is not one to mess with. I notice Lissie shooting a wink in the boy's direction. At first sight, it looks like he doesn't react, but then he lowers his head and I can just see the beginnings of what actually might be a smile. That would be a first.

Lissie is like a siren no one can resist. Not even my grumpy father or this distrustful young boy.

I walk her to the car, where Lisa is already herding the kids into the back seat.

"Are you sure, baby?"

"Positive. You go help your dad. Make sure he doesn't overdo it."

"I shouldn't be too late," I promise, kissing the side of her head.

"If it's easier for you to stay here, that's fine by me."

I turn her to face me and lean close. "Not by me. I'm not sleeping without you."

"Okay," she says with a smile, her hand stroking my jaw. "I should get going, they're waiting for me."

She goes up on her toes and presses her lips to mine, kissing me sweetly, before she pulls open the passenger side door.

As they back out of the parking spot, Lissie signs, *"I love you."*

LISSIE

"So MR. YUMA is your boyfriend? Are you going to get married? Do I get to wear a pretty dress?"

Kiara is asking a million and one questions from the back seat, not giving me a chance to answer any one of them.

"Sweetheart, take a breath and give Lissie a chance to talk," Lisa admonishes the girl gently.

"Women," Ezrah grumbles, making me chuckle.

He is so much like the big men he hangs out with at the club. It's cute since he's still so young, but I can already tell he's a handful.

I turn in my seat so I can see Kiara.

"Yes, Yuma is my boyfriend and if we ever get married you get to wear a pretty dress."

"Yay!" She does a little fist pump.

Her excitement wanes quickly, and by the time we get to the Riverside her eyes barely stay open. Lisa hands Ezrah the keys and sends him to open her door as she lifts Kiara from the back seat. The little girl clings to her, putting her head on her nana's shoulder.

"Night, Lisa, thanks for the ride," I tell her at the top of the stairs.

"No problem. Night."

I lean over and kiss the little girl's cheek. "Night, honey."

"Night, Lissie," she mumbles.

I watch them walk into their apartment before I turn to my door. I fish my keys from my purse and let myself inside, closing the door behind me before I reach for the light switch.

Nothing happens. The lightbulb must've burned out. I think I might have a spare in the hallway closet.

I walk into the living room and hit the switch there. Nothing.

29

YUMA

I CAN'T REMEMBER the last time I did something constructive with my father—if ever—but I'm thinking we should've done this years ago.

After decades of not seeing eye to eye on anything, this simple manual labor, working side by side with him toward a common goal, has been eye opening. He's still a grumpy old man, and I'm sure he still sees me as a pain-in-the-ass snotnose, but it's no longer all we see. For as long as I can remember, I colored every look or word my father directed at me through my expectation of him, although I didn't see it at the time. It became easy to interpret anything he said in the light I believed he saw me in.

Fucking expectations never left room for anything

else.

Not until now, with Momma gone and emotions still raw, it feels like we're seeing each other for the first time.

"Take a breather, Pop," I tell him, after seeing him struggle to get up from the floor to get another board. Fuck, my knees are killing me and he's got thirty years on me.

I don't even realize what slipped out without thinking until I see the emotion on his face.

Pop. I used to call him that a long time ago. Before I dropped it in favor of Nosh somewhere in my teens, because that's what all the other guys called him. Later it just became something to underline the division. Something to lash out at him with.

Fuck, it shames me to see what the simple three-letter word I've kept from him for so long means to him.

"We should call it a night. Go see your woman."

"I will as soon as I finish these last two rows. Why don't you start heading over to the clubhouse? I'll be right behind you."

He nods and I watch as he gingerly heads down the stairs.

Tse actually helped for a couple of hours before he'd taken off to parts unknown, and of course Wapi was here, but he's responsible for the boys' bunkhouse at night and had to go. We did manage to get all of the upstairs floors done, except for the bathroom and a few rows in the master.

It doesn't take me long to finish those before I clean up, shut off the lights, and head over to the clubhouse.

Trunk is on the porch, smoking a cigarette.

"I'm surprised you're still here." I motion for him to hand me his pack.

"Been a crazy fucking day," he grumbles.

"How so?"

"Had a breakthrough with those boys today. Started this morning when I caught Thomas calling Ezrah a nigger. Spent the morning holed up in my office with him." He shakes his head and takes a deep drag, before continuing. "Those kids have been fucked up. Boy's telling me some of the shit they were put through and I had a hard time not to ram my fist through a wall. These bastards methodically desensitized the kids from as young as three years old. That was Thomas' age when he ended up in the ANL's hands. Remember you told me what he'd said about mothers?" I nod and grunt an acknowledgment. "Apparently that's how the kids were kept in line. They were told their mother would end up in a hole in the ground if they misbehaved. Then they were told to dig a hole where they'd find human remains. One of those locations was at the fucking development right here in town."

"You're shitting me."

"Not even close. Hard to believe one person could be that fucking depraved, but a whole group of them? That's some sick shit. Talked to the older boy after school. After he realized what I'd already found out, he opened up too. Fuck, man. I don't know if I'll ever sleep again knowing there's that kind of evil in the world."

"Have you talked to anyone? Law enforcement?"

"Yeah. Went to the FBI office this afternoon. I would've talked to Luna, but she's not back from Telluride yet. I didn't wanna wait."

He lights another cigarette and I see his hand trembling.

"Brother, you need to get home. See your woman and your boy."

He stares off in the distance at the mention of Jaimie and River, a muscle ticking in his jaw.

"She's pregnant," he says in a monotone voice. I'm about to congratulate him, knowing they've been trying for a while. "Kept it quiet for a bit. Wasn't the right time with Momma dying and all." He runs his hand over his bald head. "Twelve weeks. Happiest fucking moment of my life when she told me." He takes another drag of his smoke. "Now? I can't help wonder what the fuck we're thinking bringing another kid into this fucked-up world."

I get what he's saying but he's missing a point.

"Are you kidding? It's exactly what the world needs; kids like yours, raised in a family where love is the color of everyone's skin. Parents to teach them basic human morals, without feeding them ideological bullshit."

"Shee-it, brother. Sobriety has turned you into a fucking philosopher." He chuckles, tossing his smoke in the can, and clapping me on the shoulder. "Or was it love?"

"Whatever," I mumble with a grin. "I'm gonna go in and say goodnight before heading home to my own woman." I start walking for the door when he calls my name.

"Yuma. Appreciate the sentiment, brother."

I lift my chin and go inside. I quickly check on my father, who's having a drink at the bar with Paco and Honon, and promise him I'll be back in the morning.

It's almost midnight when I pull into my parking spot. A quick glance at Lissie's dark apartment tells me she must have gone to bed. I take the stairs two at a time and pull my keys from my pocket, unlocking the door.

In the dark I kick off my boots and hang up my jacket, trying to be as quiet as I can, heading straight for the bedroom. That's where I first notice something wrong. Light from the parking lot filters into the room, something I know Lissie always closes the blinds against. My eyes drift to the bed, which looks just like we left it this morning. Empty.

My skin suddenly feels too tight as alarm bells go off, and I reach for the light switch. Nothing happens. I rush down the hall to the second bedroom and it is empty too. The light's not working there either. It isn't in the bathroom, or the kitchen, and when I reach for the bulb I notice it's been loosened. The moment I tighten it the light almost blinds me. I do the same in the living room, the hallway, and then I'm back in the bedroom, where I find the bulb loose as well. The entire apartment is lit up, but there's no sign of Lissie.

Then I notice her purse tossed on the loveseat, and that's when panic closes its cold fist around my heart.

"What's wrong?" Lisa, disheveled and sleepy peeks through the crack in her door after I almost banged it down.

"Where's Lissie?"

"What? She's home."

"She's not there. Where did she go?"

"I don't—"

Not waiting for her to finish, I pull out my phone and find Ramirez's number.

LISSIE

HAD IT ONLY been the cold steel pressed against the base of my skull, I would've taken my chances.

It is the promise of unspeakable things to be done to Lisa and her kids if I fight him, that has me comply with his demands. I figure if I can bide my time until we are far enough from the apartments, I might get an opportunity.

He pushes me out of the apartment and to the other side of the gallery, where a secondary set of stairs leads down to the garbage containers in the small parking lot at the rear of the complex. I make note of as much as I can, his unfamiliar voice, his size, his scent, but every time I try to sneak a peek at him, he presses the barrel harder into my skin.

An old, black Cadillac DeVille is parked beside one of the dumpsters and he pops the trunk as we approach. I know what's coming and I try to brace myself, but with one arm banding around my waist, he simply lifts me off my feet and tosses me in. I cry out when I land on my bad shoulder and immediately roll on my back, even as he's already closing the trunk. But not before I get my first look at his face.

In the darkness that follows I try to remember where I saw it before. I noted in my quick glimpse of him he's at least mid-forties, if not older. With small eyes set too close together and his nose clearly busted a few times, but the bottom half of his face was mostly obscured by facial hair. I know I've seen him before.

I can feel the vibrations from the engine when he starts it up. The moment the car starts moving, I use my right hand to feel around the trunk for a safety latch or anything I can use as a weapon. When I pull up the edge of the carpet lining, I encounter wiring and start pulling on it. Anything in my hands is better than nothing, and in a perfect world I may have taken out his taillights and he gets pulled over by the police.

I want to kick my feet against the inside of the trunk lid, but I'm afraid he'll hear. Instead I yank hard at the wire until it pops free.

After what feels like an eternity, I notice we've hit a more uneven road surface. Probably a gravel road, judging by the stones I hear pinging against the underbody of the car. When the car slows down, I pull my knees to my chest and brace my feet against the lid. The best defense is offense, and I'm planning to catch him off guard.

I listen for the door closing and then the crunch of dirt under his feet coming closer. I clench the length of wire I looped into a whip of sorts in my fist and wait for the latch on the trunk to pop.

The moment I hear it, I kick up as hard as I can, and note a satisfying thump and a loud "Fuck!"

I must've knocked him on his ass. Jumping at the opportunity, I scramble out of the trunk and plan to beeline it to the edge of the trees I see, but I've barely taken a step when my feet are pulled out from under me and I go down hard. My training has me ignore the sharp pain in my shoulder, and I instantly roll to my back so I can see him coming at me.

But before I can do anything he's looming over me, sitting down on my legs, his face distorted in anger. In a last ditch effort, I swing my right hand holding the wire like a whip and catch the bastard in his face. A sharp cut along his cheek opens up and he raises a hand in surprise. When his fingers come away bloody, the anger is back in full force.

"You fucking cunt!"

The last thing I see is his fist coming at my face.

Yuma

THE PARKING LOT is packed with patrol cars. Every fucking cop in Durango showed up within minutes of my call.

"Luna is on her way too, brother. She's already in touch with her team," Ouray assures me.

I called him as soon as I got off the phone with Ramirez, and he just called me back to let me know he's coming over with Nosh. I pace back and forth in the parking lot outside the office, afraid if I stop moving, the edge of darkness creeping up on me will swallow me whole.

"Okay."

"We're a few minutes out. Hang in there." Then he ends the call.

I'm terrified and feel paralyzed, as everyone around me seems to be moving with a purpose and all I can do is pace while envisioning Lissie broken and bleeding at the bottom of a hole in the ground. I don't know what to do, wouldn't even know where to start looking. I can't even.

I wish I had my old friend Jack at hand.

A squeal of tires draws my attention, as a black SUV pulls into the parking lot a little too fast. I watch as it's parked haphazardly behind a cruiser and Luna gets out of the driver's side. She clocks me and walks my way, clutching a box in her hands.

"I need your help," she says when she reaches me, and just like that thoughts of Jack dissipate and purpose takes their place. I walk ahead of her into the office, where she plunks the box on the desk. "I got that this afternoon from a cop who doesn't know his ass from a hole in the wall. A waitress at the restaurant in Telluride noticed it in the booth where Lissie had been sitting before the shooting, and handed it over to him. He had it in the back seat of his patrol car and forgot about it for two days. His ass is fucking toast."

"What do you need?" I prompt her, eager to do something.

"I just had a quick peek in there before I left, but I noticed a few pictures of Lissie's friend with a biker I don't recognize."

I open the box and grab a handful of pictures out.

Some are of Dani and Chains, her face no longer holding the happy smile it had in that snapshot from Vegas. Guess reality wasn't quite as grand as her dream had been. Then I get to a couple of images of her with someone else and before I even notice who it is, I spot the stark fear on the woman's face.

"That's Bones."

"Who?"

"Bones, Moab Reds. Nasty motherfucker. Almost as bad as his buddy, Chains." I hand the pictures to Luna, but she's reading a piece of paper she pulled from the box.

"What's that?"

"Birth certificate of one Jesse Gorman Brentwood, dated June 21, 2013." She looks up at me. "Brentwood was Chains' name: William David Brentwood."

"She had a kid with him?"

"That's what it looks like. Show me that Bones guy." I shove the images her way.

"I got into it with him not that long ago," I admit.

"With who?" Ouray walks into the office with my father right behind him.

"Hanging in, Son?"

I nod at him. I figure he can fill in the 'barely' on his own.

"Bones. Look at the pictures," Luna says, handing them over to her husband.

"Always thought it was strange he wasn't there during that face-off with Chains last year. Those two always got into shit together."

"What does any of this have to do with Lissie?" I snap impatiently.

"What if whoever killed those two in Telluride and shot Lissie did it because of something in this box?" Luna suggests. I immediately grab another handful of pictures and start flipping through them. Ouray does the same.

"What the fuck?" he says, and my eyes are drawn to the picture in his hand. It's a campground or a tent camp or something.

"What is it?"

"See that rim in the background?"

I lean in a little. "Is that Smelter Mountain?"

"Sure is," Ouray confirms. "This shot could've been taken from Wildcat Canyon."

Luna snags the picture from his hand. "The training camp?"

"Would appear so," Ouray says, putting the next picture down on the counter, tapping it with his finger. "And there's the reason someone is shitting their pants."

The picture shows a handful of young kids posing in front of the tents, with rifles slung over their much-too-small shoulders. Proudly standing behind them, like a pair of fucking misguided parents is Chains and Bones.

"Fuckin' knew it," Ouray grinds between his teeth.

Just then Luna's phone rings.

"Roosberg. You're kidding me? Yes. On my way."

"What's going on?"

She turns to me. "Tracker. Lissie has a tracker on her. Jasper has a bead on her."

3 0

LISSIE

I GASP WHEN liquid splashes my face.

"Open your eyes, bitch. I waited long enough. I need you awake for this."

I try to move but a hot pain shoots through my injured shoulder, and I realize my arms are tied behind me. We're outside somewhere; I can smell the damp earth and feel the cool night air on my skin. I open my eyes a crack. Trees, lots of them, and the large man holding a bottle of water and sporting a nice cut on his face from the wire I hit him with. Good.

What's not so good is the look on his face. I'd much rather have seen anger or rage than the excitement in his eyes.

I don't know how long I've been out, but in that time

he managed to get me away from the car, into the woods, and tie me up.

"Who are you?" I croak, hoping if I can keep him talking, I can distract him from whatever it is he's thinking of doing to me.

"You're just as nosy as that other bitch was."

"Who? Dani?" Saying her name, I suddenly remember where I've seen him before. That Vegas picture, he was in that group.

"Dani, Tammy, every fucking bitch I know. Always asking questions, sticking their noses where they don't belong. Told Chains she'd bring trouble, but he liked stickin' it to her. Kept her around longer than I woulda. Then the idiot got hisself killed, and left me to take care'a that bitch when she started diggin', lookin' for her kid." He scrapes his throat and hoarks up a gob of phlegm he lets fly just inches from where I'm sitting. "Then fucking Tammy answered the goddamn club phone, and I knew that was gonna end up being trouble too. Didn't take long either. Took care'a her and I shoulda put a second bullet in you too."

While he's been talking, I've been testing the zip tie around my wrists. It's snug, but not so tight I can't move at all. I steel myself against the pain in my shoulder and rotate my wrists to try and loosen the tie.

"Was gonna bide my time and finish the job quickly, but then I saw you with that bastard, Yuma." He laughs, working up another ball of spit. "Stroke'a luck, since him'n me have some unfinished business you're gonna help me settle first."

He doesn't have to spell it out; I know exactly how he plans to do that when he starts unbuckling his belt.

"What unfinished business? What did he do to you?" I hurry to say, trying to keep him talking while I work my binds. It feels like I have a little more room and I need my hands free if I have any hope of fighting him off.

"Sonofabitch as good as killed Chains. Came gunnin' for him last year, got hisself shot in the process, but his brothers were right behind, taking Chains out. We had plans, him'n me, big plans. Chains was gonna put the Moab Reds on the map…"

I barely hear what he's saying, but I notice his hands have stilled while he's talking. I use the reprieve to try and pull my right hand free. I grind my teeth against the pain of skin tearing and force on.

"…Figure it'll be good payback he finds his bitch was taken in every hole before she was killed right here on Arrow's Edge land."

Knowing what's about to happen is bone-chilling, hearing it spelled out in so many words sends me into sheer panic.

When his hands get busy again I push off with my legs and scramble backward, while yanking as hard as I can on the tie. It could be the blood making my hand slippery or my thumb pulling out of the socket, but with a scream I finally pull my hand free.

He clearly didn't expect that, and for a moment just stands there with his jeans halfway down his legs, staring at me with his mouth open.

The brief reprieve is all I need to get my wits about

me. Ignoring the pain, I push myself up on my feet, turn and force my legs to move. Behind me I hear him curse, but I don't stop moving, blundering through the underbrush as I try to create some distance between us.

When I hear a shot behind me as wood splinters from a tree trunk barely a foot away, I know I'm in deep trouble.

Yuma

"Can't have you running off half-assed."

Ramirez steps in front of me.

"You're out of your fucking mind if you think I'm waiting around here. You're wasting time, move the fuck out of the way."

"Don't know if that—"

"Outta my fucking way!" I bellow, shoving Ramirez aside.

"Hustle," Ouray says, already waiting with Nosh by his truck.

Luna just tore out of here after sharing Greene had traced the signal to Arrow's Edge land, just north of the shooting range, when Ramirez tried to hold me back. She's at best a couple of minutes ahead of us.

On the drive up the mountain, Ouray has the clubhouse on speakerphone. He sends Honon and Tse to grab weapons from the office, head for the gun range, and then orders Wapi to arm himself and hole up inside the boys' dorm until further notice.

Nosh taps me on the shoulder.

"Tell Ouray to drive up to the campground and take

the dirt road from there to the back of the property. No way anyone would get past the guys in the clubhouse."

"Nosh says take the back way from the campground."

"Yeah, thought about that." He looks at me. "You armed?"

"Nope."

"Check the glovebox."

I pull out the handgun and make sure it's loaded. I focus on the weight of it in my hand. Despite the fact it's been quite a few years, it feels comfortable against my palm.

Ouray's phone rings.

"Hey, Sprite."

"Ramirez called. No guns, Ouray, we need him alive."

"Babe," he mumbles, but his meaning is clear.

"Jesus. At least tell me Yuma isn't armed."

"Sorry, Luna," I answer for him.

"Fucking hell. You lose your cool and shoot, Yuma, I swear—"

"He won't," Ouray snaps. "Unless absolutely necessary. I trust him."

I file that vote of confidence somewhere deep so when I'm not sick with fear over Lissie, I can take it out and let that trust settle deep into my bones.

"Good enough. No offense, Yuma."

"None taken."

"Gotta go, I'm pulling into the compound and Gomez is already here."

"Be careful," Ouray tells his wife, but she already hung up.

We're just coming up on the turnoff to the clubhouse but keep going straight instead. A few miles up the road, we hit the entrance to the campground, which—aside from a couple of RVs—is pretty much abandoned this late in the season. Ouray drives to the southeast corner where an old logging trail runs all the way into our northern property line.

Nosh taps me on the shoulder again.

"Stop before the next bend. There's a clearing beyond, too exposed."

I relay the info to Ouray, who pulls the truck to the side where Nosh indicates.

"Rifle in the lockbox," he signs to my father.

Even at his age, Nosh is the best marksman the club has. He fetches it from the back and closes the gate carefully, while we do the same with the doors. Until we know the situation we're getting into, we'll move quietly.

Ouray leads and stops us when the trees open up. A black sedan is parked near the far edge of the clearing, and we wait to make sure there's no movement.

"Stick to the tree line," Ouray orders.

We're about halfway to the vehicle when a shot rings out.

Ouray immediately stops us with his hand up, but my entire being wants to run as fast as I can in the direction it came from. Uphill from us.

"Wait," he warns me, grabbing on to hold me in place.

I'm about to shake him off when we hear a second shot, followed by a loud yelp. That's when I take off running, hearing Ouray's footsteps close behind me. The blood is roaring in my ears, drowning out the noise I'm sure I'm making as I barrel through the trees.

How much noise becomes clear moments later, when I come upon a scene that has my heart lodge in my throat.

Lissie is on her knees, facing me, behind her Bones is holding her up by her hair with one hand while the other presses a gun to her head. Her face looks like it's been through a meat grinder but her eyes are alive and sharp.

"Looky here. Even better," that piece of filth spouts with a grin. "Now you can watch your bitch die."

"You're the one gonna be dead before you have a chance pull the trigger."

"Nobody's gonna die today," Gomez's voice sounds behind us, as he and Luna catch up.

Lissie's eyes are holding mine. I know she's trying to tell me something when she looks down and up again, bulging her eyes, before glancing down again. That's when I notice her hand forming letters.

"D...I...V...E...R...S...I..."

She doesn't need to finish; I know what she's telling me. I give her the faintest of nods, and watch as her fingers count backward from three.

"Hey!" I yell, diving to my left. Bones is briefly startled and in that moment, Lissie throws herself forward and out of his reach.

Then I hear a shot ring.

LISSIE

I SPOT NOSH while the guy is taunting Yuma and

momentarily distracted by the arrival of the FBI.

He is maybe fifty yards behind his son, mostly hidden by a tree as he catches my eye and gestures down to the ground.

With the barrel against the side of my head, I'm afraid to make any moves. I focus my attention on Yuma and silently urge him to look at my hand, while I spell out what I need with the ASL alphabet I've only recently learned.

The moment he yells and makes a sudden move, I can feel the cold steel move from my head and I immediately throw myself down.

I can feel the reverberation of the shot in my bones and am afraid to move. Even when voices start yelling out and I feel bodies move past me, I stay with my face pressed in the dirt. Then I'm carefully rolled on my back and Yuma leans in my face.

"Lissie, baby, say something, are you okay?" His hands roam over my body while I try to catch the breath I'd been holding. When he inadvertently touches my shoulder I cry out. "Fuck," he hisses. "I don't know where I can touch you."

"I'm okay," I manage.

"You're bleeding."

"Help me up." With his arm around me on my good side, he helps me into a sitting position. "All the way up," I insist, and with infinite care he helps me get my feet under me. I look over my shoulder, but all I can see are the backs of the FBI agents blocking my view of the man. "Is he dead?"

"No. Missing a hand, though."

"Didn't know your father was such a good shot."

"Steadiest hand in the county," Yuma says with some measure of pride. "Fuck, Beautiful, I've never been so scared in my life." He presses his lips against my forehead before he asks, "Can you walk?"

"Yes."

"Then let's get down to the clubhouse and call you an ambulance." I start to protest, but he beats me to it. "No arguments, baby. I'm never leaving your side again."

With his arm to stabilize me, we start walking away from the scene. I don't turn around once.

Yuma ignores the calls for us to wait and keeps us moving. When we pass Nosh, he leans in to kiss my cheek.

"Smart cookie," he rumbles appreciatively when he falls into step beside me.

"Thank you," I mouth at him, which earns me a wink.

31

YUMA

"TAKE A BREATH, brother."

I tear my eyes from Lissie, where they've been glued as she's being looked over by Sumo and Blue, two of the fire department's EMTs. The stubborn woman refused to be taken to the hospital, insisting whatever injuries she sustained are superficial; only scrapes and bruises.

Tse is leaning on the opposite side of the bar.

"Your girl's all right. Tough as shit. A little banged up, but that'll heal."

"You a fucking doctor now? She admitted she got knocked out, man." I still think she needs to be looked at properly.

"And she's being looked at. She's stubborn but not stupid. I'm sure if those guys have serious concerns, she'll go."

We lucked out with the full moon tonight; otherwise, this whole thing could've gone down an entirely different way. I can't stop thinking about what might've happened. That was a risky move by my father, shooting at that distance by not much more than the light of Luna's flashlight shining on his target.

My eyes find him sitting at the far end of the bar with Ouray and Ramirez, sipping a beer. He's staring hard at the EMTs fussing over Lissie, when he suddenly turns my way.

"Should've killed the bastard," he signs.

He's talking about Bones who's on his way to Mercy in the second ambulance, his right hand unrecognizable, with Gomez and Luna following right behind.

"Thanks, Pop," I mumble. The old man reads my lips and nods. I turn my attention back to Lissie, muttering under my breath, "Fucking need a drink."

"I'll get you a coffee," Tse, who hears, quickly offers.

Not long after Blue and her partner start packing away their supplies, I approach them.

"Everything all right?"

"Bullet didn't do more than graze her this time, but she's still coming to the hospital," Blue, who also happens to be Tony Ramirez's woman, says firmly.

"What's wrong?"

Blue raises an eyebrow at Lissie, who is glaring at her. "I'll let her tell you."

"Babe?"

Her face is scraped and swollen, already starting to bruise when she finally turns to me.

"They say my thumb has to be set at the hospital."

"Your thumb?"

She holds up her right hand, the thumb standing out at an odd angle. I hadn't noticed it; I'd been too focused on the blood dripping down her hands from her torn wrists. I ignore the mutinous look on her face and lean down, kissing her angry mouth.

"Let's go and get this over with."

I help her out of her chair, and with a quick explanation to the guys, guide her outside, and climb into the back of the ambulance with her.

"Call when you guys are ready," Ouray says, having followed us out of the clubhouse.

"Thanks, brother. Tell Nosh to get some rest."

He gives me a two-fingered salute and raps his knuckles on the back of the ambulance before closing the door.

"Yuma?" The fear Lissie had been hiding behind her bravado is suddenly starkly visible in her eyes.

"Yeah?" I reach out and gently stroke a strand of hair from her forehead.

"I don't want any drugs. Please? They were pushing last time."

Blue looks up and jumps in. "Won't be much fun without, Lissie. It's painful."

"She's an alcoholic," I explain and add, "We both are."

"Gotcha. I'll make sure they know."

IN THE END, we only spend a couple of hours in the hospital.

Lissie's right hand is in a splint she'll have to keep on for six to eight weeks. That news didn't make her happy. She'd busted a couple of stitches in the wound on her shoulder, but didn't need any new ones placed. Still, she'll be limited in what she can do, which means I'll be sticking around to do them for her. Not exactly a hardship.

"Where to?" Ouray asks, once we settle into his Traverse.

"Clubhouse okay with you?" I ask Lissie, leaning between the front seats. I notice she has her head turned to the window, but I catch the strain on her face in the side mirror. "Lissie?"

"Sure," she mumbles distractedly.

I have a feeling the adrenaline, which kept her going, is fading now and so is her resilience.

"Clubhouse it is," Ouray says. "Take the room behind the office. Lisa cleaned the sheets earlier this week."

Nosh and Tse must've gone to bed, because Brick is the only one still up when we get there.

"Almost five in the morning, brother," Ouray points out to him. "What the fuck are you doing up?"

"Just got back from checkin' in on Lisa and the kids. How are you doin', doll?" he asks Lissie, turning to her.

"Tired."

"That's my cue," I announce, and with my arm around her waist, lead her to the back.

"Wow," she says when I open the door to Ouray's old bedroom, now usually reserved for guests. I'm not about to share there've been times I've used this room, because none of that matters anymore.

Nicest room in the clubhouse, it's the only one with a decor above the frat house look of the rest of the place, plus it has its own en suite bathroom.

"It's nice."

I can feel her body start shivering under my hand. Wonder if shock is setting in.

"Sit down on the bed for a minute. Gonna draw you a bath, baby."

She doesn't even bother responding.

I rush into the bathroom and turn on the faucet. I grab bath oil I'm sure belongs to Luna and add some to the bathwater, before returning to where she's still sitting on the edge of the mattress.

"Come on, Beautiful, let's get you cleaned up."

"There's things I need to tell Tony."

"That'll wait."

"But—"

"Babe, it's five o'clock in the morning. Whatever you have to tell them can wait until you've had some sleep."

She doesn't say anymore and placidly lets me strip her out of her dirty clothes. I grind my teeth when I see more bumps and bruises, which were hidden under her clothes. Last thing she needs right now is my temper. I help her into the tub and grab some towels for her to rest her arms on so they don't get wet.

It's not until I sit on the floor beside the tub and gently wipe the remaining blood off her skin with a wet washcloth, tears start rolling from her closed eyes. At the first sob, I get to my feet, strip out of my clothes in record time, and sit down in the tub behind her, pulling her into my body.

I let her cry until she only occasionally shivers in my arms.

"Up, baby. We're gettin' out."

I dry her off and shuffle her to the bed, tucking her in. Then I dry myself and slip between the covers beside her, roll on my side and rest my hand on her belly.

"Sleep, Beautiful."

"James?"

"Mmm."

"How did you guys know where I was?"

I prop myself up on an elbow.

"You had a tracker on you."

She looks at me quizzically and then understanding floods her face.

"The heel of my boot. I forgot."

I lean over her to press a kiss on her lips.

"Good thing you did. That and Jasper Greene's presence of mind saved you."

"And your father," she says on a little smile.

"And Pop," I agree. "Can you sleep now?"

"Mmm."

I lie back down with my head on the pillow beside her, her hair tickling my nose, but I'll be damned if I'm moving.

"James?"

"Haven't moved, Lissie."

"Thank you for finding me."

"Would've moved heaven and earth. Love you that

much."

She turns her face my way so we're practically nose-to-nose.

"I know. Thank you for that too."

"You make it easy, baby."

Two minutes later she's asleep.

I'm still wide-awake when the sun comes up.

LISSIE

"I HEAR YOU did good, Bucco."

I look across the table at Joe Benedetti.

He showed up with Blackfoot, and Luna arrived shortly after. She suggested Ouray's office, smiling when Yuma refused to leave my side. He's been beside me the past hour while I was giving my statement.

"Not sure about that, sir…I mean, Joe. The lights not working should've alerted me."

"Think you're being a little too hard on yourself, Lissie."

I shrug and Yuma squeezes my leg under the table. Eager to change the subject, I ask, "Where are we at now? What's next?"

"Nowak showed up at the FBI office with his lawyer in tow. Ramirez and Gomez are talking to him now," Luna decides to share. "Luis Bonifacio, aka Bones, is out of surgery and we've got a guy on him. As soon as he can answer questions, we're heading over there."

"Bones is gonna go down for sure, Lissie," Blackfoot takes over. "I bet they'll be able to match up his prints with those from the truck abandoned a few miles away from the Telluride shooting. We've got ballistics running checks to match the shells from that scene with the ones from the gun retrieved from Bones last night."

"He killed Dani."

"I know. I'm sorry for your loss," Keith says warmly. "He'll pay for her, for Tammy, and for Officer Porter."

Joe gets up from his seat, announcing, "I think we've got all we need. You should get some rest. We'll keep you up-to-date."

I watch as the three of them walk out of the office before turning to Yuma.

"What now?"

The question is much more involved than the two words imply. I feel lost, tired to the bone, and more than just a little vulnerable. What am I supposed to be doing for the next couple of months? Where am I supposed to go? I woke up this morning in a strange bed, stripped bare to the skin, and other than my soiled clothing from the night before, not even clean underwear or a toothbrush to my name.

Yuma was able to find me a shirt and some old track pants to wear, but had to help me get dressed. He even ended up brushing my teeth, because I wasn't able to. Being so completely dependent on another person is far outside my comfort zone. It makes me realize how segregated I've kept myself most of my adult life.

My job has always been my purpose. I'm not sure how to look at myself without it to identify with. It's like the ground under my feet is shifting and I don't know where to step next.

"Now, I'm tucking you back in bed," Yuma says, looking at me intently. "Then I'm going to make you something to eat and feed you. After that you sleep." He takes my face in his hands and brushes his thumbs under my eyes. "Don't like these dark circles, baby, so your job is to rest. My job is to look after you."

"James…"

I'm undone by his gentleness. I thought hearing him say he loves me was momentous, but having him show me is beyond anything I've ever experienced.

A soft knock on the door precedes Lisa's head poking into the office.

"Sweet Lord," she mumbles when her eyes scan my face.

I haven't looked in the mirror yet—on purpose—but I imagine I'm not looking my best after last night. Judging by the tenderness and the skin pulling tight, there's some swelling going on.

"Lissie!"

Before Lisa can stop her, Kiara squeezes through the door opening her nana is trying to block. The poor girl stops halfway into the office and looks at me with big eyes that quickly fill with tears.

"It's okay, honey," I quickly assure her, as her bottom lip starts quivering. I hate scaring her. "I had a bad fall, but it looks worse than it is. Come here, sweetheart."

She stays rooted to the spot when Lisa steps up behind her, my duffel bag in her hands. Yuma walks over and picks the little girl up before coming to sit beside me, with Kiara on his lap.

"She's going to be fine, honey," he coos, melting me even more than he already has. He'll make a great father to a lucky kid one day.

My next thought is I might like to be the woman giving him one. It's a bit of a shock to the system, since I've never seriously considered kids. Not that I wouldn't want them—I love kids—the concept was just always slightly abstract, something you might add to a bucket list.

I plaster a smile on my face, looking at the little girl who almost looks scared of me, as she seems to burrow into Yuma's chest.

"It only hurts a little bit," I tell her, but she doesn't look convinced.

"I hope you don't mind, I went through your dresser," Lisa announces holding up the bag. "Wapi showed up with the keys to your place this morning and said Yuma asked to pack some things you would need. Packed what I thought you might want, and focused on comfortable clothes, I hope that's okay?"

"Perfect," I manage, touched. "Thank you."

"No problem. Let me just put this stuff away for you."

She disappears into the bedroom where I hear drawers slide open and closed.

"What happened to your hand?" Kiara's voice is hesitant as her eyes are now glued to the splint on my hand.

"I hurt it when it got stuck. The doctor says I have to wear this silly thing for a while, until it gets better."

"Oh."

"Wanna help me tuck Lissie in?" Yuma asks the girl when Lisa comes out of the bedroom. "She needs a nap."

"Okay."

"And after maybe you can help me make her something to eat?"

"Peanut butter and jelly? Nana says I'm really good at that."

"That sounds delicious," I tell her with a smile.

A few minutes later I'm in bed, the covers tucked up under my chin, which is what you're supposed to do according to the five-year-old.

"Come on, child," Lisa says from the doorway. "Let's get started on those sandwiches."

I watch as she skips out behind her grandmother, much happier than she was minutes ago. Kids are so resilient, and I have a feeling Lisa's kids even more than most.

Yuma sits on the edge of the mattress, bracing his arms on either side of me.

"What happens is we focus on the here and now, but keep moving forward. You and me, Beautiful."

He kisses the tip of my nose before my eyes follow him out of the room.

Suddenly that ground I'm standing on seems solid enough.

32

YUMA

"PLEASE, JAMES..."

I lift my head and look into those eyes I could lose myself in. I lightly kiss the sensitive skin on the inside of her thigh. She hisses at the touch.

She's primed, wet and flushed, and I'd like nothing more than to slide inside the heat of her welcoming body, but then I notice the bruising on her skin.

"Baby, you're hurt," I mumble, much like I've been doing since she was shot the first time.

The hunger I feel, I don't trust myself to be gentle, so I've made sure she got off on my mouth or my fingers—or both—and have resorted myself to living with blue balls. I'd done it for months before she came into my life.

It's only been a couple of days since she was hurt again, because of some piece of shit who was trying to get back at me.

I watch her head come up off the bed, a scowl on her face.

"*You're* hurting me," she snaps. "By withholding what I really need—*you*. Besides, there's nothing wrong with my legs or my vagina."

I press my lips together not to snicker, but somehow I get the sense that might not go over well when she's lying spread out on the bed, in all her beautiful glory.

"Are you laughing?"

"Wouldn't think of it," I lie, straightening my face as I crawl up her body, dropping kisses on her skin.

"You're laughing."

"Baby, right now I'm worshiping your incredibly sexy body."

"Don't tease me if you don't mean it," she says, her breath hitching when I find her nipple and pull it between my lips. "James, please…"

"This what you want?"

I hook a hand behind her knee and pull it up, making room for myself in the cradle of her thighs. Lowering my hips, I rub my hard cock against her wet core. She presses her head back in the pillow and whimpers, tilting her hips in invitation.

"Look at me, baby."

Her heavy-lidded eyes blink open and focus on mine.

"Yesssss," she hisses when I guide myself inside her body. Holding her eyes, I make love to her gently, but she quickly loses patience. "Honey, I'm not made of glass."

"You sure?" I ask, grinding myself deep.

"Fuck me, James."

Christ. I could feel that in my dick. She still manages to surprise me and it has its desired effect; I lose all control. It's fast, it's furious, and when she comes, I fly right over the edge with her.

"I should get up," I mumble sated, as my dick slips soft from her body a little later. I still have my face buried in Lissie's hair and my heart is only now slowly returning to a normal rhythm.

"Not yet."

The alarm clock on the nightstand shows nine forty-five.

"Babe, I promised my father I'd help him finish up the tile in the bathroom today."

"Is it almost done?"

She doesn't object when I roll off her this time. Lissie's been eager for Nosh to surprise Lisa and the kids with the house, but he won't unless it's move-in ready. The bathroom tile is the last thing on the list.

He already moved into a room down the hallway here in the clubhouse, an arrangement Lisa thinks is temporary because of the renovations at the house. The intent is for him to live here, in the clubhouse, the way it was before he met Momma.

"Should be done today," I promise.

I look down at her, long brown hair fanned out on the pillow, her face still flushed from her orgasm, and her dark eyes shining. Even with her body still bruised and battered, so fucking beautiful it takes my breath away. My chest feels too small to contain all I feel.

"What?" she asks, and I realize I've been staring.

"Never considered myself a lucky man, probably 'cause most of the time I was busy feelin' sorry for myself. Be damned if I don't feel like the luckiest fucker on the face of the earth now."

"Come here," she whispers, her liquid eyes drawing me in and I bend down. "I love you, James Wells."

It takes another forty minutes before I finally walk into the kitchen, hunting for coffee.

"Fucking finally," Ouray says, sitting at the kitchen table. "Wasn't sure your ass was ever gonna surface, couldn't fucking hear myself think in there. Got shit to do, brother."

I grin as I pour myself a coffee. We may have been a little noisy, but I'm not about to apologize for it. It does make it clear we'll have to come up with a better solution than holing up here in the clubhouse indefinitely.

"Lissie should be out shortly. You'll have your office all to yourself."

He grunts before saying, "Tse went over to the house with Nosh, and I sent Wapi to check in at Riverside."

I resist the knee-jerk reaction to interpret what he says as criticism, and take a sip of coffee before I respond.

"I'll head over there as soon as Lissie gets up. The house should be done after today—unless the old man decides he wants all new windows or some shit—and I'll get back to the regular routine."

"You plan to move back there? The Riverside?"

I shake my head. I've been thinking about the next step, I just haven't had a chance to do anything about it yet. "Things have changed."

"That's obvious."

"Yeah, well, I know what I'd like, but it's not just up to me anymore."

Ouray chuckles at that. "Good you picked up on that, brother."

"Morning."

"Lissie," he rumbles, as she walks right up to me and lifts her face for a kiss. As I bend down to comply, Ouray puts his cup in the sink and heads for the door. "Later."

"Want breakfast?" I ask, tucking a strand of hair behind her ear.

"I'm good. Go help your dad before he disowns you."

"I'll get her breakfast," Lisa, who just walks in, offers.

"Lissie!" Kiara's little voice is not far behind.

One of the many reasons why it's time to find a more permanent solution is the fact we're never alone, unless we hide out in the bedroom. Don't get me wrong, I love my club family—I just don't love them so much I want to spend every minute of every day around them. There's only one person who fits that bill and she's currently grinning at me. I don't doubt she knows exactly what I'm thinking. She already reads me like a book.

I leave her in Lisa's good care and head up to my father's house.

"About time."

"Lazy day?"

I expected the jabs, and am not about to let them get

to me and ruin what was a great fucking start to my day. So instead I flip them the bird with a big smile on my face.

"You've got an adoring, beautiful woman in your bed, worshiping your cock, time disappears, brother. Don't knock it 'til you try it."

Tse grunts and scowls before he turns back to troweling compound on floor, but when I look over at my father, he's grinning at me.

LISSIE

HANGING OUT WITH Lisa and Kiara in the kitchen for most of the day was better than lying in bed watching the TV Yuma had hauled in there a couple of days ago, but I was still glad when Ramirez and Luna show up fifteen minutes after the boys got home from school.

"Ouray around?" Luna asks.

"He's in his office."

"Trunk?"

"In his," I answer.

"Yuma?"

"At his dad's place."

"Can you get hold of him? Tell him to meet us in Ouray's office."

I look from Luna to Tony and back. "What's going on?"

"Call him, Lissie," Tony suggests. His eyes are kind, but I still have an unsettled feeling.

A few minutes later, we're sitting around the large

table in Ouray's office when Yuma walks in.

"What's this all about?" he asks, before taking the vacant seat beside me.

"The boys; Michael and Thomas," Luna starts, her eyes on me. "DNA results came back this morning. It opened up yet another layer to our investigation. Looks like Thomas and Michael are related after all."

"No shit?" Trunk sits forward in his chair.

"Half-siblings. Same dad, different mom."

"Michael matches the third, unidentified body we found in the grave, but he and Thomas also have DNA in common. Their father's." She turns back to me. "Looks like Thomas is Jesse, Lissy; Dani's son."

That boy, that confused, innocent-looking boy is her child. Suddenly my throat is closing and I have to swallow hard.

"It's clear Chains and Bones were both affiliated with the American National League, but we're just finding out the extent of that involvement," Tony adds.

"Those sick fucks!"

This from Trunk. I'm not surprised. I've heard by now how the ANL snatched his young stepson, hoping to add him to the children's army they were brainwashing and training for God knows what.

"They weren't just selecting a pure race," I mumble. "They were breeding one."

"Might still be doing the same thing somewhere else," Ouray points out.

"At least not Chains, and we're expediting a DNA profile for Bones. We've got three of the five boys matched, and Zach only to his mother. It's still a mystery where the other two boys came from," Luna explains.

"What about Thomas and Michael? What do we tell them?" Yuma wants to know.

I glance over at Trunk, who has probably spent the most time with those kids out of anyone.

"What do you want to tell Michael? We still don't know who his mother was, just that she's dead, and I wouldn't volunteer the identity of the father. That last would be the same for Thomas, but we can tell them who his mother is…was." His eyes are on me. "Did your friend have any remaining family?"

I shake my head. Dani's mother, like mine, had passed away a long time ago. It's one of the things that connected us. She never knew her father and if there was extended family somewhere, in all the years we'd been tight, Dani never bothered mentioning them.

"Just me," I state firmly. "He has me."

Beside me, Yuma suddenly shoots up out of his chair and stalks out of the room, all eyes following him. After a few awkward moments, Trunk is the first to speak.

"Then he's a lucky kid, and I think we should tell him together. You can give him back a little of what was taken from him."

All I manage to do is nod. There are so many thoughts crowding my brain right now. Including what the hell had Yuma tear out of here like that, but I shove that to the background. It'll hold, but what can't wait is letting a small boy know he's not alone in this world.

Half an hour later, we're sitting in Trunk's office, the

boy looking uncertainly between us. Trunk nods at me to take the lead. I'm nervous. I've been thinking about how to tell an almost eight-year-old his mother is dead, but I realize he's probably been told that for years already, before it was a fact.

"I had a best friend," I start. "Her name was Danielle, but I called her Dani, and she was the best friend I could've asked for. She was kind, and she was loving, and she was always looking for adventure. She left our hometown years ago, and I always thought it was because she'd found something better." I pause and smile at the boy who now looks confused. Time to get to the point. "And she had found something much better, I just didn't know it. She had a baby—a little boy. She'd become a mother."

Something flickers in those clear blue eyes staring back at me.

"Mothers go in the ground. I seen her bones."

Sweet Jesus. If I had any of those sick fucks in front of me now, I swear I'd rip them apart with my bare hands. Or die trying.

I don't bother explaining the bones he likely saw were not his mother's because at that time she would've still been alive. That's something for when he's older. Much, much older.

"Not all mothers, Thomas," Trunk explains. "Jaimie's a mother, and so is Lisa, and Luna, and Kaga's wife, and you've met my sister, Tahlula, who is also a mother."

"My best friend was your mother, Thomas." I wait for a beat until I see the truth settle in. "I'm so sad she's dead, and I'm sorry you didn't have a chance to know what a great person she was. She was family to me, so you're my family too, and I hope you'll let me tell you about her."

"What was her name again?" he asks, his voice a little hoarse.

"Danielle, or Dani for short."

He nods. "Dani," he repeats on a whisper, his bottom lip quivering.

I have to bite my own lip to keep my emotions in check. He looks so small and forlorn, and all I want to do is wrap him up, but I'm pretty sure he's nowhere near ready for that.

I watch him as he visibly pulls himself together and blinks his eyes a few times before turning to Trunk.

"Can I go play now?"

"Sure, kid," Trunk says easily. "You wanna talk some more, you come find me or Lissie, okay?"

Thomas throws me a quick glance before he walks out of the office.

I let go of a deep, tremulous sigh.

"Give him some time. It's a lot to process for the kid."

I nod. "I know. To be honest, I don't exactly know what I'm doing, but I meant what I said to him. I'm his family, and I will look after him like family is supposed to."

"Like I said before, Thomas is a lucky kid."

I smile and get to my feet. "Thanks, Trunk. Appreciate the vote of confidence. Now if you'll excuse me, I have a man to chase down so I can give him a piece of my mind."

Trunk's deep chuckle follows me out of his office.

Yuma is nowhere in the clubhouse, and when I walk over to Nosh's house, he's not there either. His father is, though, and with my minimal signing skills, and clear enunciation, I manage to fill him in on what happened. To my surprise, he chuckles like he finds all of this highly amusing. I don't think it's funny at all.

It still isn't when he coaxes me into his old, rusty truck and drives out of the compound. I don't want to insult him and question his ability to drive, so I sit quietly, noting he turns the truck left, going up the mountain, instead of right to get back to town.

We pass a lake on the right side, when he slows down and turns into a driveway on the other side of the road. I've never been on this road before, other than to get to the clubhouse, so I had no idea there were even houses up here.

At the top of the driveway I spot Yuma's truck, parked in front of an impressive log home. Massive logs make up the walls and a high-peaked roof sits over large windows, looking out on the beautiful view below. A porch covers the entire width of the home.

Nosh taps me on the shoulder, indicating for me to get out. The moment I do, he backs up the truck and takes off.

I make my way to the steps leading up to a door at the side of the house and try knocking. I try again, and when nothing happens, I push open the door.

An overwhelming smell of old booze, rotting food,

and dirty laundry almost has me turn and flee; but then I hear sounds coming from the back.

"Gonna puke. Goddamn fucking stench."

I walk into a kitchen to find Yuma in front of an open refrigerator that smells like something crawled in and died there. He seems to be tossing the contents into a large garbage bag and doesn't notice he has company.

For a moment there, I was afraid something had triggered him and he'd gone off to drink, and I'm almost relieved to find him cleaning instead. Confusing, yes, but a relief nonetheless.

"Yuma?"

His head whips around and if I weren't so pissed, I would probably have laughed at the bandana covering his nose and mouth.

"What are you doing here?" His voice sounds muffled.

"Oh, I don't know," I say with a hefty dose of sarcasm. "I just got some pretty earth-shattering news, which somehow had you running from the clubhouse without a word. I guess I'm looking for a pretty fucking good explanation."

"You can't be here," he announces, walking up and taking me by the arm to the sliding doors at the front of the house, hauling me outside on the porch.

"What the hell, Yuma? What is going on?"

"Babe, the place is a fucking pigsty. I haven't been here in months and neither has anyone else."

"So why are you here now? What was so important that you decided in the middle of something monumental, it might be a good time to do some housecleaning?"

"Beautiful," he says, cupping my face in his hands, his eyes smiling. "Can't offer you a home that reeks like a frat house on steroids now, can I?"

"Offer me…what? What are we talking about?"

"Gotta get the house cleaned up before we move here. It's got three bedrooms. Enough for Thomas, with a room left over."

I shake my head, trying to catch up with him, but his lips are already on mine, scrambling my brain again.

"Next time just tell me where you're off to," I voice dryly when he lets me up for air.

"I can do that."

33

YUMA

"WE HAD TO let Nowak go."

I catch the snippet of conversation between Luna and Lissie when Tse and I walk into the clubhouse.

We finished Nosh's house a few days ago but have since been busy at my house, cleaning and moving Lissie's stuff in there. She doesn't have a lot of furniture, but the new bed I got her took the place of the one I had in the master, and I fit her loveseat in the living room. It's as ready for her as I can get it, without her to make the house her own.

Pop still hasn't told Lisa about the house yet, but I'm guessing he's been waiting for things to settle down for everyone.

Lots of stuff going on that has everyone stretched in

different directions. Lissie is still recovering and has been spending as much time as possible with Thomas these past couple of days, either with or without Trunk. Ouray and Paco have been off on a run to pick up a runaway in Grand Junction and been stuck there; dealing with Child Protective Services, and this is the first time I've seen Luna in days.

"What the hell? Why?" I interrupt, and both women turn at my voice.

"Because all they have is circumstantial or hearsay," Lissie explains, much calmer than I'd be in her shoes. I lean down and brush her lips.

"We're not letting him walk," Luna explains. "Believe me, the FBI is going to be so far up his ass, he won't be able to scratch it without us knowing. But the reality is: we have no hard evidence to hold him on. All it means is we have to dig harder, because we all know the man is covered in shit, we just need to make it stick."

"What about Bones? Is he walking too?"

Luna laughs at that. "Hell no. He's not going anywhere. Nor is John Woodard. You'll be happy to know, we're even looking into Mayor Woodard for his possible involvement. Regardless of the outcome, his days in office are likely numbered. Already I've heard rumors some council members are calling for him to cut his term short and resign. Whoever his supporters have been through the years, I don't think they'll be backing him for another term, no matter what."

"About time that ass was booted out of office," Tse contributes.

"No argument there," Luna agrees.

"And that's enough energy spent on those assholes," Lissie announces, turning her face up to me. "How are things coming along at the house?"

I grin down at her. Ever since she walked in on me cleaning out the rotting food from my fridge, and I brought her right back to the clubhouse, I've managed to keep her away, but not without her asking about the progress at least twice a day. Pretty sure living in the clubhouse has lost its appeal, if it ever had any.

"Tomorrow I'll show you."

The smile she beams up to me is more than payment enough for my bleach-pruned fingers.

If I wasn't already invested in my sobriety, scrubbing off the visible remnants of my alcohol addiction from my house has only solidified my commitment. I owe Tse big time. He quietly followed me into the mess I left of my life before, and helped me eradicate any evidence remaining. We didn't talk a whole lot, but having him there without judgment went a long way to being able to move forward, leaving the past behind. A true friend.

Tomorrow we'll have our clean start.

"Can't wait," she whispers.

Me neither.

"Lissie!" Kiara calls out from the large sectional in front of the TV. She's taken a real shine to Lissie. "The movie is starting!"

"Quit hollering across the room, child," Lisa admonishes her, as she comes out of the back hallway with a pile of folded kitchen towels. "Get your keester off the couch and walk over if you wanna talk."

"I promised I'd watch *Frozen* with her while the boys do their homework," Lissie explains with a grin, before getting up and heading over to where the girl is waiting on the couch.

"Talking about homework..." Luna stands up as well. "...I should head home and make sure Ahiga is doing his. Ouray called earlier, they're on their way back. Let him know we're at home?"

"Will do."

I look over at the bar where Tse already joined Wapi and Honon for a beer. My father is sitting with them, his eyes scanning the club. I follow his suit, noting the boys bent over their homework at the large table; the two older kids at one end, and the three youngest at the other. I let my eyes drift to the couch where Kiara is snuggled into Lissie's side, both girls focused on the large screen. In the kitchen I can just catch a glimpse of Lisa standing at the stove, where Momma spent so many years looking after us. When I turn back to the bar, my father's eyes are on me, a faint smile on his face, his hands signing.

"What do you see?"

I don't have to think about the answer.

"Family."

He nods.

"Welcome home, boy."

"Thanks, Pop."

I walk over and put my hand on his shoulder before turning to Wapi who is manning the bar.

"Toss me a water?"

"Keep waiting for everyone to be here, but that won't happen. I'm thinking now's a good time."

"Lisa?" I take the water bottle from Wapi and catch Pop nodding.

"Lisa!" I yell, grinning.

Just then the door opens and Brick, Paco, and Ouray walk through along with a dark-haired, young kid, maybe twelve or so.

"Lord, gimme patience," Lisa grumbles coming out of the kitchen, spearing me with a look. "How on earth am I supposed to teach them kids manners when they've got you lot as examples?"

My brothers and I chuckle. Her words are much the same as my mother's had been for as long as I can remember. She used to be forever on our case.

"What's with all the yelling?" Ouray wants to know, herding the shuffling kid ahead of him.

Nosh gets up from his seat and walks over to where Lisa is standing, a fist propped on hip. He digs his hand in his pocket and pulls out the keys, handing them to her. I see the confusion on her face.

"Why are you giving me the keys to your house?" she asks, taking them from him.

"Your house now," he says, before turning around and sitting back down at the bar.

I look over at Lissie, who has her head turned, and her face crumples when she sees Lisa burst into tears.

"Good fucking Lord," Ouray complains loudly, to which Lisa's head snaps up.

"Language!" She wipes her tears away resolutely and

turns to the new boy, who looks like he's about to run out of here. "What's your name?"

He looks behind him as if there's someone else she might be talking to, before turning to her. "Ravi," he says in a raspy voice.

"Ravi," Lisa repeats. "You look like you could eat. Come with me." Then she turns around and walks back into the kitchen, not waiting to see if he's going to follow.

"That's Lisa," Ouray tells the boy. "You best do as she says." He gives the kid a little nudge to get him moving.

"You givin' us a house?" Ezrah, who got up from the table, walks up to Nosh. *"Why?"* He's learned some basic sign language, as have all of the boys. It's something Paco works on with them.

"She takes care of us, we take care of her."

"But it's your house."

"It was Momma's house. She would want Nana to have it," I answer for my father, who nods his agreement.

I don't think I've ever seen Ezrah cry until now. He's stoic, scarred and hardened by what he endured at his young age, but I guess his young poker face is no match for a kindness shown to his grandmother.

Brick steps up behind the boy, putting a hand on his shoulder.

"All you gotta do is say thank you and go about your day, kiddo," he says in a low voice.

Ezrah mouths his thanks before spinning around and planting his face in Brick's midriff.

"Dinner!" Lisa announces, coming out of the kitchen with a plate piled high she takes straight to Nosh. She sets it in front of him at the bar. "First plate at every meal," she says, kissing him on the cheek before heading back to the kitchen.

He turns to me with a shit-eating grin on his face.

"Worth it."

LISSIE

"LOOKS GOOD."

I'd forgotten about my follow-up visit with the surgeon who fixed my shoulder.

Yuma had to remind me this morning when I was up and out of bed before him, eager to get to his house. I'd barely seen any of it on my brief visit there, and most of what I remember was the stench and the mess. I really want to roam around, because judging by the size of the house on the outside, there's a lot to discover.

Of course, then he had to burst my bubble by reminding me I was due at the hospital at ten thirty.

"So can I use it as normal?" I ask the doctor, who's just had me go through a range of motions.

"Depends on what your normal is. You can, just give the muscle a few more weeks before you start swimming the butterfly stroke or chopping firewood. The wound has healed nicely. By the time your other injury has healed, you'll be good to go back to work."

I put my shirt back on, something I can manage to do on my own now without the sling hampering me, and follow him from the treatment room into the office.

"Unless you experience problems—in which case

call my secretary—I don't need to see you again."

Yuma, who had a call to make so waited outside, looks up when I come out of the office.

"And?"

I rotate my left arm to show him.

"I can dress myself." When he mock-pouts, I add, "No chopping wood, though. I'm still gonna need you for that."

"Glad I can still be of service," he says, putting a hand on the back of my neck as we navigate through the hospital to the exit.

"Lots of ways for you to be of service," I tease him, earning a low growl.

"What was the call about?" I ask when we get in his truck.

"A surprise I'm regretting now you've woken up the beast," he grumbles.

"The beast?" I snicker, but then I realize he mentioned a surprise. "What surprise?"

He looks over and grins at me. "Wouldn't be a surprise if I told you now, would it?"

"That's not fair," I protest, as he pulls out of the parking lot. "You can't just throw out the word *surprise* and then not follow through."

"Guess we're even then," he deadpans.

When he pulls into the City Market in town and announces we need stuff for the house, I don't even bother arguing. I'm discovering even something as mundane as hitting up a grocery store with Yuma is an experience I don't want to miss.

It's a Saturday morning and the store is busy. He lets me push the cart while he darts in and out of aisles, piling up the groceries.

"Are you expecting us to get cut off from civilization sometime soon?" I ask, eyeing the rapidly filling cart.

"Now there's an idea…but no. Wasn't anything salvageable left in the house, Babe. Gotta stock up a little."

A little is putting it mildly, judging by the three hundred and seventeen dollar price tag at the checkout, for which he pays with a credit card.

"I'll pay you back my share," I tell him, as we walk back to the truck. It earns me a scowl. "What? I can pay my own way."

"I'm sure you can," he says, tossing bags of groceries in the back. "But you're not gonna."

"Now wait a minute…" Right in the middle of my objection he walks off with the empty cart, leaving it in the assigned spot.

"Nothin' to say," he starts when he comes back.

"You can't just do that."

I ignore him when he pulls open my door and gestures me inside. With a deep sigh, he puts his hands on my waist, and almost effortlessly lifts me into the passenger seat before slamming the door shut. When he climbs behind the wheel he turns to me.

"I just did, and fair warning, I'll do it again. When you're well enough you head to the store by yourself and have a hankering to pay for shit, be my guest, but when you're with me, I pay."

"That's so outdated."

"Don't care if it is. It's important to me to look after my family. You're gonna give me that."

He faces forward and starts the truck; while I try to process what it is exactly he's telling me. It doesn't take long for me to figure out the why doesn't matter, it's the fact this is important to *him*. So before we even leave the parking lot, I know I won't fight him on this.

"I'm gonna give you that," I whisper, and he lifts my hand from my lap and presses a kiss on my palm.

"Thank you."

Trunk's vehicle is parked beside my truck in front of the house when we drive up and I wonder what he's doing here.

"We'll get the groceries in a bit," Yuma says, taking my left hand in his as we head up the steps to the front door.

There is no gnarly smell when we walk inside. Without it I can focus on the big open space, but my eyes get caught on my loveseat on one side in front of the flat-screen TV, opposite his large sectional. The big piece of furniture dwarfs my little couch, but I like the way they look together.

My eyes drift to the kitchen, where I spot two figures sitting quietly at the large island. One large, bald black man, and one tow-headed little boy, and my heart starts hammering out of my chest.

"He wants the spare room on the left," Trunk shares, and I swivel around to do a face-plant in Yuma's shirt.

"Why is she crying?" I hear Thomas ask.

"It's what women do when they're happy," Trunk rumbles.

I feel Yuma's chest moving with his chuckles.

"Ask him," he says, his lips by my ear.

As payback for laughing when I'm emotional, I wipe my face on his shirt before I walk into the kitchen.

"Hey, Thomas."

"Hi."

"You picked out a room. Does that mean you want to stay? Live here with Yuma and me?"

His nod is barely distinguishable as he glances behind me and I swallow down the lump in my throat.

"How long do I get to stay?" he asks, and my heart breaks.

Yuma ends up giving him the perfect answer.

"How does forever sound, Thomas?"

His eyes well up.

"Good, but can you call me Jesse now?"

34

LISSIE

"JESSE, LET'S GO, buddy!"

I'm standing at the bottom of the stairs, hollering up like I've done almost every morning since we moved in here six weeks ago.

I was a sobbing mess when he asked to be called by his real name. When Trunk and I spent a little time talking to him in the days prior, I'd shown him his birth certificate and some of the pictures I had of Dani. The fact he asked us to call him Jesse felt like I was getting a little part of my best friend back. The next day I had one of the pictures of his mom blown up. The one where she's sitting on a bike, smiling carefree, just the way I remember her. It now hangs in his room.

The boy sure likes his room, which isn't hard to

understand when you know most of his young life he's shared not much more than a bunkroom with several other kids. He's been without something as basic as a little personal space and loves spending time up there.

Trunk told us not to go crazy spoiling him with games and electronics, but instead let Jesse discover his own interests. It turns out he likes books, so Yuma hung up a few bookshelves in his room. Once a week, I take Jesse to pick out a new book at a secondhand bookstore Luna told me about. It's owned by her friend, Kerri, who happens to be married to SAC Gomez. While he rummages through the children's section, I hang out with Kerri or her manager, Marya, sipping on a vanilla latte. It's become our weekly thing.

"Jesse! You're gonna be late!"

I hear his running footsteps on the landing before he comes blundering down the stairs, his backpack bouncing behind him.

"Sorry," he mumbles.

"Teeth brushed?"

"Yes, ma'am." I give him a stern look. The whole *ma'am* thing is a bit much for me. "I mean, Lissie," he corrects with a sheepish grin.

I see more and more of those as time goes by, and when he flashes one, he reminds me so much of his mother.

"Much better. Go grab your lunch bag from the counter."

I ruffle his hair when he darts past me, the only physical touch I allow myself. Trunk suggests to resist the urge to pour out all my love on the boy at once, and instead get him used to small touches first before building it up.

Yuma left earlier for the Riverside to meet up with a new tenant, who is moving into my old apartment this morning. He's going to try and catch up with me at the hospital later, but first I have an errand of my own to run. Something I feel I need to do before the splint comes off.

Jesse grabs his coat and runs out the door ahead of me and is already climbing in the crew cab of my truck before I even get down the steps. Another thing I'll need to do something about in the near future, my transportation. It's going to kill me to let go of my truck, but perhaps I can convince Yuma to ditch his and keep the Sierra.

"Buckled, buddy?" I check in the rearview mirror.

"Yup," he says, giving me one of his grins in the reflection.

I smile as I back out of my spot. Most days I'm flying by the seat of my pants, with little control over my life, but I've never been happier.

That's in part why I end up at the police station after dropping Jesse off at school.

I've agonized over this decision after working so hard to get where I am, and as hard as it was for me at times, I know I'll miss it.

"Bucco!" Mike Bolter, our desk sergeant, calls out when I walk in the door. "You back?"

I force a grin on my face and wave my splint in his face.

"Gotta get this off first," I respond without actually answering. "Chief in his office?"

"He is."

"Thanks, Mike."

I walk down the hall to where Benedetti's office door is open and knock on the post. Joe looks up from his paperwork and smiles, gesturing for me to come in.

"Good to see you, Lissie. Have a seat. What brings you in?" He tents his fingers under his chin, and suddenly I get the sense he already knows why I'm here.

"I have an appointment at the hospital today." I show him my splint. "This should be coming off, and I'm pretty sure I'll be cleared to return to work."

"I can hear a 'but' coming."

My mouth falls open.

"How did you know?"

He shrugs, leaning back in his chair. "Easy. Been six weeks since you got injured and this is the first time you visit." I open my mouth to protest, but he holds up his hand. "You're an asset to the department, Detective Bucco, a good investigator. You have the kind of drive I'd hate to lose, but it's not a surprise you've decided your heart's not in it. Never met anyone so determined to prove herself to everyone else. Figured it would just be a matter of time before you discovered you had nothing left to prove."

When I walk out of his office half an hour later, I feel so much lighter. I voiced all my reasons for handing in my badge, and he gave me a hug and wished me good luck. That was not how I expected it to go.

Next will be Yuma—after my appointment—but somehow I don't think he'll have any objections. Not after I tell him everything.

YUMA

"HAVE EVERYTHING READY? We're on our way, I'm following her home."

I stay on her tail through a yellow light, afraid to let her get too far ahead. That had been the only possible flaw in my plan, the fact we'd have our own vehicles at her doctor's appointment.

The woman's a detective. The only way I'd be able to pull off a surprise party for her birthday next week was to plan it early enough, so she wouldn't have any reason to suspect anything. That's also why I picked a Friday when the kids are supposed to be in school.

Lisa had prepared food, Ouray had gone with Trunk to get the kids out of school early, and Tse was picking up the birthday cake in town. I'd left the house early, with an excuse, so I'd be at the airport on time to pick up her father.

She'd talked to him a few times when he'd called to check in on her. When I discovered her birthday was coming up, I found his phone number on her cell and called him. Hope it doesn't blow up in my face, but I know better than most it's never too late to mend fences with family. Lissie was pivotal to the change in my relationship with my father. Least I can do is help Lissie to bridge the gap with hers.

Her brothers couldn't make it on such short notice, but I'm hoping now that Robert Bucco is making a move to reenter his daughter's life, his sons will find their way too.

"All set, brother," Ouray assures me. "Everyone's inside the house and there are no vehicles parked out front."

"ETA is ten minutes."

"We'll be ready."

Momma's ring is burning a hole in my pocket. Pop gave it to me last week, telling me it's what Momma would've wanted. I didn't think I'd ever be asking a woman to share my life, but if these last six weeks have proven anything, it's Lissie belongs there. In my house, in my bed, and in my life. For good. It was my father's idea to pop the question at the party. I just hope to fuck she says yes, or I'll have to play my trump card and explain how much easier it'll be to adopt Jesse when the time is right.

When Lissie pulls into our driveway up ahead, I'm suddenly nervous as I quickly pull in behind her. She'd mentioned wanting to talk to me when we got home, and now I'm suddenly wondering what she wanted to talk about.

I'm out of the truck and before she has a chance to get out of hers, I'm at her door.

"What did you wanna talk about?" I ask her when she opens it.

"Can it wait 'til we're inside?"

I glance over at the house, knowing everyone is inside waiting.

"Yeah, sure," I give in, taking her hand as we walk up

the steps.

I let her go in first, and hear the loud "Surprise!" go up. Lissie stands frozen in the entrance for a moment before she turns to me and promptly bursts into tears.

Shit. That can't be good.

"Baby…" I pull her in my arms and throw an uneasy look at the crowd in my living room. "Happy birthday, Lissie," I mumble in her hair, as I watch her father walk up.

"Happy birthday, Elizabeth."

I can feel her straighten her back at the sound of his voice before she lifts her head. I'm not sure how to interpret her quick glance at me before she turns to face her father, and I'm left to wonder if I did well or fucked up royally as she greets him.

It doesn't take long for her to be at the center of a group, smiling as she receives birthday wishes.

"That went well," Tse says, coming to stand beside me. "For a minute there I thought it was gonna blow up in your face, brother."

I blow out a deep breath. "It still could," I mutter, my hand inadvertently reaching for my pocket where Momma's ring is waiting for the right moment.

Lissie makes her way to the kitchen, where the kids look to be guarding the cake sitting on the counter. Kiara is the first to break away from their huddle to give Lissie a hug. The boys seem a bit more reserved in their congratulations, until I see Jesse approach her.

He walks right up to her, wrapping his arms around her waist. For a moment her body seems to curl around the boy, before she lifts her head and her eyes find me across the room. Ignoring everyone, I make my way over to them. It seems like the perfect opportunity.

"Need a word with you, Bucco," I hear behind me and turn around.

Tony Ramirez is heading this way, looking beyond me into the kitchen. I don't much care for his tone so I move to block his way. He may be here by invitation, but that can be revoked in a heartbeat.

"Did you know?" he asks, stopping right in front of me.

All I can do is shake my head in confusion; I'm not sure what I'm supposed to know. I swing around to Lissie, who still has the boy tucked close to her side, her face paling even as she lifts her chin defiantly.

"Haven't had a chance before you came barging in, Ramirez," she snaps, taking a step forward. "And I would've liked to do so on my own terms, without you crashing my party."

"I was invited," he returns weakly before shaking his head. "Shit. Didn't mean to—"

"I know," she says in a more reconciliatory tone. "So I'm sure you understand you have to get in line for explanations."

"What's going on?" I hiss, trying not to draw more attention.

She leans down to kiss the top of Jesse's head and tells him to give her a minute, before reaching for my hand and dragging me out the back door to the deck.

"Babe?"

She takes in a deep breath before she speaks.

"I handed in my resignation this morning. Don't be mad."

"Mad? Why the fuck would I be mad about that? Would've liked a heads-up, but that's your call to make."

"I was going to talk to you this morning, but you were gone so quick."

"Then talk to me now."

She leans into the hand I place on the side of her face.

"My job always defined me. My whole identity was wrapped up in being a cop. A good cop. But since coming here, meeting you, I've discovered there's more to me."

"Could'a told you that," I mumble, earning me a soft smile.

"Living here, with you and Jesse, I started to realize I was perfectly happy being just me. I would've handled things differently, might have gone back to work for a while, at least until they could find a replacement, but I discovered something yesterday that changed everything."

"What?" I prompt her, my chest tight with panic. Is she telling me she changed her mind about us? I don't think I'd recover.

"I'm pregnant."

"You're...what?"

She seems to find my apparent confusion funny.

"We're having a baby." When I don't say anything, simply because I can't even remember how to breathe, she adds unnecessarily, "It's the Depo-shot, it messed with my periods. Didn't have one for years, and I thought—"

"I'm gonna be a father," I finally manage to force out, bending over when I suddenly get lightheaded.

"According to the stick I peed on yesterday, it would seem so." Since I'm already halfway down, I drop to my knee and lift my head up. "Are you okay?" she asks with concern.

"I've never been this okay." I grab her hand with one of mine, and with the other pull Momma's ring from my pocket. I'm already down here, might as well make use of the opportunity. "I never dreamed I'd find a woman I love so much sometimes it takes my breath away. I've lived staring at the edge of darkness my whole life, until you showed me all I had to do was turn around to face the light." I slide the ring on her finger without giving her a chance to refuse. "Shit, baby, you already give me a life so full, every morning I have to pinch myself to trust it's real. And now you're giving me more. I'm not sure how I deserve this, but there's no fucking way in hell I'll ever let you go."

Tears are rolling down her face, but she's not saying anything.

"Babe, this is the part where you answer," I finally tell her, getting up because my knee is starting to kill me.

"I didn't hear a question," she fires back, grinning through her tears.

I hook her behind the neck and pull her close, touching my nose to hers.

"I fucking love you, you smartass." I smile into her eyes. "Marry me?"

THE END

ABOUT THE AUTHOR

Award-winning author Freya Barker loves writing about ordinary people with extraordinary stories.

Driven to make her books about 'real' people; she creates characters who are perhaps less than perfect, each struggling to find their own slice of happy, but just as deserving of romance, thrills and chills in their lives.

Recipient of the ReadFREE.ly 2019 Best Book We've Read All Year Award for "Covering Ollie, the 2015 RomCon "Reader's Choice" Award for Best First Book, "Slim To None", and Finalist for the 2017 Kindle Book Award with "From Dust", Freya continues to add to her rapidly growing collection of published novels as she spins story after story with an endless supply of bruised and dented characters, vying for attention!

ABOUT THE AUTHOR